The Ghost

By
Andy Mitchell

Copyright © 2024 by Andy Mitchell

ISBN: 978-1-965138-12-0

Printed in the United States of America

Published by Book Marketeers.com

Prologue

He was inside their tent when he heard his father's heavy footsteps approaching. The flap on the tent quickly snapped open. He knew he was in for a beating.

"How have you been, son?" Oscar Blackwood asked.

"Good"

"Did you clean my make-up kit like I asked?"

It was a seemingly harmless question, but he knew better. He had seen his father's posture, how he walked at times like this, with his shoulders slumped over.

"Yes, I wiped off the spilled paint the best I could, re-arranged the paints in alphabetical order, cleaned the mirror, and rubbed oil on the outside of the wood case to make the wood shine and to help preserve it."

"I did not tell you to oil the wooden box. When I pick it up and get oil on my hands, it will mix with my paints and ruin their colors. Do you understand how serious this is? This could damage my work. I don't want to harm you, son, but your actions leave me no choice."

"Sorry, Father. I didn't…"

Earlier that same day, before the beating, for no particular reason, he was thinking about the early days. He had a vague recollection of his father beating him with a rubber chicken, slowly at first and then as hard as he could. His memory of it was so vague that he had started to wonder if those early beatings had actually happened. He tried not to think of the early days.

Occasionally, like today, when he did think about it, he figured that the beatings could have happened, but with each passing year, he wondered a little more if he had made up those early beatings in his mind. Maybe he was just being delusional. He wasn't sure.

His father was a floor acrobat in a traveling circus. Part of his act was putting on makeup to look like a clown. He and the other floor acrobats, most of them also made up to be clowns, had their established routines and performed various surprise gags and tricks. The audience never failed to respond to their act with raucous laughter. It seemed that his father admired that part of his life.

Still, his father's moods followed a predictable cycle, bringing a sense of routine into his life. Most people found routines to be a good thing, easy and comforting, but in his case, his father's mood changes were not only predictable but ominous. Each day, he felt that things were going to become worse for him. He couldn't help but feel that way. As a new day passed, he was another day closer to his next beating.

His father, Oscar, was listless and quiet after a beating. The next few days were a time of healing and safety for him. His father's anxiety would start to build up inside him soon enough, but it was hard to notice at first.

The cycle continued like clockwork. There was no escaping it. He would be beaten, there was a lull, and then his father's symptoms gradually became more pronounced. The changes were clear to him and his trained eye. He saw the signs. He knew when his father's demons were starting to take bigger and bigger bites out of his soul. When Oscar could take no more, something or someone would trigger another beating.

His mother left the family when he was very young, and he

only had vague memories of her. He didn't remember her face. He had more of a vague recollection of how he felt when she was around him than any specific memory of her.

She could be both warm and distant at the same time. She was protective of him like most mothers were of their children, but at the same time, Oscar must have greatly intimidated her.

He had mastered the art of enduring a blow to minimize visible damage the next day. He remained relaxed, flowed with the force of each strike, and shielded himself by placing his forearms protectively over his face.

Today's ritual of punishment began and ended almost abruptly. He had survived another one.

His job at the circus was to man the ticket booth. He was young, a teenager, but not seen by circus management as suited to do any other work, so he ended up there. He didn't mind it. It was an easy job. Sometimes, familiar customers came up to the booth and paid. All of the new customers were predictable. They walked up to his booth, took a moment to read the sign on the front explaining the ticket prices, and then stepped up to order their tickets. He quoted them the price, gave the people their tickets, and sometimes gave them change back. That was it. Each time it was the same.

Occasionally, some people tried to intimidate him into giving them free or discounted tickets. They probably thought they could get away with it because he looked so young and vulnerable, and he wouldn't put up a fight. They didn't know the circus had a security service that dealt with those people. He felt a guilty pleasure when the offenders were punished by security. They were not shy in handing out their punishments.

As much as he tried to avoid it, he had many cuts and bruises after one of his father's beatings. This was embarrassing for him when he was in the ticket booth. People would stare at him briefly, then quickly look away. This used to happen all day long. One day, he thought of a solution to this problem.

While his father was away practicing his act, he experimented with his father's paint kit. After some trial and error, he finally developed a flesh tone that matched his own. He used his concoction to cover his bruises, prominently on his face and neck. He was careful never to use too much of the paints to avoid suspicion from his father. Before returning to their tent, he carefully and methodically wiped the paint off so his father wouldn't notice it.

He learned that a long-sleeve shirt was the best solution to cover the cuts on his arms, as long as the cut was not bleeding through his shirt. Over the years, he became very good at using make-up paint to change his appearance. He also learned how to use light and darkness to his advantage.

He tried to keep nasty cuts or bruises partially hidden in shadows whenever possible. He would take advantage of anything else he could use, too. A standard prop was a hat to cover a cut on his head that wouldn't stop bleeding. Another trick in his ever-growing arsenal was to bend his body in a way that both hid a wound and made him look crippled. People were not interested in either looking at or talking to a cripple.

They both knew there would never be an end to the beatings. This cycle of abuse would continue. It was their life. Nothing could change it. He wasn't sure if others lived like him, but he doubted it. Either way, it didn't matter. He couldn't change his life. After a beating, he could enjoy simple things like smelling flowers, hearing birds, and feeling safe while his injuries began to heal. They both knew the next beating would be coming soon enough.

Table of Contents

Chapter One

Prescott, Arizona Territory

1895

Will Martin Junior, or simply Junior to those who knew him, was restless in the hour before he would start another day; a day like yesterday was and just like tomorrow would be. He dressed and went out to the west-facing covered porch and sat down. The coming dawn would inspire most people, but he didn't feel inspired. He felt oppressed. Junior enjoyed hard work but despised the monotony of working on the family farm.

Soon, he was called in for breakfast.

Junior went inside the cabin and saw his two brothers sitting at the table.

"Who's the toughest buckaroo in Arizona?" Junior asked, looking at Lee.

"I am," Lee said

"What?"

"I am." He said, a little louder

"WHAT?"

"I AM"

"You don't have to yell." Junior snickered.

He gave his eleven-year-old brother Lee a slight shove on the shoulder, and they both laughed. It was one of their time-honored rituals. Junior loved to tease his brothers, and they didn't seem to mind it that much.

Junior sat across from his two younger brothers as they looked at the large, steaming stack of pancakes in the middle of the breakfast table. Junior kept one eye on the pancakes and one eye on his youngest brother, Paul. Paul loved to eat and always seemed to be hungry.

The game was on. Paul took his fork and started to stab a pancake, but Junior was too quick and stabbed it first. Paul, frustrated but patient, waited his turn, then went for the next pancake. Junior quickly put the first pancake on his plate and stabbed the next one before Paul could get at it. Paul hesitated but backed off and gave Junior a frustrated look. True to form, Junior thought. He always knew what Paul was thinking. Paul had no malice in him, probably typical for a six-year-old boy, and Junior could read Paul's face like a book.

Junior released the second pancake back onto the pile of pancakes, sat back, and then said, "Go ahead. You saw it first."

Paul cutiously took his pancake and put it on his plate.

"Have another if you want."

Junior didn't move. Paul looked at him, gave him a quick nod of thanks, then took another pancake and smiled.

Junior admired how his brothers enjoyed each day, one at a time. They didn't have his problem, at least not yet. They were too young. Junior craved a future, even though he had no idea what that future might look like. Everyone was at the table now, and they ate their breakfast heartily.

Junior had heard the stories about his parents, Cora and Will's younger days - when they met. He listened to the stories repeatedly and knew them all by heart.

They met back in eighteen eighty and married down south in Wickenburg at the end of that year. They settled here in Prescott, in Cora's cabin. A short time later, Cora asked, "Will, back when we first met, you said putting up some crops along the creek would be a good idea. Do you still think so?"

"Yes, I do, and I'm excited to get it started." He told her his plan. Fifty acres, give or take, with plenty of room for expansion later if they wanted to. Cora had a two-hundred-acre spread with a cabin, outbuildings, and Walnut Creek behind the cabin.

The first year was the hardest. Will underestimated how much work was involved in tending to fifty acres. They bought a plow, and Will used his horse, Jake, to drag it through the dirt. It was easy to get water from the creek, which ran most of the time. Will put up a small windmill for an auxiliary water supply if needed.

Will spent nearly every waking hour maintaining the farm. It was almost too much for one man, and he looked for Junior to help. Increasingly, he began to look to Junior's younger brother, Lee, for help, too.

Junior got into trouble frequently when he was younger, especially with Will. Cora seemed to accept and understand him better. When Junior didn't do what Will told him, Will would ask, 'Why not?' Often, but not always, Junior would counter with 'What if?' and suggest another solution to a particular problem be explored.

Will was rarely inclined to stop working and reconsider an alternative solution. Work needed to be done, and only so much time was available each day. Junior knew if he pushed it too far, Will would give him 'the stare.' Junior would then be forced to get back to work. He didn't want his father to think he was lazy or a complainer.

Will came to the breakfast table, grabbed some pancakes, and started his breakfast. When he was about halfway through with his stack, he said, "It's time to expand again - about five acres. I have a spot picked out. It'll be a little harder this time, but I have a plan for how to get it done."

Junior's heart sank. Was he being punished? Did Will sense his growing frustration with being tied down to the farm and want to commit him to it? Junior knew for sure that there would be no discussion on the expansion. It would happen and add to the effort required to maintain the vegetable farm. Worse yet, Will would not stop there. After the five-acre expansion, there would be another expansion and then another. What Junior thought about the expansion was of no consequence to Will.

Junior did not begrudge Will's accomplishments. The second year the fields were in, they produced more crops than he or Cora imagined possible. Everyone, including Junior, got involved on Saturdays in taking the harvested crops to the weekly Farmer's Market in downtown Prescott. They had good, quality produce to sell, and they usually sold out. They also had standing orders for vegetables from four restaurants in town and two stores.

The larger-than-typical size of their vegetable farm was a definite advantage against their competition. They had the capacity to grow many different varieties of most of the vegetables. If most other growers had two or three varieties of peppers, they would have ten or more. The same advantage held true for tomatoes, potatoes, corn, and others. They sold three varieties of corn. The family was able to charge a little more for the more unusual vegetables they offered.

With a twinkle in his eye, Will often said that the family's finances were fueled by the horse manure they used. Everyone else in the family knew that Will's hard work was the key to their success. Good for him, good for the rest of the family, bad for me, Junior thought.

"When will the farm be big enough?" He asked his father, trying not to let his frustrations show but knowing that they did.

"Don't exactly know what you're askin', son. We'll know when it's over."

Sometimes, when Will offered advice about a particular problem, it sounded like a riddle. Understanding his meaning often required some pondering and reflection. Junior sometimes laughed to himself after figuring out what Will meant, and he was surprised when years later, he still remembered some of Will's sayings. Today, he didn't see any humor in what Will said. None at all.

When Junior was younger, one day, Cora said, "Will, I'm with child."

"That's wonderful." Will wasn't much of a talker, but he had that twinkle in his eye when he heard the news. Cora pointed out to Junior more than once that Will would get a twinkle in his eye whenever he heard good news.

A few months later, Cora and Will stopped talking about the new baby, and Junior never asked about it after that.

Then, a few years later, Cora said, "We're going to need a bigger cabin."

Will looked at her, thought about what she had told him, and answered, "Yes."

"We have some savings we can use for it, enough to buy some logs from the mill." She said.

"I'm going to need some help. I'll ask Charley if he wants to help."

Charley was Will's best friend. He ran a business taking people on guided hunting trips into the remote areas around Prescott. Back in eighteen-eighty, Will was falsely accused of murder down south in Wickenburg, and Charley was instrumental in saving Will from swinging at the end of a rope. The two remained close friends ever since.

Charley agreed to help with the cabin addition as long as Cora made him a pie once in a while to take back to his family.

They started the next spring and had the addition enclosed before winter. 'Happy,' the younger brother of Cora's friend Cat, was able to help out some days too, mostly by helping Will and Charley wrestle the longer logs into position. Happy had his own business to run, a livery stable. Other times, when he could, he would help by filling in for Charley.

Happy never asked for payment for his help. It was just what good neighbors and good friends did. They helped each other. The addition was completed the following spring. One end of the cabin was expanded nine yards, enough to add four bedrooms, making their cabin one of the largest in the area.

About three years ago, when he was eleven years old, Junior developed a new habit that concerned even Cora. He was bored at home and wanted to explore the surrounding areas. He said he needed to 'wander.'

At first, his wanderings were modest. During the school year, he would be back home in time for dinner. The wanderings gradually expanded out further and took longer and longer. He knew the town backward and forward - it was a small town, after all. Still, he liked to go to some spots repeatedly because he usually met interesting people there. The downtown plaza was his favorite place to go. He met a variety of folks there and was able to have interesting talks with many of them.

Eventually, he began searching the outskirts of Prescott and often did not return home until well after dark. On these trips, he sometimes met people who were not used to seeing visitors, and they were not always friendly.

Will would say, "He eats our corn and our vegetables but doesn't do his share of the work around here." True enough, Junior thought, but he couldn't stay home to work on the farm forever.

His mother would say something like, "I worry about what the neighbors will think when they see him walking around after dark. I've tried to talk to him, but he won't listen."

"The boy is selfish and'll never amount to much." Junior once heard Will say. The more Junior thought about his life, the more trapped he felt.

Chapter Two

He dreaded the thought of tomorrow. He would have to get up early and start helping to gather enough produce for the Farmer's Market, then pack everything into the wagon, help set up the stands, sell the produce, dismantle the stands afterward, and make the weary journey back home.

It would be a day of drudgery, and he would feel like an indentured servant. He did not like standing around at a vegetable stall, waiting for the customers to decide what they wanted to buy.

The only good news was that today, he expected a light load in the fields, although that could change. Will had a knack for finding odd jobs that needed to be done immediately.

He was fourteen years old, and it wouldn't be much longer until he was treated like a man, like an adult. He felt like one.

He liked the joking around while they worked in the fields, how even an average meal tasted good with a healthy appetite, and how his dad sometimes smiled at him and patted him on his back after a long but successful work day. His parents certainly didn't seem to understand him, and he worried they never would. He needed space.

There was an area up and down Thumb Creek he wanted to

explore. The trouble was that it was too far away for him to walk there. He needed a horse. He remembered yesterday when Will mentioned his horse, Jake, would be at Happy's Livery for a shoeing today. He hatched a plan, dressed, left a cryptic note, and headed out of the house into the cool morning air. It was still dark when he left.

When he got to Happy's Livery, he watched from the outside for a few minutes, heard nothing, and saw no activity, then went into the barn. Stupid Happy didn't lock anything. If he were lucky, Happy would not even notice Jake was missing. He planned to go to his friend Raymond's house to get him to ride along with him.

He could have the horse back by noon, which gave him plenty of time. If he saw Happy when he brought Jake back, he could come up with an excuse to tell Happy why he had to borrow Jake. He began to get the gear ready to saddle the horse.

Happy liked to start his work days early. He was almost always at the livery around dawn and almost always there before any customers showed up. He started to go inside, then stopped suddenly. He heard a noise. Someone was inside. Cautiously, he approached the door, cracked it open, and then deliberately and quietly opened it more and more until it was open enough for him to walk inside without making much noise.

He was relieved to see that it was only Junior who was putting a saddle on Jake. Why was he doing that? Jake was here for a shoeing today.

"What are you doing, Junior?"

Junior jerked a little, like he was surprised, looked at him, then proceeded to saddle up the horse without saying anything.

"I said, what are you doing?"

"I'm borrowing Jake for the morning. I'll be back in plenty of time for you to do your work on him."

"Did you ask Will about this?"

"Don't have to. He's a family horse."

"That's not how it works, Junior, and you know it. That's Will's horse. Stop what you are doing and put the saddle back in the tack room."

"Sorry, I need to meet with my friend Raymond soon. We have something important to do today."

"I know of only one person your age named Raymond, and he's always chasin' mischief. You should have nothing to do with him."

"I didn't know you were my father now. Raymond's OK. You don't even know him."

He was having a hard time getting through to this kid. Junior didn't listen. Happy was starting to lose his patience. In a loud voice, not quite yelling, but loud, he said, "Stop what you're doing. You are not taking that horse out of here today."

He was surprised when Junior yelled back at him, "I think they call you Happy because it's a nice way of saying you're stupid. I'm just borrowing the horse, you dumb shit slinger."

Now, Happy began to yell. "You broke into my livery, tried to steal a horse, and now you're throwing insults at me. You're getting to be more and more like your real father all the time."

Junior stopped what he was doing, looked at him, and said, "What does that mean?"

He knew he was in trouble. He had made a mistake. It was obvious that Will and Cora had not told Junior about his real father, not that he would have expected them to, come to think about it. He was not the one who should have told him, either, and certainly not under these circumstances. He would say no more on the subject.

"What do you mean? Will is my father, my real father."

"You have to leave. Now, and on foot." He opened the barn door all the way and waited. Junior looked confused and angry. He stopped working with the saddle, glared at him for a moment, and then quickly walked out of the barn with his head down.

Happy remembered when he was only a couple of years older than Junior. He was down in Wickenburg at the time, helping Cora. He had done something foolish, and Cora immediately straightened him out. He supposed that young people could be expected to say and do foolish things.

He was fond of Junior and remembered seeing him as a baby. But a moment ago, Junior angrily stormed off because of what Happy had said. He accidentally and unintentionally told Junior that Will wasn't his real father. It was a stupid thing for him to say. Now, he wondered if perhaps he deserved to be called 'Stupid' instead of Happy, after all.

He had a young helper, Adam, who would arrive soon and start his day by cleaning up after the horses. Happy started with the first thing he did every day, feeding the horses. At that time, he only had four in full-board status, plus Jake, so it didn't take him very long. He decided to clean the stalls himself to help him get his thinking straight. He began to reflect on earlier times.

Five years ago, he went to the annual parade in downtown Prescott. He went every year to try to get new business. A few years earlier, he bought the livery stables from old man Whitlock using his savings and a loan from Sharlot, Cora's friend. That year, like always, he waited at the end of the parade for people to get off their hot and hungry horses. Then he would talk to the people and pitch his services.

Happy remembered that bright, sunny day because it was the day he met Marie. He had talked to several people when they finished their part in the parade. They listened to his sales pitch and usually promised to remember him if they needed his services. It was a common response, and he understood he would not get much, if any, business from most of these people.

A serious-looking young woman got off her horse that day and brushed off her fancy riding dress. He walked up to her and soon had a funny feeling, like he knew her already.

"Have we met?" He asked.

Years later, he was able to piece together the basics of what she said then. It was something like, "I doubt that. My family moved here a couple of months ago. We're from Kansas. My mom needed a warmer climate, so we ended up here. We've bought a piece of land, and my father will build a cabin on it next year. He's the new foreman at the lumber mill."

Happy remembered that at the time he tried to process all this information, but it was too much. All he could do was blurt out, "You look so familiar, that's all."

"Since you said that with a smile, I'll take it as a compliment."

They continued to talk, and then Happy offered her his pitch about his livery business: "We offer you half off your first grooming, including new shoes if needed, and fifty cents off your first week's boarding." Happy worked with the blacksmith in town to help him fit the horseshoes. He didn't profit much from the shoeing, but it was an important part of his full-service horse care business. He enjoyed grooming a horse properly.

"Does your boss know about this generosity?"

"I am the boss. I own the livery stable."

She seemed impressed and, for the first time, smiled a little. "My name is Marie, what's yours?" She asked.

"Everyone calls me Happy, and yes, it is because I smile a lot.

Can't help it."

"Well, Happy, I like your smile."

They spent a lot of time together that year and the next. Marie seemed to thrive in a traditional type of courtship, and he didn't mind. He wanted to be around her. It was that simple for him. He liked treating her like a special woman because, to him, she was. At the appropriate time, he proposed to her. They married in the spring of the following year.

Those were the good days, he thought. Today was a different kind of day. He hoped he could explain things to Will and Cora. It was an accident, after all. He didn't plan on saying anything to Junior about his real father. Cora had done so much for him over the years. The Martin family had become his family - as much, if not more, than his older sister Cat. He would try to explain himself the first chance he could. He owed it to them. It wouldn't be easy, but he made his bed and now he had to lie in it.

Chapter Three

Junior couldn't go to Thumb Creek without a horse, but that was the least of his problems. He needed time to get his head right. There was a spot he went to occasionally when he felt like this, and he needed to go there today. The spot was west of town, at the end of a gradual westerly incline. There was a steep drop-off at the end of the incline, and from near the edge, he had a good view of the distant mountains. The nearest cabin was miles away. He walked up to the area and spotted his favorite tree. I was a huge Ponderosa Pine. He walked over, sat down with his back to the tree, and began enjoying the spectacular view.

He had known Happy his entire life, and not once had Happy lied to him. At the same time, he had never insulted Happy before, either. Would the insult be enough for Happy to lie to him this morning about Will not being his real father? Probably not. It wasn't like Happy to lie. There had to be something to what he said about his real father.

Why did Will and Cora keep this from him? He couldn't come up with an answer. People told him all the time he resembled his mother. Same round face, they often said. No one ever said anything about him being like Will, who seemed like his complete opposite in many ways. He was thoughtful, and Will was headstrong. He could be talkative at times, and Will was quiet almost all the time. He could admit a mistake, and Will rarely did.

There were other differences Junior could think of, but in truth, he soon became bored thinking about it. There was no denying he was very different than Will. He wondered why they didn't tell him about his real father when he was much younger. He would have been more naive and needy of his parents, and he would have accepted the news much easier then. What were they trying to hide? Was he an orphan? Not that, he thought; he always felt a closeness with Cora and knew in his heart she was his real mother. What had happened to his real father?

He pondered these questions for a good while. Then it hit him. There must have been something bad about his real father - something they wanted to hide from him. Maybe it was something they wanted to protect him from. For all he knew, they may have planned on never telling him about his real father at all.

These thoughts left him feeling disappointed. He started to question himself. Was he bad? Was there something wrong with him? He closed his eyes and smelled the Ponderosa Pine sap from the big tree, a pleasant smell similar to vanilla, and was buffeted by the cool breeze while listening to the birds chirp and squawk. Time would provide the answers to his questions. Ten minutes passed, then twenty minutes, then he could sit no more. He got up and began the walk over to Raymond's house. When he got there, he saw Raymond sitting on his front porch, and walked up on the porch.

"Hey, Junior, why the long face?"

"You mean like what the bartender asked the horse that sat down at his bar?"

"What?"

"Never mind. I wanted us to take a ride over to Thumb Creek

today, but I couldn't get a horse for it."

"A ride out to look at a creek for fun? I thought you had a better imagination than that, Junior."

OK, then what's your idea?"

"I'm feeling like today is special. We are going to have some real fun."

Junior was ready for some fun, that was for sure. "I'm up for that. What did you have planned?"

"Stay right there," Raymond said as he went into a storage shed, rummaged around for a minute, and then emerged carrying a medium-sized bag.

"What's in the bag? It smells funny."

"This is my little bag full of fun things, for a fun day. You'll see."

"OK then, let's go. Walking or riding?"

"Walking. Into town." Raymond answered.

They walked into the downtown area, which was only a few minutes walk from Raymond's house, then casually walked over to the town plaza. They sat down on a bench and watched a few people come and go, seeming to be completely consumed with their lives. Nobody acted like they noticed the two of them at all.

"Let's move," Raymond said. Montezuma Street bordered the west side of the town square. A row of whiskey saloons were located on the west side of Montezuma Street and faced the town plaza. They walked south until they were in line with the southern end of the row of saloons, crossed the street, and went to the southern side of the last saloon in the row, the Royale Saloon. They kept walking until they reached a narrow alley behind the saloon. Raymond turned into the alley, Junior followed, and they stood there in silence.

"Can't imagine having more fun than this," Junior said as he stared at Raymond.

"Be patient. You'll see." They waited and waited for fifteen minutes, and no one walked past the alley in all that time.

"It's time to have some fun," Raymond said.

"I'd like to see that."

Raymond said nothing to that, then grabbed his bag and took it over to the back of the wooden building. He took a metal pry bar out of his bag, and after a minute or two, he had removed a couple of the lowest horizontal boards on the side of the saloon. This exposed an open space under the floor level of the saloon. He took out some rags from the bag and put them and everything else he had brought under the building. Junior could smell the oily rags clearly now and immediately got a bad feeling.

"What are you doing? Are you insane?" he watched as Raymond first lit the rags and then stepped back to admire the fire. They watched it grow rapidly. Junior was stunned by how fast the fire grew. The fire consumed the rags and the sack, and soon, the flames began to leap up the back of the saloon.

Raymond seemed to be in a trance. He went to the end of the alley, looked around, then yelled, "Fire! Fire!" They both ran to the front of the Royale Saloon and then went inside. There were a few customers casually drinking and a couple of workers visible.

"There's a fire in the back," Raymond yelled

"A fire?"

"Yeah, a fire. We walked by and saw it. I'll get some help."

The two of them worked their way from saloon to saloon, yelling for anyone and everyone to help stop the fire. Soon, there was a small mob of people at the fire. A bucket line was formed, and everyone began to work franticly. Some progress was made.

People yelled encouragement and pressed harder. The work continued, but the fire had progressed to the roof and the situation became desperate. There was a staggered brick wall that rose a couple of feet above the roof line of the saloon in steps, that separated it from the adjacent saloon to the north. This was the last line of defense against the fire, which would easily spread to the whole row of saloons if they didn't stop it.

People, including Junior and Raymond, continued to work furiously to try to save the building, but it soon became obvious it was too late. Water sizzled against the bricks as it was thrown up to stop the fire from spreading. Several of the bricks cracked but miraculously stayed in place. No one quit. More and more water was thrown up to the bricks.

The fuel from the dry wood that minutes ago had been the Royale Saloon was almost gone. The work slowed, and the exhausted workers eventually stopped and stared at the smoking rubble.

Junior walked across the street to the town square, fell to his knees on the ground, rolled over on his back, and stared up at the sky. It was the worst moment of his life. He felt hollow and dirty. Raymond suddenly came into his vision.

"I never thought the whole saloon would burn down," Raymond said.

"Go away."

Raymond left without comment and he lay there for a couple of minutes. He didn't want to believe it but couldn't escape it either. A part of him, a part he would never reveal to anyone, was ever so slightly *excited* when he saw the flames leap up the side of the building. What was wrong with him?

He rolled to his knees, got on his feet, and willed his tired and sore body to begin the walk home.

He made it to the cabin, and trudged up the steps and fell into a porch chair with his head down. After a few minutes, Will came in from the fields, walked up to him, and said, "What happened to you? Are you alright?"

"Yeah. There was a fire at the Royale. Raymond and I tried to put it out, but it burned down. All of it."

"Raymond was with you?"

"Yeah."

"What were you doin' before the fire started? Why were you in that part of town in the first place?"

"We were having lunch downtown when we walked down the street and saw the fire. We alerted people to the fire, but it was too late."

"You and Raymond just happened to be there and saw the fire start?"

"Yeah." He looked up and could tell that Will was becoming agitated. This situation was quickly going from bad to worse.

"I've warned you about that Raymond boy before, Junior. Trouble follows him around like stink on a skunk, son. Why do you keep puttin' your mother and I through this? To tell you the Lord's truth, I don't believe you. I think there's more to it. I think you're lyin' to me. You are goin' to stay here, at the house, work in the fields, and do exactly what I tell you to do. If you try to leave, I'll track you down and drag you back here by your ear. DO you understand me?

Junior said nothing.

Do YOU understand me?"

Junior lowered his head and said, "Yes, sir. I understand." There was nothing else he could say.

Chapter Four

"How could you do that?" His mother said loudly enough to wake him up.

Junior opened his eyes and looked around his room. He was alone. He looked out his window; the sun was already well up in the sky, and the realization hit him that he had overslept. There was a faint but definite smell of breakfast in the air. He dressed, left his room, and began to eat his cold breakfast.

There were cracks between some of the logs in the cabin overdo for repair, and combined with the thin windows, Junior could hear most of their conversation. He doubted if they knew he was listening.

"It just happened. I was angry, and he wouldn't listen to me." Junior recognized Happy's voice.

"I'm very disappointed in you, Happy."

Silence for a moment.

His mother rarely got angry, and Junior knew she couldn't stay angry for long. "What's done is done. I know you, Happy, and you never would have said anything like that on purpose. Thank you for telling me about it."

Happy left at about the same time that Junior finished his

breakfast. His mother stayed on the porch. He braced himself. It was time to get some answers. Junior quietly made his way outside to sit on the porch.

"Morning Junior. Have a seat by me."

Junior sat down and said, "Morning, Mother. Are you alright?"

"I'm fine. Worried about you some."

"Yesterday was an awful day. I heard disturbing news in the morning, watched a saloon burn to the ground; then Will had a bit of a fuss-up with me."

"Your father loves you, you know."

"Yeah. Happy told me something yesterday. It's hard to believe and even harder for me to talk about it." He paused for a moment. "I heard yesterday morning that Will isn't my real father. You just told me my father loves me. Will loves me, I think, but is it true I've never met my real father?"

She looked at him but said nothing.

"What happened yesterday at the saloon?"

"Raymond started the fire."

"Were you involved?"

"No. I watched him start the fire, then worked with the other people there to help put it out."

"You watched? You did nothing to put the fire out before it got out of control?"

"I should have done more, but what he did surprised me. The fire grew very quickly. Maybe any other day, I could have done better."

"I can understand that."

After a brief silence, Junior asked again, "Who was my real father?"

"His name was Jesse, and he died years ago. He was not like us; he was a bad man. You are not like him at all, Junior."

"How can you know that?"

"I know you – I'm your mother. You know the difference between right and wrong. You try to do the right thing, or at least you did before yesterday. You do have a powerful lot of growing up to do. I would be glad to see you start working on that immediately."

"I'm trying."

"At the moment, you're very trying for this family, Junior. She saw his pained expression, then continued, "Maybe that's not all your fault. We should have told you about your real father a long time ago. Things are always better when brought out into the open. Secrets are harmful. I feel some better myself already, having told you."

"I can't shake the fact that Will is not my real father. He's been pretending to be my father my whole life."

"That's enough. Will has not been pretending to do anything. His feelings for you are real. He is your father, and he loves you. You're never going to have any other father besides Will, and believe me, you could do far, far worse than to have Will as your father."

"Today, he probably wants to ask you more about what happened at the fire. You are going to tell him everything, and you are going to speak nothing but the truth. You owe it to him, to me, and you damn sure owe it to yourself. Think about it." She walked into the cabin, and he was left with his thoughts.

Another day, another lecture. He could count on one hand the number of times he had heard his mother curse. He understood what she said, but she and Will weren't interested in his side of the story. He had nothing to do with hiding the identity of his real father. They did. He didn't start a fire. Raymond did. But he was the one getting lectured. *They don't respect me.*

Will and Lee were working in the fields. Paul dragged himself out of the cabin and sat down next to him. "Did you start the fire?"

"No, someone else did."

Paul looked confused and worried. Junior put his head down, contorted his face, then looked at Paul and gave him his 'funny face.' Paul giggled. *I'm glad he's so easily entertained, especially today.*

Will came in from the fields and sat down on the porch. He looked tired. They didn't talk. Someone was riding up to the cabin. Sheriff Herman Lewis tied up his horse and began walking up the steps to the porch.

"Mornin' Sheriff," Will said.

"Good morning, Will. I need to speak with you and Junior." Paul went inside.

"Have a seat, Sheriff," Will said. Lewis hesitated, then moved a chair and sat opposite them.

"Will, Junior, as you know, the saloon was a total loss. The owner has other businesses in town, and he has the resources to rebuild the saloon. I'm relieved no one was hurt or killed in the fire. Junior, I am going to ask you a question, and your answer is very important - Remember that. "What happened yesterday?"

He remembered his last lecture from Cora about telling the truth and told Sheriff Lewis everything exactly as it happened. He left out his talk with Happy, then recounted the events of yesterday that related to the fire. Will said nothing. The reaction he received from the Sheriff was not what he expected.

"Is there anything to your story you forgot to tell me? Something you left out?"

"No, sir, that's exactly what happened. Just as I told you."

The sheriff stood up and walked down the long end of the porch with his back turned to Will and Junior. He turned around, faced them, and walked up to Junior but remained standing.

"We have a problem. I caught up with Raymond yesterday and asked him the same question. He told me you started the fire, and he tried to stop you, but you kept him from putting the fire out before it was too late. What do you have to say to that?"

"He's lying. I did not start the fire."

The Sheriff stared at him for a long moment, then said, "The truth will come out in time. It always does. Lord help you if you are lying to me, son. I'm going to get to the bottom of this. In the meantime, you stay put. Chances are I'll need to talk to you again, and probably soon. Goodbye for now." Sheriff Lewis walked over to get on his horse, then rode away.

He looked over at Will, who was giving him a hard stare. "Did you tell the truth?"

"Yes, I did, Will."

Will's eyes twitched a little when he was called by his first name, but his expression soon returned to a slab of granite. Junior couldn't tell if Will doubted his statements or not.

"I'm disappointed with all this, Junior. The Sheriff will do his work. Time will fix things. For now, I want you to work extra hard in the fields. We're diggin' a new water ditch today, and you're going to do most of the diggin'."

He understood why Will wanted him to work extra hard that day, but he felt like he was being punished. He felt like fighting back, but he knew he had no choice. All he could do was keep his head down and grab a shovel.

He worked hard all day, but his bitterness grew throughout

the day. His Mother had just told him Will loved him, but he didn't support him like a real father should. Instead, he was 'disappointed' in him. That was the last straw.

After everyone fell asleep that night, he gathered some of his things and left. Will had promised to track him down if he left, but he knew of several good places to hide that Will didn't even know existed. He was leaving home to start the rest of his life - And now it would be on his terms alone.

Chapter Five

The circus life was hard for those who chose it. It was a constant grind with only a few benefits. Most agreed the best part of a circus life was the traveling. The circus workers visited places they otherwise would never have been able to on their own. The only problem was that most of the time, they were working and never had much time to explore a town and see its sights.

They had precious little free time. They had to set up, rehearse, put on the shows, break down the tents and the booths, then travel to the next town. If management felt there was good business in a town, they would book two shows a day on the weekends the following year and sometimes extend the side shows' regular hours. For those who worked in the circus, doing two shows a day was not a popular option, especially for those who had acts that required a great deal of physical exertion. But, at the end of the day, it was all part of their circus life; they had no choice but to take the good with the bad, and those who lived it wouldn't have it any other way.

Once in a blue moon, the circus workers had a morning or an afternoon of free time. Some older performers would use these rare times to relax in their tents and get some well-deserved rest. For the younger workers, though, it was different. Leisure time was their fun time.

Some of the circus boys had steady circus girlfriends, and these boys loved to show them off. When they had free time, they usually went to a prominent part of their town to unwind. Sometimes, the girls would go shopping. The couples would lead the group, stragglers would tag along, and eventually, they would settle somewhere the locals could see and admire them.

The couples loved to hug, kiss, and otherwise make a scene. Some of the more established couples could sometimes be seen caressing each other. It was all great fun, especially if their antics occasionally upset some of the stuffier old ladies who saw them, because the stuffy ladies made their objections to their raunchy behavior very clear. Getting dirty looks from women with small children also gave the circus crowd a good chuckle.

For the stragglers, especially the boys without girlfriends, a different type of activity took place, a kind of game. They loved to show off by trying to impress the random girl or girls they saw who did not have a boy with them. Each circus boy would try to make the biggest impression on a new girl. The winner earned bragging rights until the next opportunity to show off came around.

He tried to impress a girl once, only once, then he quit for good. It was a disaster.

A pretty girl walked his way, alone and with an attitude. One of the other boys saw her first and put himself where she would have to walk right by him. The boy waited, and as she came close, he said, "Hey there. Want to go to the dance with me?" Everyone knew there was no dance. It was a standard line used by almost all the boys. Sooner or later, someone would come up with a line seen as being a little more clever, which would be the popular thing for everyone to say until someone came up with an even cleverer line that the key players agreed was an improvement over the last. As the girl walked by and heard the boy's sales pitch, she said nothing, smiled and kept walking.

Now, it was his time. He was ready. She was walking his way now, and his chance was near. "Don't listen to him. Go to the dance with me." He said the words, then wished he had sounded more confident. He felt deflated but tried to put up a good front. The girl stopped to look at him. Did she like him? He could feel a bead of sweat running down his cheek and over his face paint. She looked at him and gave him a disgusted look.

"Stay away from me, you circus freak," she shouted, then gave him a hard shove on the shoulder.

The other boys laughed at him for weeks. He left the arena of youth that day, at least for the time being. He had no choice but to put his head down, blend in with the crowd, and observe the flirting action that took place by the other boys. He returned to manning his ticket booth, hid his wounds, and stayed out of trouble. At that time, he didn't know when or even if he would get back in the game.

He was interested in girls. At seventeen years old, he had developed muscles and had some hair on his face. It was his time now for his personal growth with the fairer sex to improve, or at least it should have been his time. Month after month went by, and he did nothing to try to interact with girls. He dreamed about someday being kissed by a girl, but the cycle of abuse that he shared with his father wore him down more and more after each beating. The beatings dominated his life. Someday, things will change for the better, he thought. For now, the only thing new in his life were welts and bruises in different locations on his body. He was not a quitter and looked for another chance with a girl as the weeks and months passed.

It was a break-down day when he saw Rebeca again. She was the daughter of one of the elephant trainers. No one would describe her as being pretty. Most agreed she was homely, and at least partly due to her looks, she had effectively discouraged all the circus boys who had ever approached her. He noticed that she kept sneaking glances at him while he was working. She didn't know that he had been practicing flirting for months with some pretty girls who came to his ticket booth. He had developed a killer smile that sometimes drew a return smile from the girls. He felt good when a girl showed even the slightest interest in him.

He was removing stakes, pulling poles out of the ground, and helping to fold tents. He had been working for about one hour when he realized she was working directly in front of him. When she turned around and saw him, he was ready. He flashed his best killer smile. She smiled back briefly, then nervously lowered her head and turned around. Nothing happened for a few minutes.

"Would you help me lift this board? It's too heavy for me." She said.

"No problem." He was happy to oblige, and afterward, they shared an awkward moment looking at each other.

She patted him on the side of his arm. "Thanks."

The brief encounter with Rebeca was their interaction's beginning and end. By late afternoon, he was back in his tent, lying on his cot, thinking about her. Tomorrow was a traveling day, which was always an easy day. He was in an excellent mood, feeling things were finally going his way. The experience with Rebeca had left him with a new emotion - happiness. He closed his eyes and replayed every moment they had spent together.

With a snap, the flap of his tent swung open, announcing Oscar's presence. That familiar expression was on his face, the one he dreaded above all others. *Not now. Not today.*

"How are you, son?"

"Good."

"I saw you talking to a girl today. Do you think that's wise?"

"We just talked, and not for very long."

His father, Oscar, swung his fist at his face without warning and without showing any of his usual tells. His instincts kicked in, and he narrowly dodged the blow. Another swing came, and again, he dodged it.

His father lost his balance after the second swing, then quickly straightened himself. His face was red, "You're making me angry, boy."

"I'm not a boy anymore, father." He said. From somewhere deep, after years of being beaten by his father, he reacted in a way he never thought he could. He stepped forward and pushed his father hard in the chest with both hands. He surprised himself with this reaction but had no time to think about what he did. His father fell to the floor, rose, and charged at him. His face was even redder now. Once again, he had no time to think about what he should do and could only react to Oscar's charge. He was in full-on self-defense mode. He did his best to dodge the charge, then swung and hit Oscar in the side of the head, knocking him sideways.

It was the first, and as it turned out, the only time he ever hit his father. Oscar began to go down, hit his head on the side of a short wooden dresser, fell to the floor in a heap, and did not move.

"I'm sorry, father. I didn't want to hurt you."

No answer.

He lowered himself onto the edge of his cot and shut his eyes. Images flickered into his mind, only to vanish as swiftly as they had come. His father relentlessly strikes him with the rubber chicken, the blows landing forcefully. Then, just like that, his father disappeared. A pretty girl approached the ticket booth. He smiled at her, and she returned the gesture. Then, she vanished. Other images drifted in and out of his mind, all in shades of black and white.

He tried to remember his mother. All he knew about her was that she was a circus performer. Sometimes, he recalled, she was good to him. She could be kind, but too many times, she was sullen and didn't want to be touched. These times were hard for him. He didn't understand what he was doing wrong that would make her act that way. Try as he might, he couldn't remember her face.

He suddenly realized the sun had gone down, and it was now nighttime. He had somehow lost track of time. Then he remembered what had happened.

Enough moonlight filtered through the tent that he could see his father had not moved since he fell. He was in the same position he had been hours ago, and a pool of black liquid surrounded his head. He stared at his father, disbelieving, for a long time. Eventually, he got up off the cot, knelt, and felt for a pulse. There was none.

He sat back down on his cot again and stared at the floor. His mother appeared in front of him. Her face was strangely blurry. "What have you done? You'll pay for this, son." She vanished. The next thing he knew, it was nearly dawn. He had lost track of time yet again. Feeling dead inside, he grabbed some of his clothes and put them in a bag. He knew where his father kept his money, so he dug it out and put it in his bag. He walked to the front of the tent, opened the flap, carefully looked left and right, and left the circus life forever.

Chapter Six

He picked a direction at random, north, and started walking. It was all new and unfamiliar territory. He had no idea what was over the next rise. He kept walking. Soon, he would need some food and a place to stay. Fortune smiled upon him, and he happened onto a small town. It didn't take him long to find the hotel. It was a typical two-story wooden hotel, and he wanted a room on the ground floor. He walked inside and spoke to the man behind the counter.

"I want a room with a bed. Ground floor, please." He said.

The clerk stared at him. "You need to pay ahead. How long are you here for?"

"One week." He said but didn't know why he said it.

He paid and went to his room in the front corner of the hotel. He collapsed onto the bed and woke up the following day. The room had one window facing the street. He parted the curtains, looked out the window, and noticed a restaurant across the street.

He was starving, so he walked to the restaurant for a hearty breakfast. He ate his breakfast, then paid for it with the only cash he had, a five-dollar bill. The waiter returned and gave him his change, or part of it. He had been short-changed.

"You still owe me. I gave you a five-dollar bill."

"No, you gave me a one-dollar bill."

"Check your register. It was a five."

"You calling me a liar, boy?"

He immediately put his head down and said nothing. It was a habit he had developed over his entire life. The waiter stood there, looked at him momentarily, then left.

Leaving the restaurant, he returned to his room with a hint of panic, a familiar feeling. Though anxious, he managed to think clearly, realizing the need to protect his money from being stolen. Quickly, he drew the curtains shut and started a search for a hiding spot. After some thought, he settled on putting most of his money under the bed, carefully hiding it beneath two loose boards. With a sense of relief, he felt his money was now secure. Later, he grabbed supper across the street before settling in for the night, bracing himself for the usual nightmares that plagued his sleep.

He ended up staying in his room almost all of that week. He had nothing else to do, and there was no one to talk to. He tried to talk to the waiters at the restaurant, even the one who cheated him out of his change, but they were not interested in talking to him.

When he had been at the hotel for one week, it was time for him to either leave the hotel or pay ahead again to stay longer. He wanted to think about it over breakfast. He left his room, walked over to the restaurant to get breakfast, went into the restaurant, and was met by a U. S. Marshall. "You're coming with me, son." He said. He was taken away and put in jail.

Weeks later, he found himself standing trial for the murder of his father. As the proceedings unfolded, the judge determined him to be mentally incapacitated. Consequently, he was sent to the Santa Fe Mental Hospital for further evaluation and treatment.

The mental hospital was a strange place to be. He was surrounded by people who constantly acted very oddly, day after day. For the first time in his life, he did not feel he had to hide his problems from anyone. Sometimes, he wanted to share his thoughts with someone, but he couldn't carry on a serious conversation with any of the other patients. He had a doctor assigned to him who visited him regularly. The guards were approachable, but the amount of communication he received from them was disappointing. Most said nothing to him at all.

He had control of his thoughts most of the time. That was good. He wasn't losing track of time. He liked that. Most of the people there were worse off than him, and he found that to be comforting. His body didn't hurt all the time. He liked that, too.

One patient at the Hospital drew his interest. The man appeared to be completely normal. It didn't make sense. The man never did anything unusual or strange. He waited patiently, and he finally had the chance to talk with him one day. They were both outside for a walk and crossed paths.

He stopped walking, looked at the man, then said, "I can't figure it out. You're not like the others here, are you?"

The man was surprised, but he stopped walking and looked at him. "I'm glad to hear you say that. That makes me feel good. I want to get out of here."

"How did you get in here in the first place?"

"Good question. I was working on the railroad a couple of years ago when they said I froze and couldn't do anything. The job put a lot of pressure on me."

The man hesitated momentarily, then began to open up again, "One day, I curled up in a ball and started crying. I don't know why. I wouldn't let anyone touch me. The next thing I knew, I was in this rat hole. I found out later that there is a way you can get released from here."

"All you have to do is prove that you're normal. You have to prove you're cured and shouldn't be here. I haven't froze up in the two years since I've been at this damn place. This week, I'm supposed to talk to some people and prove to them that I'm cured. I will tell them the solitude and security provided here gave me a new outlook on life."

"Thank you for telling me that. Good luck to you." He said as they began to go their separate ways.

The idea of getting out of the hospital simply by convincing people he was cured sent a jolt through him. He wondered if there was any way he could do the same thing.

Another week came and went, and he began to look everywhere for the same man he had talked to on his walk. He was nowhere to be seen. The man must have gotten out. He was excited and knew what he needed to do next.

He soon found out that acting normal was more challenging than he thought it would be. He had to appear to be unselfish, calm, and otherwise completely normal. He had never spent much time just talking to people before, not really. He had never made small talk with anyone before, never even told someone a joke. Over time and with practice, he became better at acting normally. He kept trying to improve.

Eventually, he found two guards who would listen to him. He practiced with them and asked them to tell him jokes. He did not find any of their jokes funny, but he still tried to remember all of them that he could. He didn't bother trying to tell jokes to any of the other patients.

His regular doctor visited with him for a few minutes each week. The doctor always carried a little book and took notes. Talking with his doctor was especially important, he felt. He didn't want to rush his case. He didn't want to seem to be too needy or too anxious. That would give the wrong impression, and he would need the doctor's help to get out of there, so he tried to be as friendly as possible.

On his last doctor's visit, he asked him, "Someone told me there is a way to prove to the people here that I'm cured and don't need to be here anymore. Is that true?"

His doctor seemed caught off-guard by the question, then said, "There is a way, yes." He consulted his little book, then said, "It might be harder in your case because of the…uh…death of your father."

"That was an accident. I can explain everything."

"Alright, you are eligible to meet with the panel in five months. I'll set you up with them as soon as you become eligible."

This was encouraging, but five months seemed like a very long time from now. "Thank you, doctor." He said. He had no choice, so he resigned himself to five more months of finding new ways to convince people he was normal.

Five months passed slowly. He continued to improve his act. When his time finally came, he found himself sitting in a chair facing four people at a table directly across from him. All four stared at him at the same time. He felt overwhelmed but did his best to stay calm.

"Your doctor said you are petitioning for release from this facility. How are you feeling, in general?" One of them asked.

"I'm much better now. I feel safe here, and I have had a lot of time to think about how to be a better person and get over the things that bothered me in the past."

Another member of the panel spoke, "You stood trial for the murder of your father. Did you kill your father? Do you sometimes think about the day your father died?"

"I did not kill my father. He used to beat me all the time. The day he died, he swung at me, lost his balance, fell, and hit his head. It was an accident."

It was relatively easy for him to say that because most of it was true. He hoped his words would convey honesty to the panel, even though he omitted the part where his father lost his balance after he struck him on the side of his head. It was self-defense, after all.

"I think about that day sometimes. It's a sad memory. I left the circus to clear my head and begin the rest of my life. My life with my father was all I knew, and my whole world up to that day revolved around my father. It seems odd now and hard to explain, but I found out that I didn't know what to do with myself without my father."

"We've talked to the guards about you and got a favorable response. That is in your favor. Please wait in the next room while we discuss your case." He waited outside for a few minutes and was then asked to return to face the panel. The same person who spoke up first before began again.

"Your case is compelling, young man. Your file indicates you appear to have been beaten repeatedly as a child, which is an important factor for us to consider, and we certainly have done that. Your behavior has improved steadily in the time you have spent here. This was also a big factor. Unfortunately, yours is a serious case involving the death of your father, and as a result, your petition for release has been denied. Good luck to you, son."

It felt like another beating, and this time, it hurt as much, if not more. He composed himself, thanked them for their consideration, and returned to his room.

It took him an entire month to recover, and then his doctor

told him he would be eligible to reapply for release in eleven more months. He had no choice but to wait it out.

He liked to go outside to get some fresh air whenever he could. He looked at the trees, watched the leaves fall when they would, listened to the muted sounds of distant conversations, and smelled the clean air after a rain. It felt good and helped him gain some perspective but didn't make time pass any faster.

He watched the other patients as they came and went. One man stood out to him because he reminded him of his father. As the days passed, this patient appeared to be less talkative and more withdrawn until he began to slump his shoulders and started to look like Oscar used to look before he administered a beating. True to form, the man started a fight with the guards several days later. One of the guards was seriously injured. The same thing happened again two months later, and he got an idea.

He carefully watched the man for the next several weeks and then saw the signs that told him it would only be a short time before the man would explode again. He brought this to the attention of both of the guards he talked to regularly. They believed him, passed on the word, and were ready for the attack this time. One of the guards was able to avoid getting injured when the assault came. The man who tried to attack the guard was said to have been put in a holding cell somewhere, and he never saw him again after that.

The seasons came and went, and after a long eleven months of waiting, he was allowed to go in front of the panel again to seek his release. He repeated, almost word-for-word, what he had told them a year ago, that his father died as the result of an accident.

"I understand that earlier this year, you were able to help the guards avoid being assaulted by one of the other patients here. Very commendable."

"Yes, sir. The man acted like my father used to before he would beat me."

"I see. Your behavior has been stellar again this past year. Please wait outside while we discuss your case."

When he returned to the room to face the panel, he was informed that his release petition had been approved. He was further informed that the judge who presided over his murder trial for the death of his father had been contacted earlier that week.

The judge, after consulting with his colleagues, had stated that no further charges would be sought against him related to the death of his father under one condition. The Panel would need to be the ones to release him. The Panel ruled that his father's death was an accident, and decided to release him. He was suddenly a free man. At first, he couldn't believe it and didn't know how to react. He quickly decided to do the same thing he had done for most of his stay there. From now on, he would try to act normally.

The first thing he did after leaving the hospital was to find the same hotel he had stayed in for that one week before he was taken away. He managed to get the same room as before, in the front corner of the hotel. That night, he retrieved the money he had left there and began to think about his next move. He had a pocket full of money, and his future was his, and his alone, to make. He was scared.

Chapter Seven

He paused in the moonlight at the top of the low ridge to look back at his family's cabin. Would this be the last time he would look at it? Probably not. He needed to go, to find his own space, but he knew his mother was right. He had a lot of growing up to do.

He would never forget that moment. After he had walked a good stretch, he stopped and waited for dawn. All his senses seemed to be more alert. The sound his footsteps made was louder and crisper somehow. The sweet smells of the forest as dawn arrived were better that day. The birds had started to wake up, and their chirping was louder and more varied than he could ever remember.

He had started his new life as an adult. It was stimulating at one moment, and just under the surface, it was terrifying. He left in anger, with no plan. He had a bag of clothes and a small amount of money. That's all. His future was unfolding, minute by minute, but he had a growing sense that he should have planned his exodus much better. He was a fledgling adult, at best. His emotions had gotten the better of him. He expected much more from himself.

The family followed a wagon trail, not quite a road, every

Saturday to haul their harvest to the farmer's market and at other times during the week. Their wagon made two shallow ruts in the grass as it passed over it, loaded down with people and vegetables. He saw the occasional horse droppings between the ruts as he walked.

He was making his way in life now, so he moved away from the wagon trail, ten or fifteen yards to the side, where he still had an easy walk. It felt good.

As he approached town, he saw an acquaintance out for his morning walk. He was an older man, maybe fifty years old. He had stopped to talk with the man more than once before, when Junior was on his wandering journeys around town. The man was easy to talk with and seemed to understand and support him in the past.

"Morning."

"Morning, Junior. Where are you off to so early this morning?"

"Just out for a walk."

"I see. You have a travel bag with you, too." The man eyed him up and down, and Junior thought that the man somehow knew exactly what he was doing.

"You okay?" The man asked.

"Yeah."

"Be careful out there. You need any help, just come see me – You here?"

"Thanks. I'm good. Enjoy your walk."

At that moment, Junior knew he could make it work. It was easy for him to make friends. He would use that to his advantage somehow. Right now, he had no food and no shelter. He needed to fix that, and fast. He could do that if he put his mind to it.

The most important thing for him was to get off to a good start. He needed a base camp, regular food, and at least a small, regular income. This would provide him with a minimum amount of stability in his new life. He could build upon that, and things would get better, gradually. He was confident he could make it work. All he had to do was keep trying, keep learning, and make new friends along the way.

Junior continued heading west towards town. He wasn't worried about the man telling anyone which direction he was headed. When he was out of sight, he would change direction and go confront Raymond.

Junior approached Raymond's house. He knew they had no dog and only one old horse. When he entered the barn, he was immediately hit with the foul odor of a barn that had been neglected for far too long. He didn't know how Raymond could tolerate it.

Junior thought about breakfast, knowing he wouldn't receive a warm meal that day. He observed Raymond's father leaving for work through the cracks in the barn walls. Junior found the man's predictable routine joyless and resolved never to let his life fall into such a monotonous pattern.

Raymond emerged from the house shortly after his dad left and, as Junior suspected, headed straight for the barn. Junior had seen him riding his old horse around town before. He waited off to one side of the barn and confronted Raymond as soon as he entered.

"Morning, you lying son of a bitch."

"Are you talking to yourself again, Junior?"

"I thought you were my friend. Then you told the sheriff I started the fire."

"You don't understand, do you?"

"I understand the sheriff came to my house yesterday, thinking I was an arsonist."

Raymond noticed his bag filled with clothing. "Did you leave home to become a full-time wanderer? No one will pay you a wage for that, you know."

"That's none of your business. You need to explain yourself."

"There is a simple explanation. Most people would understand it right away. Maybe I should write it down so you don't forget it?"

No response.

"OK, here it is. I knew you would blame me, so I blamed you. No one saw us. The Sheriff has no way of knowing which of us started the fire, and they never will unless one of us admits to it. Simple, right? I won't admit to anything, and I know you aren't going to either. By blaming you, we both become innocent. Do you understand now?"

"Your thinking is twisted. You're twisted. You dragged me into your mess. I don't like being under suspicion from the sheriff."

"You blamed me for it. You just said so, and you claim to be my friend? Anyway, it's unfortunate, I know. It's not the best situation now. I've had some bad experiences with the Sheriff before and needed a new way to throw him off my track this time. You shouldn't be complaining – it worked, or at least it has worked so far..."

"Do you have any other friends besides me?" Junior asked.

"I know plenty of people, but you're my best friend, I must admit."

"It's easy to make friends, but you're never going to keep friends if you use them like you used me to get you out of the mess you made."

"I can't argue with that. I…I'm sorry. As you know, I'm inexperienced with fire and had no idea the whole saloon would burn down, which was never my intention. Next time, I hope I can do a better job."

"Next time? Next time? You haven't learned anything, have

you? People told me you were trouble, and I've always defended you. Your idea of fun seems to be to destroy things."

"It hasn't been fun for me, not at all. You don't know everything that has happened. They found the metal pry bar in the wreckage, and yesterday, the Sheriff came here and asked my father if he owned one. He said he did, and when he went to get it and show it to the Sheriff, it wasn't there, of course. The sheriff asked him about it, and my father said he had forgotten something. He said he had loaned it out to someone last year, but he couldn't remember who he loaned it to. The sheriff had no choice but to leave. I was worried for a while there."

He knew Will would never lie for him like Raymond's father did, but he needed to think about that later, when he wasn't so tired, to figure out how he felt about it. Will would have told the sheriff the truth. Was that a good thing or a bad thing?

"You're twisted, Raymond, and until you recognize that and straighten out, I don't want anything more to do with you."

"What a little girl you are. You run away from the slightest problem."

"Leave. Now. Stay away from me."

"Alright. Goodbye, Junior." Raymond saddled his horse and left.

He needed to get some rest. He considered his options and proceeded to the location along Granite Creek up north. He had partial shelter there, at least. It was far away from town, about another five miles, and no one would think to look for him there, especially Will.

Chapter Eight

1883

Arizona Territory

He could have used his real name, but wanted to live under an assumed name. He was a free man, after all, cleared by the authorities. He didn't expect to ever run into any people from his past. No, he would take on an assumed name because he needed a clean cut from his childhood. He had the opportunity to become whoever he wanted to be, so he changed his name and made a fresh start, at least he hoped to.

He chose a new first name, Tim, because that was the name of the man at the mental hospital who showed him how he could leave there by petitioning the panel. He was partial to the name. He chose White as his new last name because it represented a clean slate. He was still young and hopeful that he could build a normal life. Maybe he would start to feel better someday. Maybe his hatred would subside.

Just below the surface lived another reality that he was very familiar with. It dominated all of his thoughts. His anger was fierce, and Mr. Tim White would have difficulty keeping it under control.

Most of his thoughts were about administering justice to those who had it coming. He was used to taking a beating but not very good at giving out one. He wished that he were better. He knew there were children out there suffering, and he wanted to save the ones who were in dire distress. He deserved some satisfaction, some success.

Unfortunately, his initial efforts would be failures, resulting in him moving from town to town each time. He first settled in a newly established small town. He liked living in a small town because life was simple, and the new Mr. White needed peace and quiet. This first town worked well for him for a couple of weeks.

He was restless and decided to go to a saloon. He figured that would be the place where he would blend in the best. He ordered his first whiskey and was savoring the last sip when someone pushed him hard in the back, spilling his whiskey. His glass fell to the floor and shattered. He stood up and turned around to see who had pushed him.

"I am very sorry, my friend." The man behind him said. He was serious at first, then he started to smile and then laugh. "Did your puppy just die?" He said as he began to laugh harder.

Tim became angry and hit the drunken man in the face, which caused him to collapse on the floor. This created a big scene, and he was soon escorted out the door.

It felt good to hit the man, but lashing out angrily, he knew it was not a smart move. People in this little town would talk. He would have an uphill fight now to be seen as being normal because of his actions in the saloon. The wisest course of action for him now was to move on, seek a fresh start elsewhere, and try again.

Tim found another small town to try out and was able to make this one last longer than the first one. He found it hard to blend in but still avoided the saloons. Someone suggested that he say 'Hello' to the people he met. He liked the idea and started saying "Hello" to people he met on the street. One day, he went for a walk and ran into his neighbor, who he knew from previous encounters to be very unfriendly.

"Don't talk to me." His neighbor said when he saw Tim.

"Hello," Tim said out of habit.

The surly neighbor began to insult Tim. When he was finished, the man pushed him to the side to get by. Tim took the abuse, but that night, he had a dream where he soundly whipped his neighbor with a stick. The next morning, he knew what he had to do.

Tim laid out his plan and surprised his neighbor when he was out for a walk.

The man looked surprised at his presence and said, "You again?"

Tim was holding a branch behind his back. As he brought it forward, the man saw it and reacted. Tim was immediately made aware that he was standing too close to his neighbor when he received a punch in the nose that sent him sprawling backward. He put his hand up to his nose as he fell and was sure it was broken. Tim found himself flat on his back, looking up at the angry man, who moved sideways and picked something up off the ground. Tim thought about his whipping stick. Where was it? Then he saw it. Tim absorbed another beating.

It took him a full week to recover, so he used that time to consider his future. He had to leave again because the situation with his neighbor would only worsen. He packed up all his belongings and left at first light one day in search of the next town.

If he became involved in another fight in the next town, which deep down he knew that he would - a part of him wanted it more and more now - he would have to be smarter next time. His frustration consumed him. He needed to satisfy his rage. He didn't deserve a clean slate. The time had come to fight back and win.

He moved to Bisbee, Arizona, in the southern part of the territory. It was a hilly and surprisingly pleasant place to live. The ground sloped steeply in most places. Many of the buildings had to be carved into the sides of small hills, and as a result, most of the homes and businesses were two-story buildings built to save on construction costs.

It was a quaint town in a small mountain range that provided an above-average climate for the area. Once outside the mountain range, it was a barren and bleak desert.

Tim began to realize that he had another problem. Each day, he became more isolated and withdrawn. He had no friends or family, like normal people did. His problem was that he didn't know how to make friends, and he doubted that he ever would.

Tim was not religious, but as time went on, he began to feel he was only one player in a much larger endeavor, one he didn't fully understand yet. He didn't have to feel normal because he finally realized that he was special. He was on the side of justice - righting wrongs.

Sometimes, he tried to deny it, but he had committed himself to righting wrongs and, as a result, was no longer in control of his life. He wasn't the one in charge, the one who gave the signals and pushed the buttons. He was merely a soldier for justice. He did what he was supposed to do to deliver the final punishment for those who deserved it. There would be no debate, no going back, and little remorse.

He was halfway through eating his lunch at a restaurant in town when he saw them. A plain-looking man came in with his wife and son. He saw the signs on the boy. Thoughts meshed in his brain. He wondered who gave him so many opportunities to right these wrongs.

His next assignment had presented itself. He took it as a good sign that it was such a clear and pleasant day when it happened. He dawdled with his food and then ordered another coffee. When the troubled man left with his family, he waited a moment, then followed. Following people without being noticed was a new skill he had mastered.

Tim followed the father and the boy as they walked down the main street in town, turned onto a side street, up a hill, and entered a large, expensive-looking home. Tim thought they must live in one of the best homes in town. How did they get so fortunate? Who did they have to hurt to be able to live there? Sinful people can prosper, but not forever. Sooner or later, they would have to pay for their ways.

He went into disguise for the next three days and followed the man. The man had a routine, and Tim had a plan. There was a saloon on the corner of the main street in town and the side street that led to the man's extravagant home. He would wait for the man there. His disguise was a simple one. He sat outside the saloon and pretended to be a drunk, trying to sleep it off. He kept one eye open all the while. Tim was willing to start early and finish late - whatever it took. A dedicated soldier took no half-measures.

For this man, his routine was to take walks at dawn each day, then go back to his monument of a home. The man walked on the opposite side of the street from where he sat. Nevertheless, he varied his costume every day to avoid arousing suspicion. On the third day, after the man returned to his ill-gotten and lavish home, Tim walked around the area and spotted a good location for justice to be delivered the following morning.

He was in place and ready, sitting on the opposite side of the street from where he had sat the three previous days, across from a narrow alley. He sat and waited. It was dawn, and the man was walking his way. The man hesitated slightly when he saw Tim, then sped up to get past him. Tim timed it perfectly, rose, and pushed the man into the narrow alley.

"What's wrong with you? Let me go."

"Too many people have already let you go."

"What?"

Tim stepped towards the man and, with one smooth motion, took out his club and struck the man across his face. There was a crack, and the man's face became covered in blood. He put his hands up to his face but remained standing. Tim hit him on the face again, and he went down and stopped moving. He hit him several more times, all over, until his job was done. He then went to the entrance of the alley and looked around.

An older man walked quickly from the tormentor's big house and headed straight towards him. It was time to run. He ran out of the alley, then onto the side street, and turned down the main street. Instead of stopping to check on the beaten man like he expected him to, he looked back and saw that the older man had kept moving, turned the corner, and was now following him. Tim was a fast runner and younger than his pursuer, but the man behind him looked possessed.

They ran up hills, down hills, straight out of town, and into the hills beyond. As he ran, he saw only the occasional large bush or small tree that he would be able to hide behind. He kept running, periodically looking over his shoulder to see where the man was. The man was slowly falling behind but not giving up. Tim kept running for twenty, thirty, forty minutes. Eventually, he was far enough ahead of the man to where he could stop to hide behind a tree and wait. He stopped, tried to control his breathing, pulled his club out, and watched.

It was not part of his plan - his assignment - to hurt the older man, someone he knew nothing about. There would be no justice in that unless, of course, he was forced to defend himself. Then he would have no choice.

A few minutes later, his pursuer came into view. He was barely running but wasn't stopping. The man looked left and right, searching for him. Tim crouched behind the tree and watched the man run past him and over the hill. When he was entirely out of sight, Tim began to run back into town towards his rented home.

He made it back safely. His mission was accomplished, but it could easily have been a disaster. Next time, he would have to be much more careful. He would need to have at least two good escape routes planned.

Tim remained in town for two more weeks and stayed out of sight as much as he could. He was surprised when he read in the newspaper that the man who he punished was expected to survive his beating, but he would be blinded for life. The man who chased after Tim turned out to be the beaten man's father.

Tim was glad the blind man could no longer beat his son. The newspaper article went on to quote the man's father as saying he would not rest until the man who attacked his son was found and prosecuted to the fullest extent. It was time for Tim to leave - again. The following morning, he left town disguised as a hunched-over old man with a long beard. He was headed to Casa Grande, Arizona.

Casa Grande was another small town, but unlike Bisbee, it was located in a flat part of the desert, and it was hot there. He decided he could cope with the heat and rented a place in town. He was not there for very long. He was in Casa Grande for a few weeks, laying low and mostly staying inside his house, when he decided it was time to go out to a restaurant and enjoy himself a little.

When he came home from eating supper at the restaurant and approached his house, someone caught his eye. It was the father of the blind man from Bisbee, hiding and watching Tim's front door. He had a gun.

A club was no match for a gun, and he didn't even have his club with him. It was inside the house. What a close call he just lived through. If he had not gone for supper and were still inside and happened to come outside for any reason, he knew the man would have shot him dead.

He turned around and left to find a safe place outside of town to wait out the old man. When it was later in the morning but not yet dawn, he returned to his rental house and cautiously approached. The man with the gun was gone. Tim went inside, packed his things, and left. He was well out of town when he finally relaxed and enjoyed the new dawn, tired but alive.

The man knew his name and could follow him to the next town again. He did not want to underestimate this man. If he followed him from Bisbee, he could follow him again. The only solution was not what he wanted, but he had to do it. He had no choice. He would be forced to change his name. His journey would continue with him using a different name. He had heard about a quiet little town up north called Prescott. A calm, peaceful town was just what he needed.

Chapter Eight Point Five

The man who had previously called himself Tim was at the general store in Prescott, getting some supplies. The vegetables they sold there were always fresh and tasty. They had good quality meat there but a little expensive, so he rarely bought any meat there.

He turned the corner to enter a new aisle and saw a boy standing in the middle of the aisle. The boy looked disoriented and like he was about to cry. Right away, he noticed the boy had bruises on his face and neck. He tensed when he saw the marks on the boy.

He approached the boy and asked, "Would you like some candy?" The boy looked up at him, fidgeted, said nothing, then nodded yes. He led the boy to the front of the store and let him pick out two candies. The boy put one of the candies in his mouth and smiled. He wondered if it was the first time the boy had ever tasted candy.

"What are ya doin' there, Mister?"

He turned to see the angry, distorted face of someone who must have been the boy's father. He immediately disliked him and said, "I bought him some candy."

"You stay away from him. I'm his father, and I'm tryin' to raise him good. I don't know ya. Who are ya?"

He said nothing and continued to look at the brutish man standing before him, disliking him more and more every second.

"Stay away from my boy." The man finally said.

The brute paid for his purchases and left the store with the boy in tow. He followed the two out and watched as they walked down the street.

"Throw it away."

"But father…" The brute slapped the boy on the side of his head hard enough that it knocked him down to his knees.

"You do what I say ya to do, boy."

The boy stood up slowly, put his hand up to his mouth, threw something to the ground, and continued walking with his dad. After the two had walked ahead, he walked up to where they had been and saw the pieces of candy the boy had been forced to toss. This brutish new Oscar was being very mean today. Don't be so mean, like my father was to me for so many years. The man and the boy walked the rest of the way home. He followed them.

The following day, he watched the father leave the house about an hour after sunrise, probably to go to work. He needed to learn their habits. He stayed and watched for another couple of hours. The father didn't return that morning, and the boy never left the house. He witnessed the same thing the next day. The father left, didn't return that morning, and the boy never came out of the house.

He couldn't seem to get away from it. Everywhere he went, evil men wanted to ruin their son's lives. Men like his own dad, Oscar, were everywhere. This man knocked his son down right in the middle of the street because he ate a piece of candy. It made his blood boil. He wasn't sleeping right. He needed to punish this brute, and soon.

He continued to watch the man and observed the route he used to walk to work. Every day, the man went through a stretch of forest about fifty yards deep to get to work. It would work well for what he had in mind. The following day, he was waiting in the forest. His disguise was one of a professional man, like an attorney or a banker. He saw the new Oscar walking his way.

When the man was close, he casually moved from hiding and approached the brute, whose reaction was predictable. In his disguise, he looked out of place for the forest, and he wanted to look non-threatening to him. The man said nothing and seemed very confused. He gave the man his killer smile, and this time he meant it.

The brute looked even more confused. He walked up to him, put his hand behind his back, grabbed his club, and clubbed this new Oscar in his well-practiced motion. The brute never had a chance.

Father Donovan was at his church in Prescott that evening. He was content with himself for several reasons. His Mass was one of the better ones he had given in recent memory. The congregation seemed to be genuinely moved. They left looking exceedingly pious and seemed very happy to be Catholic. His Bible study group was well attended, and his confessions were very productive.

His last confession of the day yesterday seemed especially memorable because it bothered him some. He kept coming back to it in his thoughts. Once again, he replayed it in his mind.

"Bless me, Father, for I have sinned. It has been many months since my last confession."

"Please continue."

"I had to punish Oscar again. He was very mean."

"We must be careful when punishing others. The punishment must be just and fair. Punishing someone unfairly is a sin. You must seek to change bad behavior with grace and dignity. Ask yourself, 'What would Jesus do in this situation? ' Were your actions such that you feel you properly changed the behavior of the one you punished?"

"Yes."

"How do you feel now? Why do you feel the need for forgiveness?"

"I feel sad. I wish he had not been so mean. I wish it had never happened."

"Talk to this Oscar the next chance you get. Show him you are there for him as a friend. Let him know you realize you are his equal and not his superior. Lavish praise on him for any improvements you witness - that is, if he acts…less mean, as you described. Does this Oscar come to Church here? I don't recognize the name."

"I don't know."

"I want you to pray for his soul."

"Yes, Father."

"Be careful in the future, my son. Be careful not to punish others too much, lest you also be punished. Remember what it says in the bible, in the scriptures of Mark, 'For all who draw the sword will die by the sword.' "Violence begets violence, remember. Now you are renewed in Christ. Go peacefully."

"Thank you, Father."

What caused the father to think about this confession was what happened at the end. He was almost positive the man mumbled, no, nearly hissed, something as he left the confessional, something like, "Yes, Father, violence begets violence. Father knows." He could only hope that the man didn't mean what he thought he meant.

Chapter Nine

Dusk began to settle on the quiet town of Prescott the following day. Most people were at home, settled in, trying to spend the last few hours of the day peacefully with their families. An old man slowly drove a wagon up the street, wheels crunching on the hardscrabble road, until it stopped in front of the church. He got off the wagon, rummaged through a toolbox, and pulled out a small hammer. With a pronounced limp, painful to watch, he walked around the wagon to the front wheel, positioned directly across from the front of the church.

There were a couple of people on the street, but no one paid much attention to the crippled old man fixing his wagon. Tap, tap, then silence. After a minute, tap, tap, tap. The old man limped back awkwardly to the other side of his wagon, put the hammer back in the toolbox, climbed back onto the wagon, and drove away.

Father Donovan's living quarters were in the back of the church. People of the congregation who needed to talk with him later in the day knew to knock on his back door if the front door was locked. These visits were rare, but those who felt the need to visit him at odd hours generally had serious problems, and he would never turn them away. He was almost sure that his work was done for the day. It was evening now, and soon, he would retire to his quarters for the night and do some Bible reading in his room.

Each night, Part of his routine was to walk outside the church to clean up any debris that might have accumulated during the day. Sometimes, he ran into a misguided soul who needed a night in jail to sober- up. He opened the front door and walked outside to make his rounds.

The moment he stepped outside the front door and saw the corpse, he started to yell. The body was on its back. There was dried blood on the arms, torso, and legs. His skin was ashen, and his face was beaten so badly it was nearly unrecognizable. It was the most horrible thing he had ever seen.

"Help. Help." He squeaked out, barely audible. He cried out for help again, this time a little louder. A man came up to the small covered porch at the front of the church, saw the body, put his hand over his mouth, and then stepped back. "Good Lord, what happened here, Father?"

"I don't know. I was getting ready to lock up for the day and found him here. This is terrible, simply terrible."

"What should we do?"

"I…I don't know. We should get the Sheriff."

"I'll go fetch him. He should be looking for drunks at the whiskey bars about now."

"Go then, please. I'll stay here."

The man left, and the priest sat down on the porch. He put his head in his palms and sobbed quietly. "Who would do something like this? Why would someone leave the body here?" Father Donovan avoided looking directly at the dead man for the rest of the evening.

Junior was hungry. He left home without a plan and was now paying for that mistake. He was in trouble. He did not bring any food from home with him when he left. He briefly considered stealing food somewhere but put that option out of his mind. It was too risky, and he wasn't that desperate yet. There were only two workable options left for getting help. Charley would always be there to help him, and asking Raymond for help was also possible.

He didn't want to be found, and if he went to Charley for help, it wouldn't be much longer before he returned home with his parents. He was no beggar and would not take food from strangers. Asking Raymond for help was the only way.

This pained him greatly since dealing with Raymond meant the possibility of being drawn back into his world when he was starting to get away from it and because he had recently told Raymond to stay away from him. Eventually, his stomach overruled everything else, and Junior returned to visit Raymond.

It was a good five miles from his hiding spot to Raymond's house, and he had to start walking well before dawn, which was dangerous. He avoided areas where he knew rattlesnakes would be - low areas with ground cover, rock piles, and fallen trees were typical locations for snakes. Junior walked slowly to avoid tripping, falling, or running into the occasional cactus.

He made the trip without incident and entered Raymond's family barn thirsty, starving, and tired. It still stunk in there, which Junior found strangely familiar and comforting. Soon, Raymond's father left for work, and Raymond walked over to the barn and entered.

"Raymond, it's me."

"What are you doing here?" Raymond said as he looked Junior

over. "You don't look so good. I thought you never wanted to see me again."

"I still don't, but I didn't think things through when I left home. I have no food."

"Was I the first person you asked for help?"

"You were near the top of my list."

"Long list, then? Having trouble keeping friends, are you?"

"Look, it doesn't matter. I need your help."

"My poor, weary, hungry friend - You're desperate, right?"

He didn't need the sarcasm, but he was in no position to make a fuss about it. Junior looked at Raymond but had nothing left to say.

"I'll get you enough food for a meal now, and while I'm out today, I'll pick up enough supplies to last you for the next few days. Of course, you'll owe me a favor, and you can't stay here."

"I'll leave tonight as soon as it gets dark. Don't worry, I'll figure out what to do after that."

"I'll be back in a minute."

Raymond re-entered the barn, left him some food, and then rode off for his daily adventures. Junior had no idea where Raymond went every day, but that was the last thing on his mind. He ate his meal with gratitude, found a spot in the smelly barn to rest, and fell asleep.

"Wake up, you vagabond. Your provisions are here."

He woke up quickly and saw Raymond standing before him, holding up a bag. When he looked inside, he saw plenty of dried beef, some biscuits, a few jars full of various foods, and even some string he could use to make traps for small animals.

"I won't forget this."

"I won't let you. Try to stay out of trouble." Raymond turned around and left.

When darkness came, he grabbed his bag and carefully left the barn. There was only one street to walk down before he was out of town. He needed to walk past the cemetery, the Catholic church, and then past a few houses. After that, he would be in the clear.

He walked past the cemetery and noticed people gathered around the church's front porch. It was strange. Two oil lanterns lit up the church porch. He slowed down and tried to walk in the shadows.

"Hello, Junior." He froze, then watched as the Sheriff walked out from behind the corner of the building ahead of him. "What are you doing here?"

"Just walking."

"You weren't just walking. You were trying to hide. You walked in the shadows like you didn't want anyone to see you. I heard you ran away from your family, which may explain why you didn't want to be seen. My question is the same: Why are you here at this moment?"

"No reason. Just am."

"What's in the bag?"

He handed the bag to the Sheriff, who looked inside and said, "Mostly food. Did you pay for this with your own money?"

He lied to Will about the fire, which got him into more trouble. He didn't want to lie again, so he said nothing.

"Cat got your tongue, eh? Listen, Junior, there was a murder here tonight, across the street, in front of the church. Right now, I have no witnesses, no motive, and no murder weapon. You're the only suspicious person I've seen around here, making you the closest thing to a suspect I have. I will ask you again, "Why are you here, and why now?"

He didn't want the Sheriff to know he had just come from Raymond's barn. He was sure the saloon fire incident was still being investigated. Both he and Raymond blamed each other for starting the fire. He put his head down and once again said nothing.

"All right, I don't see you as a murderer, Junior, but I've been surprised before. Sometimes, the most obvious answer is the correct answer. I'm putting you in jail until I figure out what happened tonight."

For Junior, this was the nadir of his life so far, which now officially turned into horseshit.

Chapter Ten

It was not the good start he wanted. In a short period of time, he was forced to ask Raymond for food, and now he was locked up in jail. At least he would be fed in jail. He sat on his bed, with its thin mattress, and looked around. Sheriff Lewis had left him his bag of provisions.

A pot was sitting in one corner, and an oak chair was sitting in the other corner. The floor was wood, elevated from the ground by a few inches; he couldn't tell exactly how high off the ground it was. The walls were brick, and the ceiling was wood. There were two small, barred ventilation openings on the back wall near the ceiling of each cell.

He wanted to be treated like an adult, and now he was. He had a grown-up type of problem, and the only thing he did wrong was to be at the wrong place at the wrong time. Fair to him? No. Not at all. He tried to imagine what kind of home-spun advice Will would give him now, but he couldn't come up with anything. It wouldn't be too long now, maybe today, the next day, or the next, before Will and Cora would visit him here. Unless they caught the real killer, that is, which he seriously doubted since the sheriff told him he was the only suspect he had for the murder. He laid down to think things over, and soon he was asleep.

The next morning, he woke up and looked at his surroundings again. There were two cells in the rear of the building where he was. The cell opposite him was presently empty. On the other side of the bars that locked him in was a shallow open area in front of both cells and a solid wall beyond that. A door in the middle separated the two jail cells from the Sheriff's Office in the front.

Junior was looking at the front office door when it opened, and Sheriff Herman Lewis entered the cell area. He had a chair with him and used it to sit across from Junior.

"You've had some time to think about things now. Are you ready to explain what you were doing out there last night?"

"There's nothing to explain. I was walking when you stepped out in front of me and started asking me questions."

"So that's all you have to say? While you were out on your walk, did you happen to see anything unusual?"

"No, nothing."

"You know, Junior, no one knows you are here right now. I plan on telling your parents today, and word will gradually spread. People will think you must have done something wrong since you are in jail. Make sense? You could earn a bad reputation in a hurry for no reason other than not telling me everything. It would be better for you if you told me the truth now. The longer you wait, the less you will be believed, and the tougher things will get for you."

"I wish I had something to tell you."

The sheriff stood up, took his chair, and left the cell area. Before he left, he looked back at Junior and said, "Yell out when you are ready to talk." He closed the door to the front office behind him.

Junior understood what the sheriff was doing and didn't fault him for it. Being locked up was harder than he thought it would be, though. Being there, where so many offenders had been before him, was starting to weigh on him.

It would be so simple to take the easy way out. He could easily devise a lie that would get him out of jail. He knew he could outsmart most people. Once he got out of the cell and away from the sheriff, he could easily be the one in charge, the one in control. He wondered if he should make up a story and then have a 'talk' with Sheriff Lewis. He would be ready if it came to that.

Soon, he would be talking to Will and Cora. They would stare back at him with questioning, doubting looks and ask him tough questions.

He began to plan what to say to Will and Cora. He didn't kill anyone, and he would tell them that first. Then he would tell them he was hungry, needed food, and was coming from a friend's house after getting some food when he walked by the church. He would show them his bag.

He was sure that Raymond's name would come up, but he would neither offer it up nor refuse to answer questions about him if asked. Hopefully, they would understand that he didn't explain to the sheriff what he was doing in the area at the time because he had just talked with Raymond.

What he wanted to say, and what he hoped they would accept, was that he would make his new life work. He would redeem himself somehow after getting off to such a rocky start to his new life as an adult. He would make it up to them for any embarrassment he caused them by being put in jail. He knew, right down to his core, that he could do almost anything he set his mind to.

It would never be the same for him if his brothers saw him

here, a common prisoner in a jail cell. He wasn't sure they would understand what was going on, and they would never respect him the same if they saw him here. Junior lay on his bed, put his arm over his eyes, and tried to imagine he was somewhere else besides where he was.

He woke up from his nap in a light sweat. The troubled sleep he got didn't help him much. He dreaded the moment his family would walk through the door and see him sitting in his jail cell.

He waited all day, but no one came to visit him, and he was relieved. It was time for him to do something drastic. He needed to be the one controlling his own future, and from that need, his plan began to form.

He looked at the wooden floor, then got up and walked-around on it. He grabbed the chair and tried to twist it. Then, he tried to get more sleep before the sheriff left for the evening.

He knew Sheriff Lewis worked at night. Raymond told him once that the sheriff's last duty of the day was to check the saloons downtown to see if anyone needed to be hauled away for excessive drinking and troublemaking.

After night fell, he heard the sheriff leave the office twice, then come back. He was in the office for about an hour after that when he heard the sheriff go out again. Junior suspected he had started his last patrol of the night.

Later, the door opened, and the sheriff came in. He was both holding up and dragging a drunken man into the empty jail cell. The man looked so far gone Junior didn't think he even knew where he was.

"Visitor for you, Junior. He'll be throwing- up before long. I'll clean it up in the morning. Enjoy your time together." Sheriff Lewis opened the cell and put the man on the bed. He walked out of the cell and locked it. Before he left, he looked over at him.

Junior put his head down and didn't look back. The drunken man reeked of alcohol. Junior hoped he would get used to the smell soon, but he didn't think so, especially if the man threw up.

Junior waited several minutes to make sure the sheriff wasn't coming back. He heard nothing, then looked at the drunk in the cell next to him, who seemed to have blacked out. He needed to see if breaking out of this jail was possible.

He picked up the chair, raised it above his head, and tried to smash it on the floor. The chair held firm. He was sure the noise from this traveled far into town. He waited, heard no response from outside, and this time slammed the chair down onto the floorboards as hard as he could. The chair broke into two main pieces, including several smaller pieces of wood and a few nails. Again, he waited but heard nothing outside of his cell. The drunk in the next cell did not move at all.

Junior needed to pry up one floorboard. Then he could use that board as leverage to pry up as many other boards as he needed to allow him to dig a hole under the floor and the wall foundation.

He needed to loosen the first board and pull it up. He thought he could use a sliver of hardwood to pry a board on both sides, back and forth, until the floorboard was loose. This didn't work because the sliver of wood he used was too thin and broke.

He sat and stared at the floor and at what he had to work with and came up with another idea. He took another sliver of wood, put it in a gap between two floorboards, tapped it, and then pounded it down using a large portion of the broken chair. He pounded more slivers of wood into the gap.

He planned to use the wood slivers as wedges to shift the board side-to-side, loosening its nails gradually in the process. Carefully, he worked the slivers out and moved them to the other side of the board, then pounded them down. Junior repeated this process many times, moving the slivers from side to side. For several minutes, he wasn't sure if it would work, but he stuck with his plan. Eventually, his efforts paid off. The floorboard loosened, and he could use a larger piece of wood from the chair to easily pry it free.

He pried and pulled four more floorboards loose, using the one floorboard he had just removed, and then evaluated his next step. Cross-beams were held up by short posts sitting on flat rocks. The short posts were easy to kick out, and the cross-beams eventually were no match for his determination.

He heard the man in the cell next to him throw- up, so he stopped and looked over at him. The man didn't seem to realize that Junior was in the next cell, and then he blacked out again. No trouble there.

Now he was ready to start digging. He could use the back of the old chair to scoop out the dirt from his side of the wall, dig under the jail wall's foundation, and eventually remove the dirt from the other side of the wall. Then he would be outside.

He paused for a minute to take a breather. A lot of ground needed to be moved, and the dirt was dense and full of little rocks. He was the only one in the downtown area making any noise at this hour, so he tried to be as quiet as possible and hoped some roving, curious night owl would not happen to be in his immediate area and sound the alarm.

After several hours of digging, Junior had a hole deep enough and wide enough that he hoped he could wiggle through it and out to the other side. He took another break and looked around. He had made a mess of his cell and caused some damage. He looked at the cell next to him and was surprised to see the drunk awake and looking at him with a blank expression.

"Good morning." Junior offered.

"Mornin'. Looks like you're breakin' out. That about it?"

"Yeah."

"Why'd they put you in here, anyway?"

"They suspected me of doing something I didn't do."

"Innocent, huh? They'll be pissed at you for wreckin' their jail, so you're guilty of that, at least."

"I'll make it up to them."

"My head hurts. Take care, son, and try not to make too much noise." The man laid back down and seemed to fall asleep again instantly. Junior gathered himself before attempting to leave his cell.

He started on his back, head first, and made some progress. It became very uncomfortable. He realized he would have to remove more dirt from the outside of the wall before he could get out.

After another hour's work, he was ready to try again. He grabbed the bag of provisions Raymond had given him, tossed it ahead in the hole, and worked his way out of the jail. He was free.

Once outside, he stood up and stretched, then took inventory. He had many cuts, scratches, and bruises. He was filthy. His hands had at least two cuts that were still bleeding. He would have plenty of time to clean up later. Junior had a five-mile walk to his hiding place near Granite Creek. It was time to get moving. It would be daylight soon. He wasn't sure how he felt about what he had done, but at least he was starting fresh again. Maybe he'd find some luck this time.

Chapter Eleven

One day earlier

Will snored all night, and Cora did not sleep well - not because of Will's snoring but because she was worried about Junior. Dawn was approaching, so she quietly slipped out of bed, put on her robe, and went to the kitchen. She made some coffee and sat down at the table. Paul walked in a few minutes later, rubbing his eyes, and sat opposite her.

"Morning Paul. You're up early."

"Couldn't sleep. Any leftover biscuits?"

"I think so." Cora got up, grabbed two biscuits, put them on a plate, and sat them down before Paul. He put some jam on his first biscuit and started to eat it, then paused.

"Where did Junior go?"

"I understand that he went to help a family build a barn. He'll be back in a few days."

"Why did he leave in the middle of the night?"

"I don't know. That's his way now, it seems. I'm sure he'll have an explanation for it when he gets back."

Lee walked in and sat down without comment. A few minutes later, Will came in, poured himself some coffee, and sat down.

"Who called this meetin'?" Will asked.

"No one. Us Martins think alike, I guess." Answered Cora. "I'm going to make breakfast so you men can get to work." After breakfast, Will and Lee went out to work in the fields.

After lunch, Will and Cora went out to the porch to talk. "Great lunch, Cora," Will said as he sat down on a porch chair.

"Thank you."

Will was strict about only taking a half-hour off work for lunch, so Cora always ensured lunch was ready on time so they could still have time to sit on the porch. Sitting on the porch each day was the reward they gave to themselves.

They earned it with their hard work. Ten or fifteen minutes after lunch, an hour or so after supper, it was their free time to enjoy each other's company. They did whatever they wanted to do in these times - talked, said nothing, held hands, argued - whatever they wanted.

Cora mentioned that her friend Sharlot gave her some seeds for a new variety of tomatoes to experiment with. Sharlot traveled to California occasionally and usually brought back some seeds with her to give to Cora. He stopped listening with any interest when he heard the word 'tomato' because growing tomatoes required a little extra attention from him. He knew she would want him to plant the seeds, and there was nothing more to discuss about it.

Junior had been gone for a few days, and there had been no word or sightings of him. Nothing. His disappearance was on their minds most of the time, but they had yet to discuss it together. It needed to be brought out into the open, especially for Cora.

She made up her mind years ago not to keep anything that bothered her bottled up inside. Now, the time was getting ripe for their problems with Junior to be thoroughly discussed – out in the open.

"I told Junior I would track him down if he left, but I knew it was just a bluff when I said it. We both knew, I guess, because he didn't fall for it. Junior knows this town backward and forward. I tried. I tried to make an impression on the boy, to keep him here at the farm where he would be safe, but it didn't work."

"You did what you could, Will."

"Su'pose. I wouldn't know where to start lookin' for him."

Five minutes were left in their lunch break when they saw Sheriff Lewis ride up.

"Have a seat, sheriff." Will offered when the sheriff was close.

Sheriff Lewis walked up to the porch, sat, and looked at them both. "Fine day today." He said.

"Yes, it is. What can we do for you?"

"It's not easy to say this, but there's been a murder in town. A man was beaten to death and left on the front porch of the Catholic church. It was an awful sight. Someone was able to identify the poor man. He had a wife and one child, a boy, and I'm concerned about both of them. The man may have verbally and physically abused his wife. There is some concern about how well she can care for the boy now. Father Donovan plans to go to the poor man's house to evaluate the situation. We need to see if anything more needs to be done for them."

Cora looked worried and asked, "You came all the way out here to tell us that?"

Sheriff Lewis lowered his head slightly, then said, "No, not really. Last night, after I was called to the church and discovered the beaten man, I saw Junior walking in the shadows across the street from the church. I approached him and asked him what he was doing there, but he wouldn't talk to me. He evaded all my questions. He acted like he was hiding something, and I had no choice but to put him in jail until we got some answers."

"You put my son in Jail?" Will said.

"What are people going to think? You can't suspect that Junior had anything to do with this…murder." Added Cora.

"I have no evidence Junior did anything wrong, but it's just that he wasn't himself last night. He seemed upset and wouldn't answer any of my questions. I'm sorry."

"Maybe he'll talk to us. Can we visit him this afternoon?"

"Of course. If he talks to you and we get to the bottom of this, maybe he can be released back to you this afternoon. I only need to know why he was in that area at that time of night. You're visiting him could end up helping a great deal." The three of them thought about all this, and after a moment's silence, the Sheriff stood up, thanked them for their time, and left.

"I can't believe my boy is in jail. It was bad enough when he started wandering around town at all hours of the day and night. This makes me sick." Cora said.

"We've been through much worse than this. We'll get through this just fine, you'll see." Will said.

She grabbed his hand, squeezed it, and said, "Did we do something wrong? He's never been in trouble before. He's a good boy. He left us, now he's in jail, being questioned about a murder. What is happening to our family?"

"Everything will play itself out, Cora, you'll see. Don't worry."

"How can I not worry?"

"He's always been a little different than most boys, and maybe it was meant to be. This is just Junior being himself. Now he knows I'm not his real father, and that has to be weighin' on his mind some."

"I'm the one who told him his real father was Jesse. I told Junior that his real father was a bad man. How stupid of me." Cora whimpered. She thought back for a moment to that night when Jesse kidnapped her. What a cruel twist of fate it was. She pictured the tattoo on the back of Jesse's hand, the one with the crude blue outline of a star. She could almost smell the chloroform on the rag the evil man used to cover her face. What a sad memory it was, one she had rarely thought about during her waking hours for years until today.

"We can figure it out. I know we can. And we have to face the possibility, Cora, the possibility that Junior has more of his real father's blood in him than we thought he did."

She must have been thinking the same thing because she began to tear up. He had seen her cry only once before. It was hard for him to watch, so he looked away. She began to cry, and then she rushed into the cabin. He knew they would not visit Junior that day.

Chapter Twelve

People were looking for him now. Many would wonder why he broke out of jail in the first place. That's what a guilty person would do. To Junior, breaking out and being considered guilty was a price he was willing to pay. He had the freedom he deserved because he was an innocent man, and he was finally being taken seriously, like an adult. All he had to do was not get caught.

After sleeping most of the day, he walked to his sanctuary. He walked up the incline to the giant Ponderosa Pine tree and sat down as he had before, with his back to the tree to admire the view. The sky was mostly overcast, and the sun tried to come out from behind the clouds.

Junior closed his eyes. He could get out of any jam if he set his mind to it. He would come up with a plan, improvise as needed, use his smarts, and use his grit. If he tried hard enough, he could solve any problem.

A raven flew overhead and squawked repeatedly. He opened his eyes to look at it. He thought about what had happened. Someone had brutally murdered a man. He was the main suspect, even more so now, since his break-out. The real killer must be found before his own life can continue as it had before before all the trouble started. The Sheriff told him he had no clue who the real killer was. How was he supposed to find him if he were to get involved? He had no experience tracking down criminals. He was scared, a feeling he was not used to having.

The weight of it all consumed him. He closed his eyes again and tried to think. A smart person takes the time to gather information and does not just jump into the middle of a situation. A smart person took the time to find out what was happening - first and foremost. To find a criminal, hard-to-get information needed to be dug up, theories had to be tested, a few risks would need to be taken, and maybe a lucky break or two would be required.

He heard the raven again, more distant this time. Junior opened his eyes. It was soaring in the sky, squawking. What he wanted to accomplish was impossible. It would be the most dangerous and desperate thing he had ever tried to do. He was a fourteen-year-old on the run from the law, up against a brutal killer. He gritted his teeth. Junior was determined to follow this quest as far as possible and still stay alive. He was not a quitter.

Father Donovan had locked up the church and was again reading his Bible. Someone knocked on the door to his quarters at the back of the church. He put down his glasses and walked over to answer the door. He thought someone must need his help badly to visit him this late. He opened the door and looked at Junior, who stood in front of him, worried and dirty.

"Junior, what are you doing here? I heard people are looking for you. You're in a lot of trouble."

"I know. Can I come in?"

Father Donovan had never before turned away a lost soul. Still, he hesitated. "Come in." He said finally.

Junior walked into his room, looked around, and took a chair in the corner where the priest did his counseling. Junior said nothing.

"Pray with me, Junior." Father Donovan said.

He prayed and read some scripture from the Book of John, which ended with, "Sin no more, lest a worse thing come unto thee." The prayer and the scripture reading did not seem to have the desired impact on the boy, who kept staring at the floor the whole time. He needed Junior to talk.

"Why did you break out of jail?"

"I'm not completely sure, Father. I just needed some time to think on my own."

"You couldn't think in jail?"

"Yes, but I needed open space to be free - to think freely."

"Have you sinned?"

"I damaged the jail when I left. I'll have to pay for that, I know, but there was no reason for me to be in jail in the first place. I didn't kill that man."

"There are people out there who doubt you, son, and will doubt you even more now."

"I see that, but I can prove myself to them, and I can prove myself to you. I was in the area by the church that night because I had been talking with Raymond before that. I had to ask him for some food. I didn't want to tell the Sheriff I had talked with Raymond because he still suspected me of starting the fire at the Royale. Raymond started it, not me."

"Admitting this to me will not help you in a court of law. You must know that."

"Father, you have to believe me. I want to prove my innocence. I need your help."

He pondered what the boy had said. He seemed sincere, but Junior had made several wrong decisions recently, starting with spending time with Raymond. Junior acted like a scared child, yet no doubt wanted to be seen as a man. Junior had no self-control.

His situation would only go from bad to worse. The Priest mused about this.

On the other hand, if he could somehow get past his current problems and find redemption, all would be well. He knew of no other youth in Prescott with more potential than Junior. *What did Junior want from him?*

"How can I help you?"

"Tell me the last name of the man that was killed and where his family lives."

"Why?"

"It's the first place for me to look, to try to find the killer."

"That's the sheriff's job, Junior. I can't tell you what you're asking me for." He wanted to test Junior to see how he would react to rejection. Would he act like a child again?

"But Father, you must. You must help me."

He said nothing and continued to look Junior straight in the eye. Junior put his head down again, and after a couple of moments of silence, he said. "Thank you for your counsel, Father." Junior rose to his feet and walked towards the door.

"If I tell you, would you act in a reasonable manner? You must know that you have little chance of succeeding in your mission. Could you make good decisions along the way, ones that would be good for both you and for others at the same time?"

"Junior turned around and faced him. He thought about his answer, looked like he took the question seriously, and said, "Yes, Father, I will."

He told Junior the family name and address.

"Remember your promise to a priest, young man."

"I will." Junior thanked him, then left the church.

Chapter Thirteen

Junior was in his temporary hiding spot near Granite Creek, thinking about his next course of action. Tomorrow morning, he would walk over to the family home of the man who was murdered. Hopefully, he could talk to his family members and try to understand what was happening with them. He would deal with whatever he discovered there but had no idea what to expect. He thought about different scenarios that could happen and how he would react to them.

His visit with Father Donovan had a calming influence on him. For the first time in recent memory, he had talked with someone he trusted completely. The Priest could not help him directly, of course, but he had given him a change in direction for his thoughts - consider how to help others as well as yourself. He would try to live up to his promise when he could. Sleep came grudgingly that night.

The time came for him to move again, much sooner than he wanted. His eyes fluttered open, and he roused himself awake. He ate a quick meal and began walking under the cover of darkness to the family home of the murdered man.

Junior arrived around dawn and found a place to watch the house safely. He watched for a good hour and saw and heard nothing. Then, he thought he heard something. He quieted himself and listened more intently. He thought he heard a woman crying from inside the house. He waited, then heard crying again.

He needed to talk to the woman and her family, so he cautiously stood up, walked to their front porch, and knocked on the door. There was no answer, so he waited, then knocked again. The door cracked open, and he found himself looking down the barrel of a shotgun.

"My name is Will Martin Junior, and I would like to talk to you."

"Will Martin Junior? You're the son of a bitch who killed my husband."

"I did no such thing, I swear to you. I'm trying to find out who did. I was in the area near the church when your husband was found and was held for questioning, but someone else killed him. You must believe me. If I were the one who hurt your husband, I would be long gone by now and not standing here looking at your shotgun from the direction I'm looking at it now. Consider that, please. I'm also unarmed. I need your help and don't know who else to turn to." Junior slowly raised his hands, palms forward.

"Go sit in that chair over there." She pointed to a chair in the corner of the covered porch with the shotgun, where he would have no easy escape, and kept the shotgun pointed at him the entire time. She eased her way outside, wearing a long robe, and sat down in a chair nearest to her front door, with the shotgun still pointed at him.

"Talk." She said.

"I'm trying to find out what happened and to bring the real killer to justice."

"You the law now?"

"No, ma'am. I'm sure the Sheriff is also working hard to find the killer. I happened to be in the area when they found your husband, as I said, and they were required to question me. That's all. All I want to do is to help solve this crime."

"Why?"

"I've been under suspicion and want to clear my name."

The women seemed to relax a little.

"Did your husband have enemies?"

"Not that I know of. He was a hard man, that's true. He drank too much. You didn't want to be around him when he drank."

Junior carefully asked his next question: "Ma'am, my next question is personal. One that I don't want to ask you, but I feel it is important, and I must ask you. You don't have to answer if you don't want to. Did your husband ever hit you?"

She tightened her lips together into a sad expression and said nothing. Junior had his answer.

"The sheriff said he would come here today to talk to me. You should work with him."

He watched her eyes tighten. "Ma'am, please understand. I want to solve this crime as much as you do. Can I speak with the rest of your family?"

"My boy is all I have left now, and you can't talk to him."

"I'll be careful. I know he must be very upset."

"He gets home from school at about two o'clock this afternoon. Don't know exactly when the Sheriff will be here, but I'm sure he'll want to talk to my son when he's here."

Junior decided to leave it at that. "If you want to, you can go back inside the house. I'll sit here until you are inside and then leave. Thank you for your time." She seemed to like that idea, so she cautiously went inside while he remained seated in the chair.

Once she was inside and locked the door, he got up and left.

He wanted to speak to the boy and would attempt to do so even though the mother didn't want him to. He left the area to wait in a remote and safe location for several hours. He would return when it was time.

He found a quiet place to wait and thought about what he had learned. It wasn't much. The man drank too much, beat his wife, and may have beaten his son as well. That would be reason enough for the wife to harm her husband, but Junior didn't see her as being capable of doing something like that. It didn't make sense because she seemed genuinely sad and was mourning her loss. Still, he wished he had thought to ask her if she had a good friend or family member who could have committed the crime. He took a nap, and then it was time for him to return.

He positioned himself down the street from the family house, where he could see the son walking home from school, yet not be easily seen from the family's house. Two o'clock came and went. He waited.

The boy slowly walked towards him on the street, looking dejected. He looked down at the ground as he walked and focused on only a few feet ahead of him. He was dragging his feet, creating a small cloud of dust as he walked. Junior knew right away this was the boy he was waiting for. The boy was about forty yards away when Junior stepped onto the street. The boy kept walking and didn't see Junior until he was about ten yards in front of him.

Junior held his hands up, palms forward, just as he had done this morning. "I just want to talk. I won't hurt you."

The boy stood still and looked indecisive. Junior saw some old cuts and bruises on his arms and neck and a couple of new ones.

"Can I walk you back to your house? We can talk on the way. I promise I won't get too close."

The boy turned and ran back in the direction he came from. Junior followed him and tried to stay the same distance from him as before. He didn't want to scare the youngster.

After a short distance, Junior stopped and watched the boy run away down the street. It was time for him to leave. He would not be able to get any information from this scared child. The Sheriff would be in the area soon if he weren't already. He left the neighborhood as quickly and as discretely as he could. Progress in his investigation would proceed slowly, he knew. Chances are, he would fail. The odds against him succeeding were overwhelming, but he could not allow himself any time to dwell on that. He had backed himself into a corner somehow, and now he had no choice but to keep trying to find the killer.

Chapter Fourteen

Detective Mathew Williams worked in downtown Phoenix's U. S. Marshall's Office. He liked his job and was gratified when he was able to solve a crime. He worked hard and had carved out a reputation around the office for being a determined investigator, a bloodhound. He was dogged in following up on all leads and wouldn't quit on a lead if he felt it had promise. Despite this, or probably because of this, Detective Williams often butted heads with his boss.

His boss had no feel for solving crimes, and Williams had to deal with that fact every day. Everyone in the office knew his boss spent almost all of his time trying to make himself look good. Detective Williams was just another pawn in his boss's grand plan for personal advancement. Sometimes, he thought his boss gave him time-wasting and useless assignments to keep him out of the way of whatever his boss was scheming up at that time.

Detective Williams had a brother who was also a detective and lived in Rochester, New York. A few weeks ago, he received a letter from his brother that included a newspaper article. The article was about a crime in Argentina that had been solved using a new science called fingerprinting. Detective Williams was intrigued. Apparently, every person in the world has a unique set of fingerprints.

His opportunity to experiment with fingerprinting came sooner than he expected when he landed a case involving a Hopi girl who was murdered at the Phoenix Indian School.

When he got to the scene, he saw she had been attacked in her room at the school. Her window was broken, and there was glass everywhere on the floor. There was also a lot of blood at the scene. The wounds on the victim looked to have been inflicted by a knife.

One item in the victim's room caught his interest - a lampshade with blood markings. He removed the lampshade from the scene, careful not to touch the markings, and set it aside. When he left the crime scene, he took it home with him and placed it in a safe place before going back to the office. He didn't dare share what he had in mind with his co-workers, and he especially didn't want to share his discovery with his boss.

He spent many hours experimenting with various techniques for transferring his fingerprints from his hands to paper. For one whole week, the tips of his hands were black. Some people asked about his hands, but most stared at his hands first, then back at him curiously. A few people gave him dirty looks. He didn't care. He was determined to figure it out.

It soon became apparent that there was a prime suspect in the Hopi girl murder. A young man with a very troubled past had been placed at the scene of the crime by several witnesses. Under questioning, he almost confessed to doing it, then changed his mind.

Detective Williams wanted to try to use fingerprints to get the young man off the streets. Still, he was aware that fingerprint evidence would be supporting evidence only and probably would not be enough to convince a jury of innocence or guilt in any crime. After his work with his own fingerprints, he had an effective way to get the images of the ridges at the end of his fingers transferred to paper, using just the right amount of ink on the fingers.

He went to where the suspect was being held and attempted to get a copy of his fingerprints on paper. This took some effort because the young man did not want to cooperate. In a battle of wills, Detective Williams eventually wore the suspect down, and after several attempts, he finally got a set of usable prints. Later that night, he compared the prints from the suspect to those on the lampshade. It took careful work, and he eventually concluded that several prints matched. He had hard evidence that the suspect was at the scene at the time of the murder.

When he came to work the next day, it was time to present his case to his boss. Detective Williams was prepared, had all the evidence, and wanted to get off to a good start.

When his boss's office was clear, he walked in to talk. "We wrapped the Wilson case yesterday. Big case and a feather in your cap, I would think." Williams offered.

"What do you want, Williams?"

He started by discussing the new science of fingerprinting, explaining that no two prints are the same and how useful using fingerprints as evidence could be in court. He then explained the work he had done on the Hopi girl case. He did his best to present his case but knew convincing his boss would be an uphill battle.

"You did what? What a colossal waste of public funds you are. I've never heard of this thing you call fingerprinting. It certainly can not be called a science. No court in the country would convict someone based on this magic trick."

His boss continued his tirade, "The enrollment at the Phoenix Indian School has increased dramatically over the past couple of years. The mayor and my boss wanted this case solved yesterday.

It's important for the growth of the school. I want you to focus. Forget this goddamned fingerprinting nonsense. Be productive. Be a detective. Do your job if you want to keep it."

It was a long shot, he thought as he walked over to his desk, dejected. He knew that fingerprinting science had great potential, and that made his defeat even more bitter, but at the same time, he expected it. "Good Lord, I hate working here." He mumbled as he sat down at his desk.

Junior spent a few days carefully watching the town, with nothing to show for his efforts. He learned the Sheriff's routines and, so far, was able to avoid running into him, although he kept an eye out for the unexpected. One thing still weighed on his mind, so he went back to the home of the man who was killed to ask the victim's wife an important question. He knocked on her door twice, as he had before. The door cracked open, and he was happy not to be looking down the barrel of her shotgun this time. She looked thinner to him than she had before.

"What do you want?"

"Ma'am, I'm making some progress on the case, but I need to ask you a question."

"Ask."

"Please don't misunderstand me, but I need to ask if you have any family in town or friends that would have been upset with your late husband."

"It didn't take her long to answer. I have a brother in Tucson. We're packing up right now to go live with him. I don't have any other family members around Prescott, no. As far as friends, well, I spent most of my time dealing with my family, trying to solve our problems, and didn't have much time to spend making friends."

Junior thought about this momentarily, then said, "Thank you, ma'am. Have a safe trip."

Cora had a heavy heart as she prepared for her weekly get-together with her friends Sharlot, Lillian, and Cat. She heard Junior had escaped from jail and was now on the run and possibly in danger. She wanted to convince the family to go to Mass today instead of to Sharlot's, but she had already promised Sharlot. She got ready, said goodbye to the boys and Will, and left at mid-morning.

When she arrived, her three friends and a man she had not met before were inside.

"Everyone, this is my friend Samuel. He's been a great help to me around the house." Cat said.

Everyone said hello. Cora thought back and remembered this was Cat's fourth man-friend in the past five years. Like all the others, this one was quiet, too.

"I've got to do some chores outside. It's good to meet you all," Samuel said, then walked out the door.

"He's got some inheritance from somewhere back east. He rents a place in town and comes to help me once or twice a week. He's a looker, that's for sure. Who knows, he could end up working for me all the time or maybe working with Happy at the livery." Cat said.

Sharlot decided this was a good time for her weekly reading of the *Prescott Prospector* newspaper.

"W. R. Willis is remodeling his drug store to make a separate place for the cigar department. A. P. Culver can be on the streets again."

"Oh, I know Arther. Good for him." Said Lillian.

Sharlot continued, "The hose-running fire department team has been organized. Cory Wells was elected to be the trainer."

"A little too late for the Royale, I'm afraid," Cat said.

Several more personal notices were mentioned. Someone was leaving for school in San Fransisco, someone else arrived last night from Denver, and so on.

"Oh, I almost forgot. I have something for you, Cora." Cat said.

"For me? Why?"

"To acknowledge our friendship, for turning Happy's life around all those years ago, and just because I want to. I saw this a few days ago and thought it would be perfect for you. Sharlot and Lillian, I plan on giving both of you gifts, too, just not today.

Cat reached into her purse and pulled out a lady's comb made of pure ivory. She handed it to Cora.

"I can't accept this. It's too much." She said as she admired the comb.

"You're going to take it. You deserve it. If you don't, my feelings will be hurt."

"OK. Thank you so, so much, Cat."

"You're welcome."

They finished discussing the light news. It was time for the more serious discussion they all needed to have. It came out.

Lillian asked, "Cora, we're all thinking about Junior. Have you heard anything lately?"

"No, not a thing."

Sharlot added, "He's a good young man. Anyone who knows him knows he's no killer. He's young - that's his crime. Young people do foolish things sometimes. He probably thinks the world is out to get him, so he went into hiding. He'll turn up and be cleared of any wrongdoing."

Sharlot's stature in the community had steadily risen over the years. Cora was grateful to have such strong support from an influential friend.

"Thank you, Sharlot. I don't know if the sheriff has made any progress in finding this evil man, the killer. I hope things will get easier for Junior when the killer is caught." Said Cora.

"He'll do his job. He's the best sheriff we've had in years." Said Cat.

Samuel came into the cabin and smiled at Cat.

"I thought I smelled apple pie earlier. I didn't want to miss anything."

Cora laughed and proceeded to get the pie and dish up a piece for everyone. After they enjoyed the pie, they all sat on the porch.

"Samuel was upset when he heard about the murder at the church," Cat said.

Samuel shook his head. "What is this world coming to? We all need to be careful. The killer may still be out there. We need to be extra vigilant. I wish there were something I could do to help stop this murderer."

Everyone nodded their heads. After another few minutes of small talk, it seemed to Cora that they were pretty much talked out, so she said her thanks, told Samuel it was good to meet him, and left for her short ride home. She was glad to have the comb but hoped she would not forever link it in her mind with Junior's current troubles.

Chapter Fifteen

Raymond got dressed and came into the kitchen for breakfast. He didn't say anything. Why should he? His parents were not talkers, at least not to him. Thank goodness his mother was a good cook. Today's breakfast was eggs, beef, beef gravy, and biscuits. He dug in. As was their way, his parents kept their comments to a minimum.

"I'm going to the Farmer's Market today. I hope to get a chicken for dinner," his mom said. Raymond loved her fried chicken.

"I'm going to the lumber mill for a half-shift this morning. I'll be back a little after noon." His father said.

His parents were partly talking to each other, partly talking to themselves, and partly talking to no one. Raymond felt invisible, as usual, and he longed to have a real conversation. For all of her cooking skills, his mother only saw the bad in everything. It was hard for him to have a conversation with someone who complained about almost everything. His dad was a steady man and a good provider, but he didn't have much capacity for conversation. He was always in his own world, as if everything else did not exist.

His mother said, "Are you expecting another visit from the Sheriff today, Raymond?"

Raymond took this as a statement meant to diminish him, and he felt that today had started badly like most days around here did.

"No, Mother."

Without another word, both of his parents got up from the table. His father left for work. He helped his mother clear the table, and then she left. He sat in a chair, and a familiar emotion took hold of his thoughts - disappointment. He knew that his friend Junior had conversations with his parents, especially his mother, who was very thoughtful. *Why couldn't he?*

It seemed impossible to please his parents; he had given up years ago. Soon, he would have to go out into the world and make his own way. He did not have the slightest idea how he would do that. Being angry most of the time took a lot of energy, and there wasn't much time left for thinking about his future. The world was wrong, and his thoughts were dark. He wondered if his parents loved him. Probably not. Maybe a little. He got ready and left the house. Today, he would be walking.

Raymond was looking for trouble, as he usually was. He walked a good distance from his house. People in the homes closer to his house would suspect him immediately if something went wrong, so he had to go where there would be less suspicion drawn to him. As he walked, he wondered why he wasn't more popular with the girls. He tried to talk to them, but too many times, they acted like he was creepy and disgusting. It made no sense and bothered him. Junior, his only friend, couldn't really understand him. Junior knew nothing of his parents. Everything he thought about was depressing. He hoped he wasn't becoming like his mother.

He found himself at the Smith's house. The Smiths were almost always at the Farmer's Market on Saturdays and had no children. He hid for a few minutes and watched. The nearest neighbor was fifty yards away. There was no movement, so he stood up and entered their barn. They had two horses and one pig.

He opened the stall doors and shooed the horses out. He then opened the gate to the pig pen, shooed the pig outside, and left the barn. He wanted to hit the pig for some reason, but it moved too fast.

What a poor way to start the morning, he thought. Ten years ago, it would have been great. He would have gone home, laughed at what he thought the Smiths' reaction to their missing animals, and hoped to see their pig running down the middle of Main Street. Today, it lacked excitement. He would need to do something more spectacular to make this day worthwhile. He had a long day ahead of him, with plenty of time. The ideas would come to him.

He spent much time on the street, observing without being observed, constantly on the lookout for a new Oscar. 'I have a duty to protect the youth of this town,' he said to himself at least once daily. Today, he was in his most common costume, that of a ne'er-do-well, someone with nowhere to go and nothing to do, who only wanted a small donation. Today, he had chosen a blond wig.

He wandered around town aimlessly, or at least that is what he wanted people to think. He happened to see the youth he recognized as Raymond go into a barn and turn two horses loose. Then, a pig came darting out of the farm. What in the world? What a waste of talent, he thought. The boy had no purpose, no mission. He had seen Raymond up close before and had never seen any cuts or bruises on him. Still, he spent most of his time causing pointless mischief like this. A troubled young man - but a kindred spirit, perhaps? The boy needed direction, a mentor. Yes, someone like Raymond could become very useful to him.

Junior planned his visit to the Catholic church so that he would arrive there just after dark. He knocked on the back door, and Father Donovan opened the door.

"Junior, good to see you. Come in."

Junior entered the room and sat in the same chair he had sat in on his last visit.

"Father, I've been thinking about the family of the man that was killed."

"Yes, of course. I'm pleased you are thinking about others, as you promised. I have also been thinking about your mother and father, your brothers, and your parents' friends. They are all such good people. If you thought about it that way, I'm sure you would come to realize that they would gladly take you back with them. Your family and their friends are a tremendous resource for you, Junior. All you have to do is let yourself return to them."

Junior didn't tell him that Will was not his real father. "That's all true, Father, but if I go back now, things will soon return to how they were before. Will would want my help in the fields, which I don't mind doing, but that's his life - not mine. Plus, I would still be under suspicion for both the fire and the murder, like I am now. I broke out of jail, too. I need to clear my name and my family's name for the murder. The only way I can do that is by finding the killer. Responsibility for the fire is between Raymond and the Sheriff. I would consider returning to my family once the crimes are resolved."

Father Donovan thought about this for a moment. "I admire your ambition, Junior. What you say does make some sense, but you are taking on too much. What can I do for you today?"

"I tried to talk to the son of the man that was killed. He wouldn't talk to me. He was scared and ran away. I noticed he had cuts and bruises, some of which looked newer. I think that he had been beaten regularly. That would explain why he ran away from me."

Father Donovan thought about this. "Now that you mention it, I remember seeing bruises on him when the family was in church, but I never thought much of it. All boys like to play outside and get bruises from it sometimes."

"I don't think this boy had many chances to play outside, Father."

"I've been counseling the family regularly since the tragedy. At first, the wife and the boy grieved as I would have expected them to. More recently I have been a little surprised when they seemed more relaxed and at peace the last two times I talked with them. I did not expect that, considering that they have lost their main source of income now."

"I need to know more about the man that was killed. Why was he killed? Did the fact that he was beaten mean anything? He could have been killed any number of ways, the poor fellow." Junior said

"That brings up an interesting point. The Sheriff told me that he was beaten all over his body, not just in one location, like his head. It would have taken some time and a great deal of anger for the killer to hit him repeatedly like he did."

They both thought about this.

"The devil certainly possessed the killer. What would make someone hit the man like that, over and over." Father Donovan said.

"Revenge. It had to be revenge. The man was beaten because he beat his wife and son." Junior stated.

"Again, what you say makes sense, unfortunately. There has always been evil in the world, and there always will be. It is also possible that this was a random act committed by a very, very sick person. It may or may not have had anything to do with revenge."

"The wife and son were both beaten regularly. The father was beaten. I suppose it could be a coincidence."

"We have no way of knowing right now. More information is needed. I'm afraid that finding out what made someone commit this terrible act of violence will be unpleasant and hard to understand." The priest lamented.

"You tell the truth, Father, and I appreciate your counsel. Thank you." Junior shook his hand, then left the church.

Regardless of the killer's motivation, Junior was keenly aware that it would be difficult to find him. He would need to spend more time around town, looking for people and things that seemed out of place, and he would need to take more risks. He needed to learn how to think like a killer.

Chapter Sixteen

He was a master of disguise by now. Over several years, he has developed new techniques and improved his craft. Everyone should be good at something, he thought, and *he was good at many things*. When he was at the top of his game, he felt he could make people do exactly what he wanted. He could make people walk in this direction or that direction. He could make people look at him or not, and he could do all of this without revealing his true identity.

He provided justice in an unjust world and took his duty to protect women and children very seriously. To keep his power, all he had to do was to remain hidden and focused.

He also realized that along with his growing powers came a good deal of responsibility. He felt the burden that was his alone, giving him a unique, if limited, authority over the masses. His was not an easy task, and it weighed on him constantly. He gave up long ago, thinking that no one would understand him. He had to press on to keep up the fight.

Sitting with his legs hanging over the front walkway of a row of stores, just across from the row of whiskey bars, he looked up and focused on the amateur who stood out like the true beginner he was. The young man across the street tried not to be noticed, but he was as obvious as he could be to a trained eye like his. He could not make himself respect amateurs.

The young man was clever, he had to admit. He had a few good moves. It was amusing for him to watch for a while, but ultimately, the amateur became a distraction and an irritation. He wondered what the young man was trying to accomplish. What or who was he looking for? He stayed in position and continued to watch him. Eventually, the young man walked down the street and out of his view.

The next day, he wore a new disguise and positioned himself with a clear view of the Methodist church. For now, he was content to hold back and wait. He wanted to stay out of the way and not look out of place by spending too much time directly in front of the church. He would move in closer when he spotted someone going into the church who appeared promising enough to expose himself so he could get a closer look. It wasn't Sunday, but he had found that any day is good for discovering guilty, wayward beasts lurking around churches.

The same young man from the day before presented himself, casually walking down the street like he didn't care what he was doing. He had no disguise on and would certainly draw attention to himself. What a clown. This young man walked over near the church and sat on a bench. He was unsure what to do about this turn of events. One thing for sure was that he was irritated at the interference. He tried to stay calm. *What was going on? Was he being tested?*

Soon, a young couple walked toward the church with their children. He was too far away and couldn't see the children very well. The four of them went inside the church. Any other day, this would be the time to move in closer to get a close-up look at the family when they came out. Not this time. The young man was sitting at precisely the place he wanted to be. This fellow was getting in the way and was becoming a big nuisance. Something had to change. He couldn't stand being played with like this. First, he would follow this family to see what he could learn. Tomorrow, he would use an accomplice and take this infuriating young man out of commission. How dare he? This young man will pay for what he has done.

Junior tried to blend into his surroundings and notice as much as possible, but it was a boring, thankless task. He did not like this work. Day after day, he felt like he had accomplished nothing. He was not meant for this. Working with Will in the fields was just as tedious, but at least that came with good meals and an occasional bath. He would have to brave the cold water of a creek to clean up soon enough. He decided to put it off until tomorrow.

He had ruled out a family member or a friend of the family as the possible killer. He believed what the wife had told him, and he felt fortunate he was able to talk with her before she left. The killer had to be someone else. Someone else looking for revenge - and someone who didn't know the family well, if at all. Junior had no idea where to find such a person or if it was even possible. It was the ultimate long shot.

Junior was chasing an elusive and brutal killer, or was it killers? He had no way of knowing. As the hours and the days wore on, he began to doubt if he would ever solve the murder. He didn't know what to do next. He just hoped that doing something was better than doing nothing. No guarantees. Junior felt it in his bones that the killer was among the crowds somewhere, here in Prescott, looking for his next victim, and if Junior could spot him first, he just might be able to stop him before he killed again. He steeled himself to continue his search.

Each day, he positioned himself as discretely as possible, away from where he thought the sheriff would be and as far away as possible from people who might recognize him. Yesterday, he was at the Methodist church in the morning and then went to the southern part of town in a residential area in the afternoon. Once again, yesterday he saw nothing out of the ordinary all day.

Today, he was hidden behind bushes in front of the road that led to the lumber mill. To his right was a grouping of homes on both sides of the road. The mill was to his left. He heard a variety of loud sawing noises coming from that direction. Behind him and immediately to his right and perpendicular to the main lumber mill road was the old mill road, which was no longer used or maintained. He sat and sat until his backside began to hurt. His afternoon observation post would be far from here, he resolved. A long walk would do him good.

An old man with a bad leg came up the road from the mill towards him. The man looked downtrodden. Junior stayed motionless and watched the old man. He thought he smelled a sour whiskey odor. He was surprised when the old man turned up the old mill road to Junior's right and started to walk up the road, increasingly moving behind Junior's location. He turned, watched the old man walk, and wondered where he could be going. He continued to watch him. When the old man had walked enough of the old mill road to be out of sight from the lumber mill, he began to speed up. *That's strange.* Then, the man began to run, and he no longer had a limp. It was time for Junior to find out what was behind this odd behavior.

He got up and walked quickly after the man, then jogged and soon ran at full speed. He would spot the man, lose him, then spot him again as the narrow road weaved left and right. Junior didn't know why he was running. Was it a trap? Was he being led somewhere? The man's actions were beyond suspicion, like that of a criminal, but the man also had no way of knowing Junior would be hiding where he was and watching him that morning. He decided to keep running.

There must have been a root or something else protruding out of the road because he tripped and fell. He got up to continue his pursuit. His right ankle hurt a little, and he limped for a few strides, then he was able to continue the chase.

Junior began to get winded but kept on running. He ran past a tree and felt a blow to his chest. Someone had clubbed him. He immediately went to the ground and tried to assess his injury. It was serious. He was hurting. He needed to take loud half-breaths to get enough air. That was a priority. He couldn't do anything until he could calm down and get enough air. A full breath was not possible - it hurt too much. He couldn't move, and he was vulnerable. The killer would finish him any moment now. He was utterly defenseless. He rolled over, slowly and painfully, to look at his attacker.

He saw no one. All he could do for now was find a position on the ground where he could breathe easier and was not in as much pain. He found a decent position and lay there for a few minutes to gather himself. The pain was severe. He closed his eyes and tried to let the pain subside.

He heard a dog barking loudly, and then the animal began to lick his face. "Apex, stop barking and come here right now. You'd better listen to me."

Junior opened his eyes and realized it was much later in the day.

"Oh my, what happened to you? Are you OK?'

"No. I need some help getting up. Get me some help."

He heard a couple of familiar voices: "Wake up, Junior, please." The woman said, and the man said, "Wake up, son."

He opened his eyes and saw Charley and Elizabeth's worried faces. He was lying in a comfortable bed.

"A friend told me some people found a young man who matched your description and needed help on the old mill road. I went to check on it, and there you were. We brought you back here, to our house. You've got a huge, puffy purple bruise on your chest, and I think you broke a rib. How do you feel?"

"Like I've been kicked by a mule."

"The good news is that no bone broke the skin. The area is very swollen, which I've seen before with broken bones. I think one of your ribs is cracked but still in place. It will heal just fine if you take care of it. We can't find any huge lumps or dips on your skin that would be expected if your bones were pushed out of place. You don't seem to be bleeding anywhere, either. You are lucky, even if you don't feel that way right now."

"Thanks, Charley, for helping me. I want to keep this whole incident quiet…" He felt a sharp pain in his side.

"Don't worry about that. When you're in less pain, we'll talk. Maybe in a week or so. Right now, you need to take a bath."

Junior was able to climb into the bathtub slowly and then let the warm water soothe him. He reflected on when Charley and Elizabeth decided to move back up to Prescott a few years ago. They said their guided hunt business in Wickenburg had started to slow down. When they returned to Prescott, they couldn't get over how much the town had changed since they visited their good friends Will and Cora four years ago. The lumber mill had been busy cutting down trees to provide lumber for the new homes people wanted to build.

He remembered Charley once told him everything in the

world was constantly changing. His own life had undoubtedly been full of change lately. Junior was starting to understand how fast things could happen. He would have to slow down now and be patient if his rib was going to heal right.

A week passed, and he was still in constant pain, although he did detect minor improvements each day. Sleep was still difficult. That morning, he slowly walked to the kitchen table and sat across from Charley.

"The Sheriff doesn't know you're here."

"Thank you for not telling him."

"Tell me more about why you were running on that road in the first place."

"I was looking around town trying to spot any suspicious behavior, to get any information I could about the killer." Junior repeated what he had said about the man's unusual actions on the old mill road earlier in the week.

"So you said, but I still don't understand it. You have no advantage here. The killer holds all the cards. You're not being smart about this, Junior. What if getting hit in the ribs was only a warning? If you keep this up, it will be much worse for you the next time you're attacked."

"That's what I have to avoid somehow. I ran right into his trap. The next time, I need to turn the tables on him. I'll never underestimate the man again. Nothing matters now, though, because I can't do anything until I heal up."

"Maybe your time spent recovering will help you to come to your senses."

Junior looked at Charley but said nothing. They were at an impasse, and there was no point in arguing the point further.

"Your parents know you are here and have agreed to stay

away for a few weeks."

"How did you manage that?"

"It took some time. The first thing I told them was you were looking for the killer, saw him, then chased him. That's why you were clubbed. I thought your mother was going to faint when she heard that. Your dad looked worried, too. He demanded I turn you over to Sheriff Lewis immediately. He said you would be safer there."

Junior considered that last statement but didn't buy the part about him being safer in jail. When he was hurt and needed help, Will demanded he be turned over to the sheriff - some father.

"How did you talk him out of it?"

"I just kept trying. I explained that you would not be able to heal very well if you were in jail. It's a dirty place. At least with you here, Elizabeth and I can look after you when we're not busy."

"I don't see that as enough to sway Will if he demanded the Sheriff be notified."

"Your mother rarely puts her foot down once your father makes a demand, but when she does, it has a big impact on Will. She put her foot down and held her ground. I've never been able to change your father's mind once he sets his mind to something. In fact, I think she's the only person in the world who could ever change his mind. You're lucky to have two good parents like Will and Cora."

Junior tossed that statement around in his mind for a moment, then tossed it out again as quickly as it had come in.

Chapter Seventeen

His daughter was a princess, his son a constant irritation, and his wife cried too much.

He fully acknowledged that he had a temper. At his wife's insistence, the whole family went to church every Sunday, and every Monday, the three of them - him, his wife, and their son went to see the Methodist pastor for family counseling. Today was a Monday, and the three joined the pastor in his office, sat down, and got comfortable.

"Pastor Taylor, thank you for taking the time to see us."

"I'm happy to see you all once again. How are things at home?"

"This week was like last week, just like the week before, just like every week for the past six years. The boy will not change his ways. He does not understand that I have to discipline him because I want him to change. I want him to be a better son, to quit causing problems, and to behave better, like my daughter does." the man said.

"The Bible teaches us that children need discipline and guidance, and they also need our love. He read a passage from the book of Proverbs: He that spareth the rod hateth the son, but he that loveth him chasteneth him in good season."

"What does that mean, In good season?" The wife asked

"It means there are limits to punishing a child. When children stray, they need to be redirected righteously so they can understand where they went wrong. Nothing more than that. The punishment must befit the transgression. Consider the grace of God in knowing when to stop."

"That's easy to say. It's hard to do. The boy makes me angry. He doesn't get better when I punish him, so I have to punish him all over again sometimes."

"Try not to be angry. Do you love your son?"

"Yes, that's why I want him to grow up right."

Pastor Taylor turned to the son and asked, "Do you want to say anything?"

The boy glanced at the pastor, then looked straight ahead and said nothing.

The Pastor offered a short prayer and a warm smile, and the three Scott family members got up and left.

Junior never realized how much a cracked rib could hurt. When possible, he tried to find a comfortable position in his chair and remain as still as possible. He wanted the bone to heal correctly.

He thought about what had happened to him and was encouraged because he was the only person who had seen the killer - or was he? The man had a limp at first, then he didn't, and later, he showed he was a fast runner. Junior never really saw his face. Early on he smelled alcohol on the man, but it was obvious that the man was not drunk.

He surmised he had probably made more progress than the

Sheriff had. If the man he chased was indeed the killer, then he knew about how tall he was, maybe, but even that was unclear. The man he chased may not have been the killer at all. He may have been working with the killer and was used to draw Junior into the open. The man who ran down the road could easily have been someone whom the killer wanted Junior to think was him. Why were they going to so much trouble just for him? They must have seen him around town. Junior saw that as a good sign, that he must be making some progress.

Junior thought at least two people were involved in his attack. What if the man who killed the man at the church was the same man who clubbed him on the old mill road and, as Charley said, only hit him once as a warning?

He didn't understand many things but still felt satisfied that he had made at least some impact on the killer. As soon as his body healed, there were many missing pieces to the puzzle to be sorted out, and he had much more work to do. While he was laid up, he was still trying to think like a killer to hopefully gain insights into his motivations and actions.

Pastor Taylor was pleased with his weekly women's get-together on Tuesday afternoon. He had selected a good discussion topic, listened as most of the women were able to participate in the conversation, and finally shared a lovely prayer with them. He especially liked this women's group because they always brought good food. He wasn't married and always looked forward to good home-cooked meals. After the meeting, he strolled outside with the group to an area in front of the church, where he said his goodbyes and gave his well-wishes.

There was always a clean-up necessary after a group of people visited the church. Paster Taylor set about picking up after the women's group. He was almost done sweeping the floor when he heard a knock on the back door. Strange, he thought. Nobody knocks on that door. Paster Taylor walked the short distance to the rear door and tried to push the door out. A heavy weight was blocking it. He tried to push the door open again, but it wouldn't budge.

He went out the front door and immediately noticed an old woman sitting in a wagon in front of the church. She was severely hunched over and didn't look well. "Can I help you?" He offered.

"I come to see… 'bout joinin'…the church."

Her voice cracked and popped like something sharp was caught in her throat, making it difficult for her to speak. He looked at her and couldn't help but notice her fierce, penetrating eyes. He thought then that there was a reason the Bible teaches us to be kind to our elders. She must be in a lot of pain. "All you need to do is to come to our service on Sunday at nine o'clock. We'd be happy to have you join us. I could introduce you to some other women there if you'd like."

"God…bless you, Pastor," she said. She picked up the reins and slowly moved her wagon away from the church.

He watched her leave, then walked around the side of the church and the rear to look. He was stunned. What he saw horrified him. A badly beaten man was propped up with his back to the rear door of the church. Pastor Taylor couldn't walk any further. He put his hands on his knees and threw up. He would have to get the Sheriff. The man's face was distorted, unrecognizable. He was the same size and was dressed like Mr. Scott, the man he had counseled yesterday about punishing his son. Still, he couldn't be sure.

When the Sheriff arrived and saw the victim, he looked disappointed. The Sheriff inspected the body of the beaten man for a few minutes, then walked back to Pastor Taylor.

"Have you seen or heard anything suspicious today, pastor?"

"Not a thing. We had a women's get-together earlier, and maybe a half-hour after the meeting ended, I heard a knock on the back door here. When I couldn't open the door, I walked back here and saw him. What a tragedy."

"That's the truth. I'll look for witnesses, but this killing looks very similar to the recent killing at the Catholic church. No witnesses were found then, and I'll be shocked if we find any witnesses to this crime, either. The Sheriff returned to the corpse and studied the surrounding area for several minutes. Apparently, he saw nothing important because he walked over to the pastor again and said, "Would you wait here until I come back with the undertaker? It shouldn't take too long."

"Sure, sheriff."

In forty minutes, the Sheriff returned with the undertaker, and he was surprised to see someone who looked like a newspaperman was tagging along with the two of them. He knew that sooner or later the newspaper people would hear about this, but it turned out to be much sooner than he though and he wasn't happy about it. What scavengers they were.

The man introduced himself to Pastor Taylor. "I'm a reporter with the *Prescott Prospector*. Can you tell me anything about this terrible crime?"

He didn't want to at first, but he eventually relented and told the reporter the basics of how he had found the body. The reporter thanked him and then turned to speak with the Sheriff.

"Do you have any ideas about who could have done this, Sheriff Lewis?"

"Not at this time. This victim looks to have been killed in the same manner as the victim recently found over at the Catholic church. I'm working the case hard and am open to any useful information your readers may have concerning either of these killings. The problem with that murder, and possibly this one too, is I still have no motive, no murder weapon, and no witnesses. I haven't searched for any witnesses yet for this crime. I will, but right now, it looks like both of the victims appeared suddenly, out of nowhere, and the killer seems to have vanished like a ghost."

"A ghost. Interesting, and how very sad. Good luck to you, sheriff, and thank you for your time." The newspaperman left the area.

Junior wondered what he would do if the killer's identity were discovered. What if the killer confessed? If he went back home, would Will think of him differently now? Would things be better for him there? Probably not, he thought. At any rate, Junior wanted to be the one who solved the crime. He wanted the credit for finding this criminal. Being a hero would be the perfect way to start his new life.

He was overthinking it and eager to get started again on solving the murder when Charley opened the door and came in with a puzzled look on his face.

"How are you, Junior?"

"A little better than yesterday. Still hurts."

"Takes time. There was another murder, this time at the Methodist church. A man was severely beaten, just like the man at the Catholic church. The Sheriff has no clue what happened. There should be some mention of it when the paper comes out. Sheriff Lewis hopes someone will read the notice in the paper and step forward with some information. If someone like that were out there, they already would have spoken up. I hope I'm wrong. I hope the story about the killings doesn't cause people to get scared or panic. Things like this are not supposed to happen in a small town like ours.

"Charley, I have to ask you. Do you know if the man who was killed was a child-beater?"

"No. I haven't heard that. I talked with Pastor Taylor, and he mentioned that the man, his wife, and their son had all been to the church yesterday for counseling. So, yeah, it's possible he was."

Junior explained how he had talked with the wife of the first victim and how he had come to believe the man who murdered him did it for revenge, even though there was no evidence the murderer knew the family. Also, there were no known family members or friends around who would have been motivated to take revenge. The killer had to have been someone else.

"Revenge, but didn't know them? That's odd. Some kind of vigilante killer, then?"

"Yes, I think so. I'm laid up here and can't do it myself. Could you ask around to find out if the man beat his son? The first victim beat his wife, too."

"Yeah. I can talk to the Pastor and the Sheriff again."

"If it turns out both of the victims were child-beaters, I think you should point that out to the sheriff, and the killer could be, as you say, a vigilante."

"I will. You have given this a lot of thought, obviously."

"I've had a lot of time to think about it."

"I like that you're here and not out there chasing this lunatic and putting yourself in danger. Plus, people who don't know you won't think of you as a killer anymore once they find out that you've been here trying to recover from a cracked rib."

"I don't want anyone to know I've been here until I can move around better. I'm still responsible for the damage to the jail. I could still be suspected of starting the fire, too. I'm not sure."

"We won't tell anyone you're here if you don't want us to."

He picked up the paper and started to read it. He saw the article he was looking for and laughed. *'Ghost', huh? Ghosts don't strike down wicked men like I do, and they don't have the authority and the power I have to do so.* In the past, he would have packed up and ran away. Not now. He was strong enough to finish his work here, and there was much more work to do in this backward town. He read the full article.

'GHOST KILLER' STRIKES AGAIN

S R Scott was found deceased last week, beaten in a similar manner as the man who was found recently at the Catholic church. Sheriff Lewis said the murderer vanished from the scene 'Like a Ghost,' and the sheriff is asking anyone who might have information about either one of these killings to report directly to him. This murderer does not seem to have a conscience and puts our calm, quiet community in grave danger. This 'Ghost' killer must be found out!

Chapter Eighteen

"Williams, in my office - Now."

Matthew Williams was almost finished with his latest assignment, which had proved to be a total waste of time, so he was not surprised his boss called him in for what he suspected would be his next time-wasting job. He walked over and sat down, facing his boss.

"I'm sending you to Prescott on assignment. They've had two killings up there with enough similarities to be linked. The local sheriff has no clue as to what's going on. They need a professional, our best, and I've decided to send you up there. You will only be on loan to them, of course, until you solve the case. You leave first thing tomorrow. Here's everything you need."

Williams was handed a folder that included summaries of the two homicides, as well as other information about his ride to Prescott, his accommodations there, and so on and so forth.

"Go easy with your questionable ideas about hand prints or anything else you may have come up with lately."

"They're called fingerprints, sir."

"Of course, fingerprints. Now, remember this: I want you to solve these crimes, and the sooner, the better. You're representing this office. If you look good, then we look good. Don't mess it up. That's all. Dismissed."

Detective Williams walked back to his desk. Finally, he thought, a chance to leave this dungeon and prove himself. He would be the top man in Prescott, unofficially, of course, but he knew he could dance circles around any local-yokel Sheriff in Prescott.

He went to the tiny stage stop for the Black Canyon Stage to get on the route between Phoenix and Prescott. It was quickly becoming a warm day, and he was glad when he heard the stagecoach would be on time and he would soon be on his way. Once he started the trip, he was reminded why he hated riding stagecoaches. Dust was everywhere, and he knew it would only get hotter inside the coach as the day wore on.

He could handle the dust and the heat, but the rough ride jarred his bones. It took the better part of the day to get to Prescott, and by the time he finally got there, he was utterly spent and sore all over. He went to his hotel and ordered a bath. He then ate at the restaurant adjacent to the hotel, returned to his room, collapsed in the bed, and fell asleep immediately.

The following day, he went to the Sheriff's Office and walked in to introduce himself. There was only one man inside, sitting behind a desk. "Sheriff Lewis?" he asked.

"Yes, and you are?"

Detective Matthew Williams from the U. S. Marshal's office in Phoenix. I've been assigned to work with you on the two recent murders you've had here."

"Yeah. I got word yesterday that you would be reporting. It's good to have you. We could use all the help you can give us on this one. It's a head-scratcher."

"Tell me about it. I've read the summaries, but little detail was provided."

Sheriff Lewis gave him an overview of the murders and explained how both bodies were those of child-beaters who were found at local churches, badly beaten, with no witnesses found in either case.

The sheriff told him that last night he had to deal with a fight in a saloon, and four of the participants were still sleeping it off in his jail. "Last night was a long one, and I didn't get much sleep, detective. My mind is still a little foggy. I may have omitted a few details, but I'll fill you in as soon as things come to mind."

"The newspaper here published an article after the second beating and asked for anyone with information about either case to step up. Two people came forward with leads, but neither lead amounted to anything."

"What have you come up with for a motive? Who would benefit from the murder of these two men?"

"I haven't figured that out yet. The only connection we have is that both of the victims beat their sons. The victim's families didn't know each other, and there weren't any known friends or family members locally, in either case, that might have taken the law into their own hands and become suspects in the murders. One well-respected man in town here brought up the idea that the murders were the work of a vigilante killer. That idea makes the most sense to me, and it's my current theory."

"Who exactly is the man who gave you this idea?"

"His name is Charley. He's a good friend of Will Martin, the father of the young man I told you about, the one who was seen near the Catholic church when the first victim was found."

"Tell me more about this young man."

"He's a good young man, this Junior, with a good head on his shoulders. Let's see, I forgot about something. In the last year or so, he's been seen around town, mostly walking around observing things. From what I've heard, he spent some time talking to people, was friendly with the folks he met and saw when he was out and about, and never caused any trouble. The young man was curious about things, is all."

There was a fire recently at a saloon downtown. He was at the scene when the fire happened and helped put it out. Unfortunately, the saloon burned to the ground. At first, I suspected him of starting the fire, but he told me another youth named Raymond had started the fire, and I believed him. So far, I haven't been able to prove Raymond, or anyone else, started the saloon fire."

The sheriff continued, "I saw Junior at the scene of the first murder, walking In the shadows. He wouldn't tell me what he was doing there, so I put him in our jail. He broke out and, in the process, ruined one of our cells. No one has reported seeing him since.

I got the mayor involved and showed him how easy it was to break out of our jail. He was surprised, and a little embarrassed by that, and he told me he would help me get the funds to build two new jail cells, only much sturdier this time."

"Let me get this straight, Sheriff Lewis. Junior, barely a teenager, spent a lot of time walking around town last year, and this year, he was at the scene of the saloon fire, and he was at the scene of the first murder but refused to cooperate with you. He broke out of your jail, and he has been at large ever since, including during the time of the second murder?"

"Yes, that's all true."

"We had a case in Phoenix a couple of years ago that turned out to be very sad. It involved an intelligent young man with a promising future who seemed normal. He came under suspicion for a crime, so we followed him. We wanted to talk to him, and when the time was right, another detective and I moved in for a talk. He pulled out a knife and threatened us with it. He said we were all out to get him. We were all shocked by this. Fortunately for us, we were able to subdue him and bring him in, but he ended up being placed in a mental hospital. His parents were devastated, but this kind of thing has been known to happen before, and it can happen in the best of families."

"I don't see that as the case here with Junior."

"That's my point - exactly. Most of the time, these sick people seem normal until something snaps in their heads. Why do you think he broke out of jail?"

"Good question. Young and stupid, I guess."

"I thought you said he has a good head on his shoulders?"

"Yeah, he is smart, but he's definitely young. Fourteen years old, if I remember right."

"That is young. With the normal fourteen-year-old mind, it would be too young for someone to commit these well-thought-out and brutal crimes. For a sick mind, it's a different story. It would be unusual at that age but not unprecedented."

"Junior's no murderer. I'm sticking with the vigilante killer theory for now. It fits what little evidence we have."

"Right, the idea given to you by a friend of Junior's father."

"Yeah, so? It makes the most sense."

"Look, I'm new to this case, and I'm not in a position to have a firm opinion about it yet. I'm not trying to upset the apple cart here; I'm only trying to put the facts together. I'm starting from scratch and want to keep all possible options open.

That said, I must confess that Junior is at the top of my list of suspects. As you described them, his actions put him at the top of my list until we further develop the case. I'm just following the evidence here. He may not stay at the top of my list, but we must find him and bring him in for a talk."

"I've been looking everywhere with no luck. He knows this area well, obviously, and he'll be hard to find. I'm glad you're here to dedicate all your time to this case, detective."

"I'll start today. Hopefully, he won't become dangerous if cornered. In a confrontation, if the worst comes to worst, we may have no other choice but to take his life. I certainly hope it doesn't come to that, believe me, but if it did happen, and there were no more murders after that, then you could make a case the 'Ghost' murders were solved, couldn't you?"

Sheriff Lewis gave Detective him a stern look and said, "Let's hope it doesn't come to that."

"Let's hope. I'll get started, sheriff, and of course, I'll update you on what I find out. Williams stood up and left the Sheriff's Office.

He was hungry, so he found the best-looking restaurant in town and went inside for breakfast. He sat down and ordered his food. While waiting, he began to rap his fingers on the tabletop, thinking.

The sheriff was blinded to the facts because of his loyalty to the Martin family. He was sure of it. The evidence against the young man was overwhelming. He could probably accept one coincidence as genuine and give Junior the benefit of the doubt. Two, three, or four coincidences happening at about the same time? That was not likely. He didn't buy it for one minute. How could the sheriff not see this? There was no doubt that the sheriff was a blind fool.

All he had to do was bring the young man in alive. The best possible outcome for him personally would then be for him to interrogate Junior, break him, and force the truth to come out. But interrogating suspects was not one of his strong suits. His strengths had more to do with analyzing facts and coming to conclusions. Nevertheless, he would find a way to deal with Junior when the opportunity presented itself.

Williams tried to look at the case from the sheriff's viewpoint as any good detective would. At this early stage of his investigation, nothing he could see backed up the sheriff's position of Junior being innocent. He didn't want to shut down the idea altogether, but he needed more information before giving it any credence.

His food arrived, and he began to eat it. About halfway through his breakfast, his next course of action became clear. He needed to visit the Martins and talk with them.

It was a clear day with only wisps of clouds in the sky. Will and Cora had ten minutes of their lunch break left.

"How's the okra this year?" She asked.

"Comin' along. Cora, you were right to let Junior stay at Charley's," Will blurted out. I'm glad we didn't tell Sheriff Lewis."

She had watched him, sensed his guilt, and was relieved he was ready to discuss it. When he hurt, she hurt.

"Both of us doubted him and ourselves. Considering everything, it's the first reaction most good parents would have in the same situation. We both know he's innocent. He went out on his own, was too young, got in a tight spot, and then did something stupid by breaking out of jail. It hurts. It looks bad for him. It looks bad for us, too, but it can be fixed." she said.

"I understand why he calls me Will now. I have no choice but to get used to it."

Cora knew what her husband meant. Time heals all wounds,

but that didn't make it any easier for Will. He would bury his pain. That was his way.

Their lunch break was nearly over when they saw a stranger ride up. She was glad Will was with her. The man slowed as he got closer and gave them a crisp wave.

"Good afternoon, folks," he said as he got close.

"I need a few minutes of your time if possible."

"Who are you?"

"I am Detective Matthew Williams. I've come up from Phoenix to help the sheriff solve the two murders that took place recently in Prescott."

"Come on up and join us," Will said.

Detective William's boots made a heavy, sharp thud with every step he took as he walked onto the porch. He found a chair and sat down.

"You're Will and Cora Martin?"

"Yes." Answered Will.

"Good. I'll get right to the point then. The sheriff has very little to go on regarding these two homicides, as you may know. Your son, Junior, was seen near the first murder when the victim was discovered. Junior didn't cooperate with the sheriff and was put in jail. He then proceeded to break out of jail and was at large when the second murder took place. Is that correct, Mr. Martin?"

"Yes. He's innocent."

The hairs on the back of Cora's neck stood up. Junior was recuperating at Charley's house at the time of the second murder, but she couldn't tell the detective.

"What do you want from us?" She asked.

"I need to talk with Junior to eliminate him as a suspect."

She didn't believe him for a second. It was as clear as day to her that this detective thought Junior was the killer.

"We have no idea where he is. He left home a few weeks ago, and we haven't seen or spoken with him since," she stated.

Detective Williams gave her a hard stare, then turned his attention to Will. He must have learned nothing from looking at Will because the detective briefly looked down at the deck.

He raised his head and asked, "Do you mind if I look inside the cabin?"

"Go ahead." Said Will.

Williams went inside the cabin, with Will and Cora not far behind, and slowly looked around. He searched every room and spent extra time in Junior's room. He said nothing, then walked back out the front door.

It looked like he was ready to ride out. "If you learn anything about Junior, contact me at the Sheriff's Office. Do you understand?

"Yes," Will said.

"Good day then." Williams nodded his head slightly, turned around, and left.

"I don't trust that man," Cora said.

"I think he's a decent fella', just doesn't know what's goin' on."

"I hope you're right," Cora whispered.

Chapter Nineteen

Detective Williams had hit a dead end. The only thing he learned from his visit with the Martins was that they would be reluctant to give him any information about Junior. He asked around town about the Martins and heard mostly positive things about the family. The occasional negative comment he did hear seemed to have a strong dose of jealousy attached to it. On the outside, the Martin family seemed to be as clean as a whistle.

He learned even less in the next two weeks than he did that first day after talking with the Martins. He saw nothing, and the people he interviewed knew nothing. He had to turn the investigation around, so he changed tactics. If Junior was going to be found, there was a good possibility he would be on the move at night, under the cover of darkness. He remembered when he was young what an exciting thing it was for him to go outside at night, usually with one or more of his friends. Even now, being out at night made Detective William's senses come alive.

On his third night of walking around in the evening looking for a clue, he saw something that caught his eye. He had been slowly walking around in the downtown area. A half-moon provided him some light. He saw a young man enter the partially rebuilt Royale Saloon, walk past the large 'keep-out' sign, and enter the building. He cautiously followed him in and drew his pistol. As quietly as possible, he moved closer to the young man and watched him. He was close but didn't want to get too close.

"What's your name, son?"

The young man turned around to face him. "Easy partner, I'm just checking on their progress here. My name is Raymond. Who are you?"

"Detective Williams. I'm up from Phoenix, and I've been assigned to the Ghost case."

"Show me some identification. You could be the Ghost for all I know," Raymond said.

The detective showed Raymond his badge and asked, "What are you really doing here?"

"I'm a concerned citizen, appalled by the senseless burning of a perfectly good saloon. I'll be old enough to drink soon, you know."

"I can see why so many people don't like you, Raymond. Did you start the fire here, son?"

"Of course not. Ask Sheriff Lewis, and he'll tell you Will Martin Junior is suspected of starting the fire."

"Where is Junior?"

"I have no idea. For all I know, he's left the Prescott area altogether. I haven't seen him for weeks. He could be dead by now. Hope not, though."

"I may have to bring you in to talk some more. I can also throw you in jail for trespassing."

"I'm a minor, and you can do no such thing." Said Raymond, bluffing.

Detective Williams continued to look at him but said nothing.

"My parents would make a big stink if you put me in jail." Said Raymond, lying.

"I'm going to keep my eyes on you, Raymond. One mistake, and I'll put you in jail, and I don't care if you're a minor or if your parents don't like it."

"Well, having eyes is a good quality for a detective. Good luck to you. I'll be leaving now."

Detective Williams continued to stare at Raymond as he passed by him and walked out of the building. He had a feeling this was not the last time he would talk with Raymond.

He watched as the man followed Raymond out of town for ten minutes. Then, the man following Raymond turned around and returned to the downtown area. He knew where Raymond was headed, so he hurried to Raymond's parent's house to wait for him.

He waited, then saw Raymond approach. "Psst, Raymond, it's me." Junior said as he stepped out of the darkness from the corner of the barn.

"Junior, you're alive, or did you die and return as a ghost?"

"Very funny. Let's go into the barn and talk."

Once inside, Junior said, "This place stinks. Don't you ever clean up around here?"

"As much as my busy schedule allows me to, yes."

"What busy schedule? Forget it. I saw you go into the Royale, and a man followed you in. You both stayed inside for a few minutes, and then he followed you for a while on your way home. What was that all about?"

"He was a detective from Phoenix, working the Ghost case. He was looking for you. I told him I haven't seen you in weeks."

"Was that all he wanted to talk about?

"Yeah. My supper is probably getting cold now." Raymond said, then gave Junior a curious look, "Don't tell me you're hungry again."

"I'm not hungry, no, and I haven't forgotten when you helped me. I still owe you. I've been thinking about something else, and I wanted to get your opinion about it."

"See, you need my help again. How predictable you have become, Junior."

"Somebody clubbed me in the chest last month and cracked one of my ribs. I've healed enough to come out at night to look around, but it still hurts. Anyway, what I wanted to talk to you about is that when I think about that day, chasing that man, I think I was being set up. I ran into a trap."

I was sitting near the lumber mill, just seeing what I could see, when a man with a limp walked down the road, then turned up the old mill road. I was surprised because he began to run down the road and no longer had a limp. It was the Ghost, or someone working with the Ghost. I started to run after him, and after a few minutes, someone clubbed me in the chest."

Junior continued, "I've had some time to think about it. There had to have been a second person there that day. I saw the man running up ahead of me, and at the time I was hit, he was too far up the road to have come back to club me. The Ghost had to have had an accomplice working with him that day. My question to you is, do you think the Ghost was alone when he committed the two murders, or do you think there were two or more people involved in the killings?"

"Interesting question. Maybe two people could work together - the Ghost and his dedicated sidekick, maybe?"

"For all we know, three or more people could have been working together," Junior said.

"Now you've gone too far. The next thing you'll tell me is that all the people buried in the cemetery have risen out of the ground as ghosts so they can follow their ghost leader and rule Prescott?"

"No. I'm not saying that, but I want to ask you one thing. Do you think a revenge killer, which I'm sure the Ghost is, would be more likely to work alone?"

"Yes, that would be logical. If multiple people were involved in multiple murders, then more things could go wrong. A single killer has a better chance of controlling his mistakes. There may be at least two people involved in these killings, but my guess is the Ghost works alone."

"I think so too. Still, this accomplice who hit me in the chest… He has me confused."

"Maybe you should stop chasing ghosts."

"I'm not going to stop."

"Suit yourself. I'm going in for supper. Try to stay out of jail."

The following morning, Sheriff Lewis knocked on Charley's door and waited. Charley opened the door.

"Mornin' Charley. Junior is still missing. You've heard by now that he broke out of jail last month. It occurred to me that I haven't been to your house to ask you about him. Have you seen Junior?"

"I haven't seen hide nor hair of him for weeks, Sheriff. The boy is in trouble, I heard. I want to do what's best for him, which in this case would be to have him sitting safely in your jail. If I see him, you'll be the first person I tell, I promise."

Sheriff Lewis wasn't sure what to do. Charley had a reputation for telling an occasional tall tale, but under the circumstances, with Charley sounding so honest and forthright, for now, he felt he had no choice but to let it go.

"Good to see you, Charley. Take care."

"Good day then, sheriff, and good luck." Charley watched the sheriff start to walk away; then, he went back inside his house.

Junior was sitting at the table and asked, "Who was that?"

"Sheriff Lewis. He wanted to know if I'd seen you since you left the jail. I told him no."

Junior looked up and grinned at Charley, then shook his head.

"Junior, have you ever cooked anything?"

"No."

"Elizabeth went out to buy vegetables and some meat for a stew tonight. You are getting around better now, and it's about time you helped out around here. She will show you how to make it when she comes back."

"Sounds good."

"Listen, Junior, I know you are mad at your father, and I know how frustrating he can be sometimes. I've been mad at him, too, plenty of times. He is the most stubborn and single-minded person I know."

Charley remembered the day, many years ago, when he was exasperated with Will and called him stubborn and simple-minded. Still, he thought it was better for him to stick with describing Will as 'single-minded' in this situation.

"Junior, you need to understand that beneath his rough outside, in his way, your father is trying to do what is best for you. He loves you."

"He can love me or not. It doesn't matter to me. He's not my real father and never will be. He doesn't understand me and never will. I'm not like him."

Charley looked at Junior momentarily, serious and a little disappointed, then said, "You're more like him than you realize."

A moment later, Elizabeth returned with the makings for their stew. She showed him how to prepare the meal, and Junior started to work on it. He seemed glad to be doing something productive. When he was finished putting the ingredients together he moved it over to the top of the wood stove to cook.

"Junior, have you ever played poker?"

"No."

"I'm going to teach you how to play five-card draw."

"Why?"

"You need to get educated in the ways of the world, and this is as good a time as any for you to get started. Besides, it's fun. Elizabeth, are you in?"

"Wouldn't miss it." They all walked over and sat down at the table.

Charley explained how the game worked, including the rankings of the hands. Junior asked him some questions. Charley dealt out a couple of practice hands, and Junior asked more questions. Then they decided to play for real. Charley gave each player fifteen cents starting money, and they began to play.

Charley started strong and had an early lead. Elizabeth faltered when Charley bluffed her, and she lost a big pot. Shortly after that, she lost all her money. Then Junior started to get hot, won the game, and took all the money.

"Remind me never to play cards with you." Said Charley.

"Remind me twice." Said Elizabeth.

Charley looked over at Elizabeth, standing by the wood stove. "I smell something good. Is it ready?

"Come and get it." She said.

Charley looked at Junior and said, "Let's eat."

Chapter Twenty

Junior surveyed the area behind the Methodist church. It was early Sunday morning, well before any church activities would start, and good for what he wanted to do.

There was an open area behind the red-brick church building. Behind the open area was a forest cut straight and parallel to the church's back wall. Junior walked to the forest's edge and noticed a lightly used wagon trail in front of the forest. The forest was dense, with many small pine trees amongst the larger ones. He heard a variety of bird sounds coming from the forest. The birds seemed to be waking up, full of energy and loud. He'd seen enough there and turned and went to take a closer look at the area behind the church.

At the center of the rear wall was an uncovered wooden porch, maybe five feet wide and four feet deep. He took a closer look at it. Two black spots were on the otherwise clean wood. Junior was sure these spots were initially blood spots that had turned black over the past few weeks.

He set about taking a detailed look at the grounds behind the church. There were plenty of footprints in the area, not as many as he would expect to be at the front of the church, but still, Junior didn't see anything unusual. He turned his attention to the side of the church. At first, he saw nothing unusual. There were several footprints. He realized the second victim had been placed here at the church almost a month ago; much time had passed since then, and it would be a long shot for him to find anything meaningful here.

He saw two unusual marks. They were almost completely eroded, but they hadn't been stepped on. He got down on his hands and knees to take a closer look. They were round depressions that seemed out of place there. He lowered his head until his nose almost touched the round marks and examined them closely.

After a moment, Junior stood up, grimaced a little from the pain in his ribs, brushed the dirt off his pants, and looked up at a man he did not recognize. The man was holding a revolver pointed squarely at his chest.

"You must be Junior."

"I am"

Detective Williams flashed his badge at Junior.

"I've been looking for you. I'm Detective Williams, and I'm up from Phoenix, working on the Ghost killings. You're going back to jail."

"Wait, I have something to talk to you about and something important to show you."

He eyed the young man suspiciously, then asked, "What?"

"There is a wagon trail behind the church, which was probably used to bring the victim's body here."

"The sheriff saw the tracks and came to the same conclusion."

"There were only two small blood stains on the porch where the body was placed, indicating the man was killed elsewhere, then brought here."

"That's what we thought, too."

"Look at these round impressions in the ground here." Junior slowly lowered one arm and pointed at the impressions."

"So?"

"They look like marks left by a cane. And why would someone who needed a cane be walking here, in this dirt area on the side of a church?"

"Good question. Do you think the marks could be from kids playing with sticks or from something else?"

"No. Other explanations don't fit what went on here."

Now he was confused. This fourteen-year-old youth was trying to link some clues together here, but Williams didn't see the connection. "Tell me what you think went on."

"The victim was killed somewhere else, somewhere remote maybe, then brought here on what most likely was a wagon and placed on the back porch. The killer then moved the wagon around to the front of the church. Whoever dropped off the body was wearing a disguise and used a cane to walk around the side of the church, back to the rear porch, knock on the rear door, and then walk back along the side of the church to the front, where his wagon was. He did all this without anyone noticing anything unusual about him."

"Let me punch some holes in your theory, young man. There was no reason for the wagon to be at the front of the church in the first place. The Ghost didn't even need a disguise. It would have been much easier for him to use the wagon trail to bring the corpse here, dump it on the porch, hurry back to his wagon, and leave. No one would be the wiser." Detective Williams was surprised at how easily he could discredit Junior's theory.

"I'm sorry, son. Your theory sounds more like the desperate conjuring of something that could have happened and more than likely invented to distract me and the sheriff from what did happen. You dreamed all this up to distract from the investigation. The best answer is typically the simplest answer. Your answer to what happened requires unrelated things to be grouped together and then somehow fitted together to create a scenario that doesn't add up."

Junior had to think about that for a moment. "The round marks in the ground are from a cane, which doesn't make sense. They are out of place and don't fit here. The Ghost was in disguise when he dropped off the body, then drove the wagon around to the front of the church, got out, and walked to the rear of the church, again using a cane. I don't think that whoever dropped off the body could count on leaving the area behind the church without having been seen by the pastor or someone else. There wouldn't have been enough time, especially for someone who goes to such extreme measures to never be recognized."

He still had his pistol pointed at Junior. This young fellow was everything he had heard about. There was no doubt he had a good head on his shoulders. He lowered his pistol and decided to test the young man's theory.

"Let's have a visit with Pastor Taylor. It's Sunday morning, and he should be getting ready for the day. I want to ask him if he saw anyone outside the church that day or if there was a wagon in front of the church. You first," he said as he pointed for Junior to walk ahead. They both walked around to the front of the church.

He holstered his pistol as they entered the church. The pastor was checking the pews to ensure enough hymnals were available.

The pastor saw the two of them and looked surprised. "Junior, how are you? Are you safe?" He looked at the detective questioningly.

Junior seemed to know many people, and most of them liked him. Williams was a little surprised and frustrated by the pastor's reaction.

"I'm fine. This is Detective Williams. He came up from Phoenix to help solve the Ghost killings. We're working the case together now."

Williams started to respond, but Junior spoke too quickly, "We have a theory that on the day of the killing, the killer knocked on the back door so you would find the body. If you had responded quickly, which I heard you did, there would have been a good chance you would have seen the Ghost killer in disguise. Can you think back to that day and remember seeing anyone?"

The pastor appeared to look past his plans for the day as he thought back to the day he found the body. It took him a few seconds. "I was near the back of the church when I heard the knock on the door. I went over to open it, but it wouldn't budge, so I walked out of the front entrance to the church and saw a wagon there."

Junior turned his head sharply to look at Williams.

"An old lady was sitting in the wagon. She was in bad shape. It looked to me like she was crippled. She had a cane. When I talked to her, I remember she had a very intense look on her face. It looked to me like she was in great pain, the poor lady."

"Do you remember seeing anyone else around that time?"

"No."

"Thank you very much, pastor." He said. Junior and the detective walked out of the front of the church. A couple of well-worn benches were in the front, one on each side of the front entrance. They sat down on one of the benches to talk.

"Sorry, Junior. Looks like your theory didn't work out."

"It worked out perfectly, don't you see? The old lady was the Ghost. No one would have ever suspected it. I had no idea the

Ghost had such believable disguises and impressive abilities. Can you make yourself look like and talk like an old woman? Enough to fool anyone? This goes beyond anything I could have imagined. The man is talented."

Williams thought Junior went a little too far in his praise for this imaginary Ghost. "You're stretching the truth to fit your theory, Junior. The Ghost is the Ghost, and an old woman is an old woman. I don't see the connection."

Junior put his head down and looked frustrated. The young man was nothing if not creative. It was very inventive of him to be able to use the round marks in the dirt and the old woman in the wagon that day to try to combine these two unrelated and immaterial things and come up with his wild theory.

He didn't trust the young man. It was that simple, and he wouldn't allow himself to be tricked by this nonsense. He would not be led down a rose-lined path that led to an unlikely conclusion, especially when that path was built by this clever new acquaintance of his, his prime suspect. He thought about what he should do next and quickly developed a plan.

Look, Junior, we have no evidence to hold you on. I'm going to let you go free. Don't leave town. My advice to you is to stay out of trouble. Go, now." Junior looked surprised at this turn of events but gladly walked away.

Detective Williams followed Junior. He was confident in his basic detective skills and was sure Junior had not noticed he had been followed. The detective watched as Junior entered a house in town. Unless he was mistaken, this was the same house where someone named Charley lived. Sheriff Lewis told him he had gone to Charley's house to ask if he knew where Junior was. Charley said he had no idea. Well, well, he thought. I know something you don't, Sheriff, and I'm not going to tell you right away, either.

Charley has been helping Junior.

It would be easy to tail Junior from Charley's house every day. Sooner or later, Junior would make a mistake - they always did. He knew from experience that even the best criminals tripped up eventually, and he'd be there to catch him in the act when it happened.

Chapter Twenty-One

It had been too long since he had killed, and he felt like his mission had stalled. The annoying young man had been a distraction and slowed him down, but his plan against him had worked. The amateur was out of his way and would not bother him, at least for now. If the young man continued to harass him, then much harsher methods would have to be used. That would be just fine with him. He relished the idea of taking him out of commission forever. His source told him the boy went out only at night now because he was trying to avoid the sheriff.

He preferred working during the day anyway. He could see things easier and had complete confidence in his ability to disguise himself. His mission would proceed without interference. Good. His years of experience hunting down these bad men and his instinct for properly punishing them made him a potent force for justice.

He had started to take more pride in being called the Ghost. He liked feeling invisible and getting the credit for utilizing his skills. He had finally identified his next target, but it had taken too long for him to find this new Oscar. Justice had been delayed, and each passing day made him increasingly anxious and frustrated.

It was tempting for him to push the timetable. He would

enjoy the spontaneous killing of the evil man, but the rigors of maintaining his self-taught system, with every detail meticulously planned out, overruled that impulse. His previous experiences with failure due to poor planning were still fresh in his mind. His mission had to be flawless, and his identity had to remain a secret. Both were important for his continued success - in this town or any town. Every kill he performed was planned out well in advance. As long as he stuck with what had worked so well for him in the past, he would continue to be unstoppable.

Charley saw Junior when he came in and asked, "How did you do?"

"I made some progress. I went to the rear of the Methodist church to get a feel for what happened there. I found out something interesting. There were some unusual marks on the ground on the side of the church. I looked at them closely and, shortly after that, ran into a detective who told me he was working on the Ghost murder cases."

"A detective? Are you sure?"

"Yeah, he said his name is Williams. He showed me his badge. We talked for a while, then we went into the church and talked with Pastor Taylor, and then the detective let me go. I answered all his questions truthfully."

"I don't understand why he would let you go."

"I don't know either. I must be more convincing than I thought I was. We talked about the murder there. I think I gave the detective some ideas he hadn't thought of before. He must have known I was right or at least on the right track. Then he told me he and the Sheriff did not have enough evidence to hold me, so he let me go."

"You got lucky today. He must have forgotten about the

damage to the jail. What sort of unusual marks did you find?"

Junior explained the marks from a cane, and that the Ghost had disguised himself so well as a crippled old lady that he came across as being entirely believable. "The pastor still thinks it was an old woman in the wagon, not the Ghost."

"The Ghost will not stop killing as long as he finds fathers out there who beat their children or until someone finds him and stops him," Junior added.

"I'm going to make some coffee, then we can sit down and talk about this," Charley said.

He went over to make some coffee, then brought two steaming mugs. Charley started, "When I'm trying to solve a problem, especially if it's a big problem, I've found the best way to do it is to get other people involved to help me. Everyone has a different way of looking at things, so you get more ideas than you would if you tried to solve a problem yourself. Plus, if it becomes necessary to take action to solve the problem, people are already involved and would be more likely to help you with the solution."

"What are you saying? I can't ask the sheriff to help me." Junior said.

"I know. Hang on. I'm thinking."

Junior took a sip of his coffee.

"You said you think the killings will continue as long as there are child-beaters in Prescott. The killer must be looking for these people, or he has someone else who is looking for him. We can do our own search for them, and if we're lucky, we might be able to take action before someone else gets killed." Charley said.

Junior looked intrigued. "How are we going to do that?"

"Not sure yet." He took another sip of coffee. "This kind of information is hard to get. The families don't want to talk about it.

They're under a great deal of pressure and probably feel very bad about themselves and their situation."

They drank more coffee.

"Let's go talk to Sharlot. She has a good deal of influence in this town. If nothing else, she can work with Sheriff Lewis. You and I won't be able to get any information from him, but she may be able to. We need to know what the Sheriff and this detective are thinking. We need to know what progress they've made. She can also go to the churches to get information." Said Charley.

"Good idea. Let's ride out there and see if she's home. Charley thought it was worth the trip. He hadn't heard any mention of Sharlot being out of town. That meant she probably was in town, which meant she was probably home, taking care of her mother. As they rode up to her cabin, they saw Sharlot and her mother. Her mother had her left arm hooked around Sharlot's right arm as they walked, and she was using a cane in her right hand.

"Morning, Sharlot," Charley said.

"Morning. Who's the fugitive with you?"

"He's innocent. You know that."

"You shouldn't have broken out of jail."

"I know. You're not the first person to tell me that."

"Go up to the porch. I'll meet you there in a minute."

As they walked towards Sharlot's cabin, Junior said, "Charley, look at the impressions Sharlot's mother's cane made in the ground."

"Yeah, so?"

"These marks from Sharlot's mom's cane are similar to those I found at the side of the Methodist church."

They walked up, sat on the porch, and watched as the two

women walked up the porch and entered the house. When Sharlot returned to sit with them, she went after Junior again.

"I can't believe you broke out of jail. Your mother has been a total wreck from worrying. What were you…"

"Let's go inside so we can talk." Charley interrupted.

They went inside. "You're right, Sharlot; I should have stayed in the jail."

"Did you learn a lesson?" She asked.

"Yes."

"What was it?" She asked.

"To try to think things out ahead of time."

Sharlot raised her voice to a near shout, "Don't try - Do."

Charley watched as Junior appeared to be fuming. He was biting his tongue, but Charley doubted Junior would challenge Sharlot.

She stared at Junior momentarily, then turned and asked him, "Now, what did you want to see me about?"

Charley started, "Junior has been working to solve the Ghost murders since he broke out of jail. In fact, he has already had a run-in with the Ghost and ended up with a cracked rib as a result."

"Oh no. Is that so? Are you all right?"

"I'm good. Still hurts." Junior replied.

Charley continued, "Junior has developed a theory about the killer."

Junior picked up the conversation from there and explained his idea that the killer was acting as a vigilante.

"You might be right, but I don't see how I can help," Sharlot said.

"You are the perfect person to help us. We want to stop the

next murder from happening and catch the Ghost at the same time. We need your help in getting information," Junior said. He was glad Sharlot let Junior talk without interruption. She looked intrigued.

"There are two obvious things you can help us with right away. The first thing would be to talk to Sheriff Lewis to learn what progress he might have made on the two cases. He has a detective working with him now. Came up from Phoenix. We can't work with either of them, but knowing what they know could save us time. What information does he have? Has he made the vigilante-killer connection yet, and if so, has he found someone who could be the Ghost's next target?"

"I told the Sheriff about your vigilante theory, like you asked me to do when you were laid up. I don't know if he believed me, though," Charley said.

"I want to save the next victim from being killed by the Ghost, but I have to stay clear of the sheriff, who probably still feels it's his duty to put me back in jail if he found me. Guess I might have made him look bad."

Junior continued, "Anyway, the second way you could help, and this may end up being the most useful way, is we need to find the children or wives who are being beaten so we can protect their fathers or husbands. The most obvious place to look for these families would be the churches. Both of the bodies of the first two victims were placed at churches. We could go to the churches ourselves, but we think they would tell you more than they would tell us."

Sharlot spoke up, "I want to help. I'll go to the sheriff, acting as a concerned citizen, and talk with him. I'll talk to the mayor if I need to, to see if he can learn more from the Sheriff. I know Father Donovan very well. I'm sure when I explain what is going on, he will tell me if there are any other beaten children or wives out there whose fathers or husbands could be targets. I don't know the Methodist Pastor well, but I'll buy him lunch and talk to him. Come back in a few days, and I'll give you an update."

Chapter Twenty-Two

Sharlot always liked Sheriff Lewis, but even good men needed inspiration sometimes. She would be that for him today. She rode over to his office and went in. Sitting at his desk, he looked up at her and smiled.

She got right to the point. "Sheriff, I'm concerned about the Ghost killer. He's still out there. Who knows when he will strike again? What have you found? People are worried and constantly asking me if I know anything. Talk to me."

"There's nothing much I can tell you yet." He said.

That was not the answer she was looking for. "You know, I could ask Mayor Young about the investigation. You report to him, do you not? I'm sure he would tell me most of what you don't want to tell me. You could make it easier on yourself if you told me now."

"Alright, but don't get too excited. There hasn't been much progress on the case. We have no motive, no evidence, and no murder weapon for either crime. Our only suspect is the young man, Will Martin Junior, who recently broke out of jail."

Sharlot's back went straight as she started at the sheriff. "That boy is no killer, and you must know that. You're wasting time thinking about Junior while the Ghost is still roaming around town. Perhaps he's a vigilante killer."

"I've heard that theory. We've considered that option, as well as others."

"Think about it. Two beaten children, no connection between the families, and two dead fathers."

"It does make sense," the sheriff admitted.

"I'm not going to tell you how to do your job, and I know you have other work to do besides these murder cases, but think about it. What if you or someone else becomes aware of a child who has been beaten and then can protect the father of that child before the Ghost attacks him? Keep your eyes on the lookout for children or wives who look distressed. That information could become very important. You might be able to save someone's life."

"I will. You have my word." He said.

Sharlot gave him a sincere yet stern look, thanked him for his time, and left.

She went to see Father Donovan next, stopping only briefly to talk to a couple of acquaintances who stopped her on the street and wanted to talk. She went into the church to speak to the priest.

"Have you seen any kids who appeared to have been beaten? I just finished talking with the sheriff. He thinks there's a chance the Ghost is a vigilante who is looking for children who look like they've taken beatings so that he can go after their fathers. You may know of a wife who has been beaten, also. If we can spot these children or wives first, we might be able to save a life."

"No, I'm sorry, Sharlot. No one comes to mind. He sat expressionless for a moment; then, his face came to life.

"Wait a minute. Yes, there is a family - the Murphy's. They have a boy, maybe eight years old now. He's not always with the family at church, but when he is, he never talks. I remember that he sometimes covered up a part of himself with his hands, like his arm, or his head and neck. I thought it was unusual when I saw it, but I never thought about it much after that. The boy's dad, Bradley Murphy, is very formal and austere. Come to think of it, he could very well be a child-beater."

"Thank you, Father. This could greatly help save a life and find this Ghost."

"The Murphys live on the southeastern side of town, on Fourth Street, if I remember right. God bless you, Sharlot, and I'll keep my eyes and ears open from now on."

"Thank you again, Father."

She left and began to wonder about the state of the world. In just a few minutes, she had located someone who was probably a child beater. Maybe a wife beater. How strange. She lived an isolated life, rarely thinking about the evil in the world. It was easier for her to ignore it. Not anymore.

Sharlot walked over to see Pastor Taylor at the Methodist church. "Good afternoon, Pastor."

"Sharlot, what a pleasure it is to see you. Are you thinking of converting to my church?"

"No, I'm afraid not. I have a serious matter to discuss with you. I'd happily buy you a late lunch to discuss it."

"Thanks, but I just finished my lunch. I haven't had any coffee today. How about a cup?"

"Sounds good." They went into the Pastor's office. She sat there for a few minutes, and he came in with the coffee.

"I hope black is good for you?"

"Black is perfect, thanks."

"Now, how can I help you?"

She explained she was working with the sheriff and other concerned citizens, who believed the Ghost was a vigilante killer. She told him she and the sheriff discussed the idea, and the sheriff agreed that the theory made sense. "I need your help in finding a family, or families, who have children, or maybe wives, that look like they have been beaten."

"I'll need to think about that for a minute." They sipped their coffees, and then the Pastor said, "No family comes to mind right now, Sharlot. I'll surely be looking for that sort of thing; I can guarantee you that."

"Thank you, Pastor. Keep your eyes and ears open. You may end up saving a life or two."

They drank the rest of their coffee as Sharlot asked him how the funding program for the expansion of his church was going.

"Slowly. We'll get there eventually." They talked for a few more minutes as they finished their coffees, and then she thanked him and left.

The first thing the following day, Sharlot wanted to tell Charley what she had learned, so she rode over to his house in town. The information about the Murphy's boy couldn't wait. She knocked on his door.

"Hello Sharlot. You look like you have news." Charley said.

"Yes, can I come in?"

"Of course. She walked in and saw Junior sitting at the table. "I've made some coffee. Do you want sugar?

"No, black is perfect." She had drunk a lot of coffee lately but didn't think another cup would hurt her.

"I talked to Sheriff Lewis. He is at a loss. He hasn't found out anything yet. I also went over to talk to Father Donovan, who told me of the Murphy family. They have a son who looked like he has been getting regular beatings."

Junior listened intently.

"They live on the eastern part of Fourth Street, apparently."

"Thank you for coming all the way over here," Charley said.

"I thought you would want to know right away."

"Yes. We've got some fresh biscuits and gravy if you're hungry."

"No thanks. I need to get back and check on Momma. Good luck to you two."

She left, and Junior became animated. "The Murphys have to be the Ghost's next target."

"We have no way of knowing if the Ghost is even aware of them, Junior, or if he is, when or where he would strike next." Charley countered.

"I'm familiar with that side of Fourth Street. There are no vacant lots there. It will be hard to watch their house, but it can be done. I'll find a way."

The wheels were turning in Junior's head now. Charley said nothing. "This man, Bradley Murphy, is the Ghost's next victim. I know it, and I'm going to save him before that son of a bitch Ghost can get to him."

Charley was a little taken aback by Junior's language but said nothing. There was nothing that he could do to change Junior's mind anyway.

Chapter Twenty-Three

Junior hoped he would save a man's life today, tomorrow, next week, or the week after. He didn't ask for permission or even notify Charley and Elizabeth that he would be leaving that morning. About one hour before dawn, he went to Charley's front door, cracked it open, carefully looked out, and then went outside to walk over to Fourth Street. What he wanted to do was important. It would take him thirty to forty minutes to get there.

Today's work may not result in anything. Chances are he would learn nothing today and need to return and try again tomorrow and probably the next day. He could spend weeks without seeing anything unusual there. All he could do it try.

He couldn't be seen on his walk over. He needed to be as clandestine as possible on the way over and back to Fourth Street. He planned on walking down different side streets and varying his route each day as much as possible. As he walked, he tried very hard to look inconspicuous.

So far, it looked like the day would be another 'plain' day, as Junior liked to call them, just like the last two or three days had been. There was no weather, not even much wind. It was boring. It was not too hot or cold, and there were no clouds to speak of. It was very plain.

Junior remembered from his wandering days that a dangerous dog was on the east end of Fourth Street, so he entered from the west side. He didn't like the mean dogs, who seemed to be looking for an excuse to bite him if he crossed over what the dog saw as his invisible line - the borderline of the dog's territory that couldn't be crossed without consequences.

Most people didn't like the mean dogs, but everyone was forced to respect them. There were also a couple of dogs on the street who would bark at anything and everything. He expected that and wasn't worried about the noise they might make.

First, he needed to find out which house on Fourth Street belonged to the Murphys. He liked Charley's approach to solving problems by involving more people, but he was on his own now. He wanted to protect Mr. Murphy, find the Ghost killer, and do it all by himself.

Junior arrived at the west end of Fourth Street and began walking down the dirt road as casually as possible. He tried to look left and right without moving his head too much. He had walked about a third of the way down the street when he noticed one of the homes had a low wooden fence on one side, about three feet tall, that he could hide behind. He neither heard nor saw any activity from the house, and he decided to go for the fence.

He turned and walked over to the fence, like he owned the house, then stepped over the fence and lowered himself behind it. He waited there, motionless, but heard nothing, not even a barking dog. The yard he was in was mostly dirt, with a few weeds scattered around. It looked like the owners had made some attempt to control the weeds because most of the weeds were only about one foot tall.

He could peek over the top of the fence or look through a crack. Neither option was very good, so he looked for a better way. In less than a minute, he found a knot in one of the wooden slats that he could use to look through and see the street without risking being noticed by someone when he peeked over the top of the fence. All he had to do was remove the knot. It was loose, so he began to pull and push it as he tried to work it free. Eventually, he was able to worry the knot out of the fence. He had a good but narrow view of the street. He settled in and kept his eye on the street, looking for anything unusual.

He watched as the men left their homes, one by one, to go to work. All he could do was sit there, wait, and stay patient. Maybe he would get lucky. Perhaps he would see a boy who looked sad and down on his luck. Some light began to appear in the sky, and as time dragged on, he saw no children and no more adults coming out of their homes. He was at a dead end, and his efforts would yield no results today.

He sat there for a moment and wondered if he could become like one of the mean dogs when it became time for action. Could he protect the house and the people inside ferociously? Could he attack the Ghost without a second thought or doubt if this murderer with a seemingly endless supply of disguises crossed Junior's invisible line, his territory? Him, a fourteen-year-old against this ruthless and practiced murderer? Thinking about taking action was utterly different than actually taking action. He realized this truth and needed to build up his resolve for the decisive moment if it came, and everything would be riding on his shoulders alone to make a difference.

Junior began to get a little nervous as dawn arrived and the morning blossomed into full sunlight. He was about to start the risky walk back to Charley's house when a drunk appeared on his right. The drunk was trying to walk down Junior's side of the street, and he looked like he could fall over at any moment. The drunk stumbled and wavered but managed to stay on his feet as he slowly made some forward progress. He wore dirty-looking and no-doubt smelly clothes, long mangled hair, and a scruffy beard. Junior would have to wait until the man passed before he could leave.

He watched the drunk struggle past him, slowly moving down the street to Junior's left. He was glad the drunk had not been there earlier in the morning. He could quickly have drawn too much attention to where Junior was hiding. If he had arrived at the same time as the drunk, he might not have been able to find his look-out spot.

The morning had been a waste, so why not just sit there and be entertained by the drunk to see how far he would walk before he fell and blacked out? Junior had nothing better to do anyway, and being delayed for another few minutes wouldn't make any difference.

Why were there so many drunks in the world? Junior wondered. Even in an out-of-the-way place like East Fourth Street here in Prescott, in the Arizona Territory, in the early morning hours. What had this world come to?

He whispered his earlier thought to himself, "even in an out-of-the-way place like East Fourth Street."

What was the chance of that? *This drunk was out of place here, wasn't he?* It did not make any sense for him to be here. He could have been coming home drunk, but at this hour, where would he be coming home from? Something wasn't right. Junior's senses went on high alert.

On an impulse, he hopped over the fence and began to follow the drunken man, who was still stumbling and staggering about fifty yards ahead of him. Junior kept his distance and tried to keep his head down and look casual. The drunk made a move to the right, crossed the street, entered the front yard of a house, and walked up the steps of a covered porch. Instead of going in, he knocked on the door.

Junior saw a bush in a nearby yard that would provide some

cover. He dove for it and waited. The drunk knocked on the door again, but there still was no response from inside. He kept knocking until, finally, an angry man opened the door.

"What do you want, mister?" The angry man shouted.

The drunk quickly produced a club from somewhere in his clothing and hit the man in the head. The man who answered the door collapsed immediately. The drunk looked totally sober now, strong and agile. Junior remembered the so-called drunk he saw on the old mill road. Was it the same man? The drunk dragged the man to him and away from the threshold and quietly closed the front door. He then pulled the man off the porch and around to the side of the house.

Junior was both stunned and excited as he watched this. He stood up instinctively and ran towards the house. He ran past the front of the house, turned the corner, and saw that the attacker, who had his back to him with his arm raised high, was preparing to strike the victim again.

Junior ran as fast as he could towards the attacker. He crashed into him and pushed him hard in the back. The club fell harmlessly, and the attacker was forced forward. Junior tripped over the fallen man and fell face-first onto the dirt, with his legs on top of the man, who he was now sure was Bradley Murphy.

Junior's rib injury was taking longer than he thought it should to heal. He felt a sharp pain in his chest when he fell on the dirt. He dealt with the pain for a quick moment, then looked up, but the attacker was gone. He had vanished - like a ghost.

Junior pulled back and stood up to look at the man who had been hit with the club. He was lying on his back and wasn't moving at all. His face was covered with blood. Junior picked up the club and inspected it. It was carved from a mesquite branch, about one and one-half feet long, with a handle carved into one end.

Someone had spent a great deal of time to craft this weapon. He saw a few spots of blood on the end of it. It was a nasty and deadly-looking tool designed to kill.

"Don't move, Junior, or I'll shoot you."

Junior froze. Who was that? Nobody on this street knew him. Then he remembered the voice.

"Drop the club right now and slowly turn around."

Junior carefully pushed his arm out and dropped the club. He then slowly turned around to face Detective Williams. The man had a massive grin, obviously very proud of himself.

"You are under arrest for the assault and intended murder of this man. You're going back to jail. This time you will have an armed guard watching you twenty-four hours a day. You won't escape from the jail again, Junior. Sorry. In fact, you may spend the rest of your miserable life with an armed guard watching over you unless they decide it would be much easier and cheaper to hang you."

"This isn't what it looks like, detective. The Ghost was just here. I watched him club Mr. Murphy at the front door, then drag him around here. The Ghost would have killed him if I hadn't stopped him."

"I saw something different with my own two eyes, Junior. I'm not falling for your lies anymore. Should I start calling you the Ghost now? You ran to a hiding spot behind a bush, then timed your attack perfectly, clubbed him, and dragged the man around to the side of the house. When I arrived and turned the corner of the house I didn't see any Ghost. I saw you. There was no Ghost here, Junior. You were the only one here with a club in your hands. I caught you red-handed."

"That's not what happened, I swear."

"Swearing won't help you now. Nothing will. Let's go. Lay flat on your stomach, hands behind you so I can cuff you. If you do anything unexpected, if you try to run or make any sudden movements, I promise you I will shoot you dead."

"I'll do as you say."

Junior did as instructed and offered no resistance as he was cuffed. He was forced to stand up, and then he was jerked back a step. He looked over his shoulder and saw the detective pick up and carefully examine the club. He acted like he was looking for something.

"Let's go. Move it." The detective ordered. Junior started walking.

Detective Williams stopped the first person he saw after cuffing Junior, a woman out for a walk with her young daughter, and told her to get help for the fallen man. He told her where to find him. The women agreed, then looked at Junior as though he was a dangerous criminal. He cringed. His worse fears had become painfully real. He was returning to jail, and his search for the Ghost was over.

Everyone who saw the two of them on their walk to the jail stopped and stared. Junior thought they would never forget the moment. He knew he wouldn't. He was humiliated. He saw a few people he knew. They looked like they were more shocked than most by what they were watching. Junior was roughly hauled off towards the jail, with a gun pressing into his back the whole time. No one would believe him when he tried to explain why he was at Murphy's house at that moment, especially Detective Williams.

Chapter Twenty-Four

He entered his house, slammed the door shut behind him, grabbed his fake beard, ripped it off, and threw it on the floor. Next came his wig and all the other minor pieces he had used in his disguise. He was forced to live through a surprising and disappointing turn of events. This kind of thing was not supposed to happen to him anymore.

He relived the events of this morning in his mind. At just the wrong moment, the young man pushed him and propelled him to the rear corner of the house. Luckily, he was able to maintain his balance and stay on his feet. He could have been an acrobat, like Oscar, except he hated acrobats, and he hated Oscar.

He found himself near the rear corner of the house when he heard a loud thump behind him. He came to a stop, turned, and saw that his attacker had tripped over the body of the wicked man. He had landed face-first on the ground and raised a small cloud of dust in the process. The dust hung in the air for a moment, but he could see through it to see who had pushed him. As the young man began to stand up, he immediately recognized the face. It was none other than the boy they call Junior, the same troublesome youth who had been interfering with his efforts for weeks now. He quickly left the area and followed his planned escape route home.

The young man must be so determined to do wrong that getting clubbed in the ribs was not enough to stop him. He would not be so lucky the next time. It would be permanent the next time. Obviously, Prescott has become a very corrupt town, and the wrongdoing in the town seems to be spreading like a disease. Earlier that day, he was close to finding justice for a boy who a terrible man had repeatedly beaten. Junior had denied the boy his justice.

After all his hard work, planning, and considerable talents, he was stopped by someone half his age an instant before obtaining redemption. He hit this new Oscar in the head, a bit of a glancing blow but enough to knock him out. His moment was near, but he couldn't finish the man. Why? because of the boy who surely was sent by the devil himself.

He was in such bad spirits. It was time for breakfast, but he wasn't hungry. He used his primary escape route to find his way home. He was lying on top of his bed, fully clothed, as he tried to concentrate.

He lost one of his favorite clubs. He had spent a long time making it, too. A small sacrifice, he thought. It was an older design, and he had a design improvement in mind that he wanted to try. He liked the idea of a single knot of wood that protruded at the end of the club and aligned with the handle so the knot would always strike the target first. This time, he would use the wood of a large Manzanita bush. He liked the red color of the bark when the bush was alive, and it was a dense wood, perfect for a club.

He could look forward to that, but a real dilemma was upon him now, and he knew it would be painful. His nightmares were light and easy to endure shortly after he had properly dispensed justice to an immoral man. The nightmares would then become progressively worse and worse and would only get better after he found justice again with his next kill. Then he could relax again.

Now, thanks to Junior, his worst nightmares would be with him for many upcoming nights until he could take vengeance and protect those who could not protect themselves. It was his life. He could not change it. He hated Junior.

He seemed to lose focus and easily escape into a dream suddenly. A new and very intense nightmare invaded his soul.

He was clubbing the man, Bradley Murphy, over and over in his father's tent when the flap snapped open. The boy who pushed him earlier came into the tent, holding the rubber chicken. The sight of it made his knees weak.

"How was your day, boy? The boy asked.

His meek response, "Good," was all he could come up with.

"I don't think so. You're lying to me again, boy."

The kid stepped over and slapped him with it. He could do nothing, not even raise his head. The blows came harder and faster as he absorbed another beating.

The next day, he awoke to the sour smell of his sweat. He couldn't move, so he lay there, hoping today would be better. This boy had bested him but had escaped with his identity intact.

He had never considered the possibility that anyone would spot his disguise, identify him, and then follow him. He never saw anyone following him, and he always looked for that. If someone had followed him, they would have had to have been a top professional and an experienced man. Junior was an amateur.

Or, he wondered, was someone waiting for him there? How could anyone possibly know he would be at that location and at that time? Did they understand his mission? Maybe they did. He would alter his approach in the future, regardless. But, first things first. *Junior must die.*

Chapter Twenty-Five

He was pushed in the back and into the cell by the detective. He couldn't see the man's face, but he imagined he still had the same grin on his face that he had earlier that morning.

His jail cell had been rebuilt, and he was told more than once that it would not be physically possible for him to escape again. The changes were dramatic. He strongly suspected the floor was constructed from something he had heard of but never seen before - concrete. He wondered if steel bars were put into the concrete. This time, the chair inside his cell was metal and bolted to the floor. Escaping from here would be nearly impossible.

There still was the small, barred window, about seven feet above the floor, in the rear wall - the outside wall of the jail. This little window and the one in the adjacent cell were the only light sources for the cell room, and they allowed Junior to know when it was daytime and nighttime. During the day, if he went to the front of his cell and looked out, he could see a little piece of the sky and sometimes a cloud or two. He lay on his cot most of the day and considered his plight.

What bad timing. How did Detective Williams end up there, and at the worst possible time - when he happened to be holding the club? The Ghost had been there too - then he wasn't. It seemed like he vanished into thin air.

He heard the door open and then close. "You have a visitor." The guard said. Ten minutes, then your time's up. He had two guards now. Each worked a twelve-hour shift. This was his daytime guard, and he was a man who never smiled. His nighttime guard checked on him every couple of hours or so. He suspected the nighttime guard slept in the front office for much of his shift because he never heard much noise coming from the front office at night. The nighttime guard was slightly more pleasant than the daytime guard.

Junior saw a somber Charley standing in front of his cell. Charley held on to two cell bars and leaned his face between the two bars in front of him so that his nose was inside the cell. This seemed to give more weight to his words and make their conversation more personal.

"I hope you are not planning another escape. They are serious now and convinced you are the Ghost."

"Charley, you have to believe me. I didn't do this."

"I want to believe you. I do. I'm also worried about what Cora and Will will think when they find out about you being back in jail. I'm afraid this latest incident is going to shake them up something awful. This looks bad for you - real bad. If you escape somehow, these people here will track you down and shoot you on sight. You need to think about that."

"I'm not going to try to escape. I learned my lesson after the first time."

"OK, Junior, tell me what happened."

Junior recounted the whole morning's events leading up to his arrest. Charley listened but didn't look convinced.

"Alright then, that's your story. I want to believe you; you know I do, but this thing is going to play out in its own way. I heard that the man who was hit with the club, Mr. Murphy, has survived so far. Head injuries are hard to predict. Sometimes, it looks like people will make it, but they end up not surviving. If Mr.

Murphy recovers, the sheriff is going to want to show you to him for identification. That is your moment. God help you and your family if the man identifies you as his attacker."

"For now, just do what they tell you to do, and whatever you do, stay out of trouble."

"I will, Charley. Thank you for coming, and it was good to see you again."

"I'm going to try to keep this news from your family for as long as I can. Be good." Charley left.

Junior laid back down on the bed and closed his eyes. What a mess. His parents will be devastated when they hear of this, and they are bound to hear about it sooner or later. How did everything go so wrong?

The Ghost was free to do whatever he wanted to do now. He would kill again in Prescott or some other town. If he killed again in Prescott, Junior would at least be partially exonerated. He supposed the detective and the sheriff, who evidently are convinced he's the Ghost, would consider the possibility that another killing could have been carried out by someone who worked with the Ghost or wanted to copy him. It won't be easy for him to leave the jail anytime soon. He would be stuck in this cell while they searched for a possible Ghost helper or apprentice. He wondered if he would be forced to go to trial and face a jury. What a disaster that would be.

He was worrying too much, so he decided to take it one thing at a time, one day at a time. It was very likely Will and Cora would be visiting him, and he had to face the possibility that his brothers would come to visit him, too.

He couldn't sleep, so he sat up, put his feet on the floor, and stared at the back corner of his cell. Why had he given up on Will? He wasn't his real father, but he knew Will had always done his best to raise him right. He missed having the steady, stubborn, hard-working, frustrating old guy around to talk to. They just disagreed on things. There was a communication problem and an understanding problem, but he no longer doubted Will's intentions.

Looking back over the last few months, it seemed he had acted like a petulant child. Many boys his age would gladly trade their parents for his if they could.

"I've only been thinking of myself." He muttered.

Bang. Bang. Bang

Junior felt the first bullet as it grazed his shoulder. He was surprised, made a guttural sound, and dove to the floor. He quickly rolled over to the back wall of his cell so the shooter would have the worst possible angle to shoot at him from the small window above. He looked over and saw three holes in his mattress.

"We're coming in. Don't shoot, or it will be the last thing you do." He recognized Detective Williams' voice.

Junior put his hands up high in front of him, palms forward, then stopped moving. The door to the front office cracked open and then was pushed all the way open. No one was standing in the doorway. He saw two pistols, one high and pointed to the left and one low and pointed to the right. The Sheriff and Detective Williams came in quickly, the detective pointed his gun this way and that way. Sheriff Lewis had his gun pointed at Junior the whole time. "What happened here, son."

"Someone tried to shoot me."

"Are you hit?"

"Grazed on the shoulder, is all."

"Get up slowly and sit on the cot. A dark cloud follows you wherever you go, doesn't it, Junior? The sheriff looked him over for a minute.

"Alright, it's over, whatever it was. Get the Doc," the sheriff told the detective.

He ran behind a nearby building as he had planned and waited. When he felt safe, he took off his red mustache and wig, put on the black mustache he had brought, and tried to compose himself. After his first shot, he heard a gasp and the sound of the boy falling to the floor. Maybe I got lucky, he thought. Only time will tell. He continued to compose himself, then began to walk home, stopping casually here and there to look in the shop windows. He was in a good mood. What a blessed day it had been.

Chapter Twenty-Six

Saturdays were harder now for the family since Junior was not available to help. At least the sky was overcast, Cora thought. The early summer heat wouldn't be so bad today. Even so, working at the Farmer's Market would be a long and exhausting day. Cora spent most of her time selling the vegetables. She also needed to plan for and get ingredients for tomorrow's regular get-together with her friends at Sharlot's cabin. Maybe Lillian's husband or Cat's new man-friend would be there?

From time to time, she noticed people giving her a quick, serious look, and then, just as quickly, they looked away. Why were people acting so strange? She nonchalantly inspected her clothing to see if something was not right. No, everything was fine as far as she could tell. She ran her fingers in her hair; all was well. She didn't like feeling self-conscious.

"I'm so sorry about your boy, Cora." The lady at the mushroom stand said. Cora was a regular customer.

"What do you mean?" she answered.

"Oh, oh, I'm sorry. I thought you knew."

"Knew what?"

"I heard Junior was back in jail. The sheriff thinks he's the

Ghost."

"What?"

"I'm so sorry," the lady said. Cora paid for her mushrooms, left without getting her change, and returned to her vegetable stand.

"Lee, Paul, you're both in charge until I get back. If you need help making change, ask the folks buying the vegetables to help you." She gathered herself together, then walked over and told Will she needed to do an errand and would be back in an hour or so. Then, she left the familiar surroundings of the Farmer's Market.

She needed to talk to Charley right away. He may know something; in any case, it would be better to talk with him instead of Will, at least for now. She thought Will would be more likely to react in the wrong way. She needed to know more. When she had a better idea about what was really going on, she could come up with the best way to approach Will with the news.

She rode over to Charley's house and knocked on his door. Elizabeth answered the door, took one look at Cora, and then quickly invited her in. When she got inside, she saw Charley finishing an early lunch. She smelled fried chicken.

She asked him, "Have you heard that Junior was in jail?"

"Yes, it's true. I'm afraid Junior got himself into a real pickle this time. I talked with him about it yesterday. He says he's innocent. I want to believe he is."

Charley retold Junior's story from the day before. "Everything depends on a witness waking up after a severe beating. He hasn't so far, and he's still unconscious the last I heard."

"Let's go to the jail and talk to him and talk to the sheriff," Cora said.

The three left went to the Sheriff's Office and walked inside.

"Sheriff, you have the wrong man behind bars. My son probably saved that man's life."

"I understand you're being upset, Mrs. Martin, but Detective Williams caught him red-handed. Junior was standing over the victim with a club in his hand. That doesn't happen by accident. The detective is sure he has caught the Ghost."

Cora gave him a cold stare. "I want to talk to my son."

"You can."

Cora, Charley, and Elizabeth went into the cell room to speak with Junior. The guard was right behind them. "What happened to your shoulder?" Cora asked.

"Nothing, just a scrape."

She shook her head. "Charley told me your story. Is there anything you need to add to it? Think about it hard before you answer."

"No, ma'am, there's nothing else," Junior said quietly.

"As far as I know, the only people who think you are a killer are that stupid sheriff and this Detective Williams, who's not even from around here. You have a lot of support around town. You must know that, Junior."

"I do, and I'm starting to appreciate it more now. It seems strange for me to say this, but I miss Will. He would know what to do in this situation."

"He probably would, and I'm glad to hear you say that, but I haven't told him you're in here yet. I wanted to find out for myself first."

They talked with Junior for another few minutes about nothing in particular. "Be good, son. I know this whole thing will blow over soon," she said. Charley and Elizabeth said their goodbyes, and then they all left with concerned looks on their faces.

A week passed, and Junior heard nothing. He was used to going wherever he wanted. He was cooped up in this small jail cell, and the days dragged on and on. That morning, he did what he had done the day before, and the day before that - He sat in his cell, stewed, and felt sorry for himself.

He tried to move his bed to the opposite side of the cell, away from where the bed was when he was shot at, but of course, the bed was bolted down to the floor like the chair had been. He lay down and hoped the Ghost wouldn't come back and try to shoot him again. The night guard had promised to patrol the jail's exterior occasionally. He asked himself what Will would do if he were in his shoes. It didn't take him long to come up with the answer. Will would face this situation head-on, and that was precisely what Junior planned to do.

The door to the jail cell room opened. His daytime guard, the sheriff, and the detective all entered the room. The sheriff and the detective both had their pistols pointed at him.

"You're going outside for a while. Don't cause a fuss." He walked outside to the front of the Sheriff's Office and over to a wagon. He was then told to climb up in the wagon and to lie face-down. He got in.

"All the way up, Junior." The guard said.

Junior positioned himself so his head was near the front of the wagon's bed. A thick, rough burlap bag was thrown near his face. He was instructed to put the bag over his head, which he did. He was told to put his hands behind his back, which he did, and then he was cuffed. Someone kicked him in the leg to let him know he was being watched while he was in the wagon.

The wagon started up, and they rode for at least an hour.

Finally, the wagon stopped, the sack over his head was removed, and he worked his way out of the wagon. He found himself in the middle of a pine forest, with only one building visible, a good-sized cabin he did not recognize.

"We've got two guns on you, so don't do anything stupid." The sheriff said.

He was led onto the front porch of the cabin with a gun in his back, and then he went inside.

Sheriff Lewis told Junior, "You'll go into the house and the bedroom in a minute. You will stand where we tell you to stand, and you will not say anything - not a word. You stand there and be quiet. We'll tell you when it is time to go. Do you understand?"

"Yes."

They entered the only bedroom in the cabin and were immediately hit with a distinct musty odor. He recognized Bradley Murphy lying in a bed, sleeping. Junior still felt the gun pushed into his back, a little harder now. Sheriff Lewis went over to the side of the bed to rouse Mr. Murphy. The man gradually started to wake up and tried to focus his eyes. He looked at the four men standing around his bed but said nothing.

"Can you see us OK?" Sheriff Lewis asked.

"Yes."

"Take a good look at this young man," the sheriff said as he pointed to Junior.

Mr. Murphy looked at Junior.

After several moments, Sheriff Lewis said, "Alright, time to go."

Junior was led to the back of the wagon and told to get in and lie down like he had on the ride over. The bag was put over his head again. Once again, someone gave him a kick in the leg. He lay there in the wagon for at least fifteen minutes before the wagon began to move. He lay there in the back of the wagon for another hour. Eventually, they stopped, and he was led back into the Sheriff's Office. The sack over his head was pulled off. They removed his handcuffs.

"You got lucky this time. Mr. Murphy insisted his attacker was a shorter, older man with rough-looking hair and a dirty beard." Detective Williams said.

"Against my better judgment, we'll have to let you go; charges have been dropped for now. Rest assured, you will be watched, young man," Sheriff Lewis said, giving Junior a stern look.

Junior felt a sense of relief that he couldn't quite believe. He walked out of the Sheriff's Office, stood on the small covered porch in front, looked at the people on the street, and took a deep breath. All he wanted to do was to go home.

Chapter Twenty-Seven

"As I live and breathe. Junior! Is it you?" Charley said.

He stood just outside of Charley's door and absorbed a crushing hug. "They let me go. I'm free."

"Come in. Come in."

"Well, look at you," Elizabeth exclaimed.

"Junior, have a seat, and you can tell us all about it. You hungry?"

"No thanks. There isn't much to tell you, really."

Charley had a sly grin and asked Junior, "You didn't bust out of their new jail, did you?"

"No. They took me to be identified by the victim, Mr. Murphy, and he told them I wasn't the one who attacked him. Mr. Murphy was recovering in a cabin far away from town because I didn't recognize it. After they brought me back to Prescott, they had no choice but to let me go."

"I'm so glad it worked out for you," Elizabeth said. "You had us worried there for a while. We woke up that day, and you were gone with no explanation, then later the same day, you were put back in jail. We didn't know what to think. Now you show up here, out of nowhere, and you're free again. I'm so happy for you."

"We both are. We never doubted you for a moment. What are you going to do now?" Charley asked.

"The first thing I want to do is to go home and make things

right with Will and my mother. I have some explaining to do."

"Yes, you do. I have some work I need to get at this afternoon, but I planned to stop by to talk to Will tomorrow morning. I'll see you there tomorrow. Maybe I can fill in the gaps when you explain things to Will. Are you sure you're not hungry?"

"No, thanks. It was good seeing you both. I need to thank you for all of the support you have shown me. Someday, I hope to pay you back."

"Now you're getting too serious on us, Junior. It will take you a while to walk home. Enjoy your walk, and think of the good times you've had with your family. Don't worry about us. We were glad we had the opportunity to help." Charley said.

"Thanks, Charley. I'd better get going."

Junior stood up, got hugs from Charley and Elizabeth, and then walked over to the front door and opened it. "Thanks again." He nodded at them both and left to start his walk home.

It felt good to see the family cabin as it came into view, the tall shade trees by the creek, and the expansive, green vegetable fields. He walked up to the front door, opened it, and walked in. Lee and Paul were there, and they both ran up to him and hugged him.

"How was your trip? Did you get a lot done while you were away?" Asked Lee.

"I learned a lot, I can tell you for sure." He said.

He put his hand on Paul's head and tousled his hair. Paul looked up and smiled.

Cora came in and stopped. He gave her a relaxed smile as she quickly walked up to him and hugged him.

"Let's go out on the porch for a minute." She said. They went outside and sat down.

"Your father, yes, I said your father, still thinks you are on the run after breaking out of jail. He hasn't talked about it, but I know he is upset to no end. I didn't tell him you were staying at Charley's. I knew he would go over there and make a scene. I sure didn't tell him you were back in jail, either. I didn't have the heart to make him go through any more worrying.

Junior, It's up to you to straighten out this mess you have made. I'm proud of you, son. You need to make your father proud of you, too." She left him on the porch and went inside the cabin.

Will was working in the fields, as he knew he would be. Junior walked over, stood about ten yards away, and said, "Hello, Will."

With a bunch of weeds in one hand, Will stood up and said, "What in the blazes are you doin' here?"

"The Sheriff set me free. I'm innocent of all charges."

"What about the damage to the jail?"

"I guess they figured it needed to be improved anyway. They never mentioned it, so I don't really know."

"Why didn't you tell us what was going on? You had your poor mother in a tizzy."

"I…um…I…I'm sorry. I had to see it through."

"I hope you're tellin' the truth. Sayin's one thing. Provin's another, you know."

"I can start by helping you pull weeds."

"Can't hurt."

"I'm hoping you will let me come home to stay."

"I'll have to run that by your mother. Right now, why don't you get to work."

The two of them pulled weeds for the rest of the afternoon. Junior's hands were sore and bleeding a little when they ran out of daylight, but he didn't care. He enjoyed the work and was glad to be working alongside Will again.

Charley came to visit the next morning. He, Will, and Junior grabbed coffee and sat on the porch. Junior didn't have time to explain anything to Charley before they started talking. Junior started the conversation,

"The Ghost uses disguises. No one knows what he really looks like."

"You don't say. How do you know this?" Asked Will.

"I've seen him in disguise," Junior said

"You've seen the Ghost? Let's start from the beginnin'. Why did you break out of jail?"

"More than one reason. Mainly, I wanted to prove myself and catch the Ghost.

"You don't say."

"Yes, I just said it. I'm telling you the truth." Junior snapped back.

"The law in town wasn't good enough to get the job done. They needed your help, but they just didn't know it? They needed someone to help them do their job and show them how bad their jail was. Was that it?"

Charley interjected. "I think Junior did them a favor if you think about it. They must have known they needed to upgrade that rickety old jail Junior so easily escaped from. What if they had a real criminal in the old jail, and he escaped? Then they would have had a serious problem and uncomfortable questions to provide answers for."

"Maybe so. Let me see if I understand you, son. You busted out of jail, spent all these weeks on your own, and you show up here sayin' you've been cleared of all charges. That's not the whole story. What am I missin'?"

After a few moments of silence, Charley decided this would be the perfect time for a small lie. "I asked Junior if I could help him after he escaped from jail. He stayed with me for a while." Will looked a little surprised. Junior wondered if Charley's revelation hurt Will, but it was always so difficult to read Will's expression. He thought it had to have hurt him, at least a little.

"I'm sorry. I should have come to you." Junior said, looking at Will.

"Thank you for sayin' that," said Will. I was mad at you when I heard you had escaped. It made you look guilty, and I'm sorry to say I might have turned you into the sheriff if you had come here.

They all took another sip of coffee, and nobody said anything. Junior and Charley had put their cards on the table. Junior knew what good friends Will and Charley were, then decided there would be no hard feelings about it.

"You said you saw the Ghost - In disguise?" Will asked.

"Yes." Junior described what happened on Fourth Street but left out the part about him being arrested. Will then looked at Junior with a hint of admiration and respect but said nothing. "You probably saved the man's life - the child beater."

"I hope so. He's still bedridden. It looks like he is going to live. I hope the man can change his ways, eventually, and stop his child beating."

Will stared blankly at him, looked into his empty coffee mug, and said, "I hope so, too."

If you're still interested, Junior, we have some work to do." Will prodded, looking at Junior.

"After everything I've been through, I am actually looking forward to pulling more weeds today."

They all stood up. Will offered Charley his hand; they shook, and then Charley turned around and headed home.

"Let's get to work then," Junior said. Will nodded, and they walked over to begin working in the fields.

On the way over, Will said, "Good to have you back, son.

Chapter Twenty-Eight

Junior had been clubbed and shot at, so obviously, he had made some impression on the Ghost. To Junior's way of thinking, there were still many missing pieces to the puzzle that needed to be added before he could make any real progress. Who was the Ghost? Unexpected and unexplained things had happened. He needed to learn more about his adversary, but he wasn't exactly sure where to restart his efforts.

The Ghost using a club was dangerous enough, but the Ghost with a club and a gun was much worse. Junior didn't like how this made him feel. The stakes were getting higher and much more ominous for him. He decided to ride over to the Sheriff's Office and ask the sheriff a question he needed to ask to help him move on to the next logical step in his search. He rode over there and walked into the front door.

"Well, well. The notorious Ghost has finally decided to turn himself in." Sheriff Lewis said.

"I'm not the Ghost, and you know it, sheriff," Junior said.

"So you say. What can I do for you?"

"I need your help. I want to talk to Bradley Murphy. He's seen the Ghost – in disguise, but I need to know if he can help us catch the Ghost somehow."

"What do you mean, us? Did someone deputize you while I was sleeping last night?"

"No. Look. I have a personal interest in this case. He tried to kill me when I was in jail."

"That was a big shock, but you're taking it too personally, Junior. I don't understand why you want to be so involved. You're more likely to get hurt or killed than you are to solve the case, and then people will start to wonder why you were involved with this Ghost case in the first place. People will start to ask me what I was doing at the time. How could I have let this happen?"

"Be honest, Sheriff, who do you think gets the credit for catching him? You do, of course. All I want to do is gather some information. I'm no more than a pawn in your operation. You're the one who'll be calling the shots at the end when the Ghost is caught."

Sheriff Lewis looked like he wasn't exactly sure what a pawn was, but he did seem to like that someone would appreciate his role in the investigation. He paused momentarily, then said, "I'll tell you where he is, but in return, you must tell me if you find anything important. Deal?"

"Deal."

"OK, Junior. He's back at his home on Fourth Street. He's much better and recovered enough to defend himself if he has to."

"Thanks, Sheriff. I'll visit him, and you'll be the first one I talk to if I get any useful information."

The sheriff nodded, and Junior left.

He headed over to Bradley Murphy's house and knocked on his door. The door opened, and he found himself face to face with the child-beater.

"Good morning, Mr. Murphy. I'm Will Martin Junior, and I hope we can talk for a few minutes."

"I recognize you from the other day. They say you saved my life."

Junior smiled slightly.

After a slight hesitation, the man said, "Come in."

The place was dirty and unkempt, but Junior found a chair to sit in. Mr. Murphy grabbed another chair, positioned it to face Junior, then sat down.

"What do you want?"

Junior started, "You've seen this man, this Ghost, face to face, and no one else has. I know he was in disguise, but I hope you can remember something about him that would help me identify him."

"I told the Sheriff and that detective all about it. Ask them."

"I've talked with them." Junior lied. "They are at a loss. They have no clue who he is."

"I don't know either."

"Please, Mr. Murphy, there must be something."

Bradley Murphy started to fidget in his chair. "Why don't you people leave me alone? I opened the door, and this dirty old man with crazed, unfocused eyes pulled out a club and hit me on the head. The next thing I know, I woke up in some cabin in the middle of nowhere."

There was a knock on the door, interrupting their conversation. They both looked out the window and saw a man wearing a long coat and a big floppy hat who appeared to be staring at his feet. Mr. Murphy asked, "Who in the blazes could that be?"

He walked over to the door and was about to open it when Junior said, "Wait. This doesn't feel right. Stay inside. Do you have a back door?"

"Yes," Mr. Murphy said, pointing towards the rear.

"Stay inside. It could be important."

Junior went out the back door and walked around to the side of the house as quietly as he could. He moved up the side and peaked around the front corner of the house. The man in the long coat was still knocking on the door and looking down at his feet. Junior continued around the front and walked towards the front porch. "Can I…"

What he saw next, he would never forget. What he saw was the man's eyes - the surprised, frantic, crazed look in the man's eyes as he turned and hurled himself off the porch, a club in the air, aimed straight at Junior's head. It was everything Junior could do to avoid being hit by the club. He stumbled backward, fell on his back, and saw the sky.

The Ghost appeared, hovering over him, and raised his club in the air to strike. Junior reacted by whipping his leg into the Ghost's ankle. That seemed to knock him off-balance, but he still had his club aimed directly at Junior's face and took a swing at him as he was falling to the ground. Junior put his arm up to protect himself, and the club hit his arm midway between his shoulder and elbow. The Ghost fell on the dirt.

Junior felt the pain in his arm but did his best to fight through it and was able to get back on his feet. The Ghost started to stand up again, too. Junior used his good arm to push him back to the ground when he was halfway up. He began to walk towards the Ghost when the pain from his arm caught up with him, and he had no choice but to put a hand on the arm, look down for a moment, and grimace. The pain was intense.

He recovered from the pain long enough to look up, but he saw nothing. The Ghost had vanished once again.

He yelled, "Ahhh," and then he had to sit on the porch momentarily. Hit in the ribs and now in the arm. It was more pain than he had ever experienced in his entire life.

Junior walked to the door and knocked, "Mr. Murphy, it's me, Junior. Open the door, please." The door opened, and Junior saw that Mr. Murphy was pointing his handgun at him. He lowered the weapon.

"What happened to you?"

"The Ghost was here to pay you a visit. He's gone now."

"You're kidding."

"Not at all. Can I come in?"

"Yes, of course." Junior entered the house and sat in the same chair he had sat in before. "You saved my life again."

It was hard for Junior to talk, but he said, "Guess I did."

"You're hurt." Mr. Murphy said. Junior nodded.

"Wait here. I'll get the Doc." Junior wondered if the Ghost was still outside and was about to say something, but he couldn't react fast enough. When he looked up, he saw the front door closing.

An hour and a half later, the door opened. Mr. Murphy and the Doc walked in the front door. By then, Junior's arm was throbbing more than ever. "You were walloped, it looks like. I can see the swelling from under your shirt. Let's get that shirt off so I can get a better look." The Doc poked and prodded his wound, and Junior tried not to complain too much.

"Good news for you, son. Your bone is probably broken, but it's still in place. I'm going to wrap your arm and put you in a sling. Go easy for a few weeks; it should heal up just fine. If you try to do too much, or God forbid you get into another fight, you could end up making your arm much worse. Do you understand?"

"Yes. I understand." The Doc wrapped Junior's arm, carefully put it in a sling, said his goodbyes, and left.

Junior looked at Bradley Murphy and remembered what Father Donovan had counseled him on all those weeks ago about considering others as well as himself. Could he change the man's life with a few words? Probably not. People don't change their ways, at least not quickly. Finally, he said, "Doc's a good man. He helps others every day."

Mr. Murphy looked at Junior for a couple of moments, then nodded his head. Junior wondered if he had made a point because it was all he felt he had a right to say. "It's time for me to go. You be careful."

"I will. Thank you."

Junior soon discovered it was much harder to get on a horse with a broken arm. He kept trying and trying. Eventually, he succeeded. The pain was worth it, he thought to himself, because he had learned something valuable today. Mr. Murphy said the Ghost had 'crazed, unfocused eyes.' He had seen that same look himself. The Ghost was not just a vigilante. He was insane.

He followed his plan and found the group of pine trees behind the neighborhood, stopped running, and composed himself. The boy was still alive. He was surprised when he watched Junior ride up to the cabin. He thought about returning another day, but he gave it some thought and decided it was perfect. It would be a golden opportunity. He would quickly club Mr. Murphy, then shoot Junior.

He wondered why Junior had shown up at exactly the wrong moment again. Junior had surprised him when he was on the porch. The two extra inches on the soles of his boots threw off his balance just enough. What bad luck he had that morning when he chose his disguise.

Junior has strong, malicious powers that enable him to show up at the wrong place at the wrong time again and again. How was that even possible? He had always thought the boy was an amateur, but now he knew better. Junior was only pretending to be an amateur. He would end this threat to justice. He would be more innovative and more unpredictable next time. Junior will not only die, but he will suffer first.

Chapter Twenty-Nine

Raymond wore his Sunday best clothes when he walked into the saloon, looked around, sat at the bar, and told the barkeep, "Whiskey, please."

The barkeep returned to get a glass, paused, turned around, and looked at Raymond. He pursed his lips, then slowly began to walk back towards him.

Raymond was at the Emporium Palace. It was his next target, and he needed to go in and take a look around. The saloon was narrow in the front, and deep. Just as he had suspected. When the customers walked in, the long bar was on their right. A few small tables were set up on the wall opposite the bar. Also opposite the bar and behind the tables was a stairway that led up to the second floor.

The rear third of the saloon was an open area with several large gambling tables. There was another stairway at the very back of the saloon and a back door. He knew there were whores who worked upstairs. Undoubtedly, the rear stairway and door would be the best way for someone to discretely leave the saloon after spending time upstairs.

The barkeep arrived and faced Raymond.

"How old are you?"

"Old enough. Don't worry about that. I look younger than I really am."

"Go home, Raymond. I'm not serving you."

He didn't expect to be served, and he certainly didn't expect the barkeep to know his name. I guess I'm finally making my mark in this town, he thought with some pride.

A few days later, when he was satisfied he had planned his adventure as well as he possibly could, he walked nonchalantly down the street an hour after dark, carrying a knapsack over his shoulder. A drunk was sitting on the side of the wooden deck of the saloon adjacent to the Emporium. There was a narrow alley between the two saloons. From where the drunk was sitting, he could see the street ahead, left and right, and if he turned his head to look behind him, he could see down the alley. Raymond walked over and kicked him in the leg. He needed for the wretch to leave. There could be no witnesses to what he was planning to do.

"What?"

"Move away from here. You're stinking up the area and driving away customers."

"Sure." The drunk stood up, reeking of Whiskey, and shuffled off down the street. Raymond watched him for a moment, then went into the alley. He remembered what he had seen inside the saloon a few days before and looked around until he found the perfect spot. He knelt at the side of the building, worked a board loose, took out the oily rags from his knapsack, and shoved them underneath the wooden floor of the Emporium.

He had already picked a spot across the street to watch the fire. Maybe he would get lucky and see a naked lady running out into the night. He might even offer her his jacket.

"What are you doing, Raymond?" He recognized the voice - how could he forget it. "Pull those rags out now, or you'll regret it." Raymond looked over, and as he did, the Ghost opened enough of his jacket to show him the handle of his gun.

"I thought you were a drunk, but you're obviously not."

"Very perceptive. Unfortunately, I'm going to have to turn you in."

"No, you can't do that. I was never going to do anything."

"Yes, you were, and those oily rags and matches prove it. Burning down a building with people inside, and at this time of the night? That's a tricky proposition. That's how people get killed sometimes. I swear to you, Raymond, if there is a fire here tonight or at any time in the future, I'll tell the Sheriff what I saw you try to do in this alley tonight."

Raymond did not doubt that the Ghost was serious. He was trapped.

"OK, you got me. What do you want?"

"First of all, you don't know me, and I don't know you." He opened the other side of his coat, exposing his club. "That is the most important thing. You can never tell anyone we've met. Never. I like you, but I'll hurt you bad if you talk. Do you understand?"

"I understand."

"Secondly, I may need your help soon. You will help me when I tell you to, Agreed?"

"Agreed"

"OK, now go home."

Raymond picked up his things and gladly left the area.

Who's the smart one now? he thought. Sure, part of him would have liked to bludgeon the boy, but he had to be more careful now, especially since Oscar and Junior had joined forces. Raymond and Junior were friends. Could he use their friendship to his advantage somehow? He would bide his time and lay his trap. He took off most of his disguise, and with a smile, Samuel

Blackstone, son of Oscar Blackstone, left the alley and walked home.

Junior spent the past week giving his arm time to recover, spending most of his time resting around the cabin. He took two or three short walks every day. His ribs were still sore after all this time, and he hoped the walks would help him heal.

"Let's take a walk." He said to Paul, his youngest brother. Lee was outside, working with Will.

"Where are we walking this time."

"Same as before. Down the road to the end of the fields, then we turn around." They started on the walk. Paul had short legs and was not a fast walker, so their pace was slower than Junior would have liked.

They were at the end of the fields when they saw Sheriff Lewis and the detective riding towards them. Junior and Paul stopped and waited for them.

"Junior, how are you?" asked the sheriff.

"Good. Paul and I are out for our morning walk. We were getting ready to turn around and head home when we saw you."

"Your ribs have healed well, Junior, no trouble getting around, I see. What happened to your arm?" Detective Williams asked as he scrutinized Junior.

"Long story. I'll tell you about it in a few minutes."

"Long story, eh?" Williams countered.

Obviously, Detective Williams still mistrusted him.

Sheriff Lewis interjected, "We've got some bad news, Junior. It's better if we tell you when you're sitting down. Can we meet you at the cabin, then?"

"Yeah. My mom's getting ready for visitors tomorrow. Knock on the door and ask her to make us some coffee. She should have just about anything else you might want, along with your coffee."

They rode to the cabin, and Junior and Paul slowly walked back behind them. They made their way up the front porch.

"Paul, can you go inside while we talk?" Sheriff Lewis asked. Paul reluctantly went into the cabin. A moment later, Cora came out with three coffees. She sat them down, then gave Junior a questioning look on her way back inside.

The sheriff started the conversation. "Junior, I'm afraid another man has been killed in town. Same as before - left at the Catholic church, no evidence, no murder weapon, no motive. Brutal murder. Looks like the work of the Ghost."

Junior wondered why these two lawmen rode all the way here to tell him of another murder. He steadied himself and asked, "Was it someone I know?"

"Yes, Bradley Murphy." The detective said.

"Bradley Murphy? No. It can't be."

"I'm afraid so." Said Sheriff Lewis. Junior felt sad and disappointed beyond words. Sheriff Lewis and the detective sat, sipped their coffee, and watched him intently.

Junior said, "Sheriff Lewis, I know I told you I would provide you with any information I gathered. I have some new information, but I've been laid up here and haven't had time to tell you yet."

"I can see that. What do you have?"

Junior recounted what had happened to him when he visited Mr. Murphy.

"I'll never forget the look in his eyes, sheriff. He looked more like a wild animal than a human. Normal people don't act like that.

I'm convinced the ghost is insane."

Sheriff Lewis looked at him with a severe expression. "You never cease to surprise me," he said.

"I was lucky, I guess."

"Yes, you were. Very lucky. You need to be more careful. I mean it. This Ghost is very dangerous, and you don't fully understand how dangerous he is. He's good enough to kill you any time he wants to, and believe me - You will never see it coming."

Chapter Thirty

Cora was excited that Cat and her newest man-friend, Samuel, were coming over for an afternoon meal. It was a Thursday, and she was in the General Store in town looking for something special to prepare for the big meal.

Cat had given her a lovely pearl comb earlier in the year, to Cora's great surprise, and she wanted to make today's meal something special to pay her back for her kindness. She saw several bottles of wine on display and thought, why not?

"Can you help me?" She asked the man standing nearby.

"I know a little bit about wine." The man said. Cora soon got the impression the man knew a great deal about wine, and she appreciated his modesty.

"My husband and I are having a get-together with another couple today, and I was wondering if you could suggest a wine for us."

"You can never go wrong with this red wine." He said as he showed her a bottle. "It goes down easy and still packs a punch."

"Alright, if you think so."

"I've got a special going on today. Buy one bottle, and the second one is half-price. A second bottle might come in handy for four people."

"That sounds fine."

"Good for you. I'll even throw in a free corkscrew."

"What's that?"

"You use that to take the cork out of the bottle."

"Yes, of course." She paid for the wine, then went looking for a few blueberries.

She walked around the store for a minute. Out of the corner of her eye, she saw a quick movement, like someone had just dashed behind an aisle. Curious, she walked over to where she had seen the movement and looked around the corner. There he was, hiding. "What are you doing back here, Raymond?"

"Looking around the store, just like you."

"You're acting strange. I don't like it.

"I'm not acting strange."

"Then why are you hiding back here?"

"No particular reason, ma'am. Besides, who says I'm hiding?"

She looked at him hard and said, "I hope you're telling me the truth. Promise me you won't cause any trouble."

"I promise. Don't worry."

Cora left him, knowing he was up to no good, and reminded herself how glad she was that Junior had stopped running around with Raymond.

Samuel rode out with Cat on their way out to the Martin's cabin. He was surprised when Cat told him they had been invited to an early supper. He had no time to prepare for the encounter and wasn't sure if he could handle it.

Killing Junior would come later. For now, he had to find a way to control his emotions. The rough plan he had in his mind would come together soon. He just needed a little more time. He couldn't get ahead of himself today. He had to stay focused on the big picture.

They rode up to Martin's cabin, walked up, and knocked on the door. Cora opened the door.

"Hello," Cora said with a big smile. She hugged Cat. Samuel, it's so good to see you. Please come in, you two. I'm almost finished with the meal. I hope you both like it." They exchanged more pleasantries, and they all sat down.

Samuel loathed the boy more than anyone except for his father, Oscar. He was with Cat, so he had no weapons, no club or gun. He expected to have a knife and a fork available with his meal. He hoped he wouldn't be sitting next to Junior. He had to stay calm and stick to his tried-and-true methods. He didn't need this temptation. Damn her, damn Cat for bringing him here. He was no good at spontaneous vengeance.

"Cora, you always have one of the cleanest homes in the Territory. It's such a pleasure to come here."

"Thank you. Can I get you anything?"

"Just a glass of water, thanks," said Cat. Cora got both Cat and Samuel a glass and filled it with fresh creek water she had in a pitcher.

Paul poked around a corner and said, "Hello, Cat. Hello, Mister."

"Hello to you too, Paul," Cat said. Then she looked at Cora and said, "Something smells good."

"It's almost ready - chicken stew with mushrooms and vegetables. I hope you like the seasonings. We're eating out on the porch today. I'll go fetch the men." She left to go round them up.

A minute later, Will, Junior, and Lee came in from the fields and went inside the cabin to clean up. They came back out, and soon, everyone was sitting at the table outside on the covered porch.

Things have become too complicated, too fast. Now, there were three boys added to the mix. It would be easy to end Junior, but there would be too many other people to deal with. Cat would try to stop him. Will looked like he would be a force to be reckoned with.

Samuel looked down at his silverware and saw only a spoon and a butter knife.

"Samuel, do you want to say grace?" Cora asked.

"Uh, I must confess I don't know how…I never learned one."

"That's OK. We don't always say grace ourselves. Will?"

"OK." He said grace, then everyone dug into the food, especially the two younger boys. Cora smiled at them.

"Please ignore my two younger boys, Cat. There will be plenty of time to teach them manners later when the time is right," she said.

Cora turned her attention to Samuel. "Cat tells me you live in town and have an inheritance of some kind. What do you do with your time?"

"Ah… nothing special, but I still find the days go by quick."

Samuel watched as Cora stole a glance at Will. He looked at her with a sour expression as though he thought he was lazy or wondered how his days could go by quickly if he had nothing special to do. *They have no idea, but they'll see what I do with my time soon enough.*

"He's a keeper, I can tell you that. He's very handy around the house." Said Cat.

Soon, they were finished with their meals.

Paul chimed in, "What's for dessert?"

"Blueberry pie, of course. Can't you smell it?"

"I guess I can." He said slyly.

"Why don't you and Junior go get the pie and bring it to the table?" Paul got the pie, and Junior got new silverware. Then, they brought everything back out to the table. Junior brought over a knife to cut the pie with.

"My ribs are still sore, and I only have one arm to use, but I'm glad I can help with a few things, even if it is just carrying silverware. I've been trying to help in the fields but still can't do much." Junior said.

Junior sat down where he was before, directly across the table from Samuel. "Junior, what happened to you? How did you get hurt?" Samuel asked.

"Broke a rib several weeks ago. Last week I broke my arm. Still recovering. Hurts some." He said.

"I can see that, but how did all this happen?"

"I got into a little dust-up with that evil son of a gun they call the Ghost. I think he's a coward, really - he never seems to finish a fight. But that's good for me because otherwise, I might not be here today."

Samuel stopped talking, only vaguely becoming aware he was suddenly shoveling the pie into his mouth. He looked up and saw Cora smiling at him.

Not today, patience, not now. I must stay invisible.

"Boys, why don't you go inside for a while and let us adults talk," Cora said. She returned from inside with two bottles of wine and the corkscrew. "Who knows how to open a bottle of wine?"

"I do," Samuel said, then removed the cork from the first bottle and poured everyone a glass.

"Where'd you learn to do that?" Will asked.

"Must have picked it up somewhere along the way. I got into a lot of trouble when I was younger."

"I can believe that," Cat said, smiling at him sideways. Soon, the second bottle was opened and poured, and their tongues got a little looser. Even Will started to talk.

"Junior and I have had issues over the years, but he's coming around now. I'm proud of him." Cora smiled broadly.

Samuel looked at Will and then over at Cora but said nothing.

"Sometimes we don't know things 'til later," Will said.

It took Samuel a quick moment to understand what he meant, but he got it. *At least I won't have any trouble outsmarting Will.*

The afternoon wore on, and with only a couple of hours of daylight left, they had to leave. "You want to come home with me, Samuel?" Cat asked.

"I would love to, but I've got to get home. I need to clean my place up, or I'll catch some disease from living there. I'll be over this week to work on your windmill." He said.

Cat looked disappointed but kissed him on the cheek and said, "OK, Sammy. I'll be waiting for you. Cora and Will, thank you." They left, and Cora and Will began to clean up.

On his way back to his house, he was unsettled and angry. Cat acted like it wouldn't be long before she wanted to get intimate. He didn't know how to be intimate. He'd have to end their friendship but wanted it to last as long as possible because she was such a good cover for him.

His hate for the boy intensified. *Why did he call me a coward? I was being clever by not getting caught.* I'm going to pound him senseless, then pound him some more. Cat and the boy had bothered him that day, but he expected them to do that.

Something unexpected, something new, was getting under his skin now - Cora and Will. They seemed to have a connection, a bond, that he knew he would never have with anyone in his life. Their connection couldn't be real, could it? Maybe, but he would never forgive them for their disturbing display – all designed to make him feel bad. What was wrong with these people?

Junior will be dealt with just like the others. Everyone will pay the same price to see the show. They will all pay with their lives. Samuel was still undecided about who he would kill first but looked forward to killing Junior last.

Chapter Thirty

Cora was excited that Cat and her newest man-friend, Samuel, were coming over for an afternoon meal. It was a Thursday, and she was in the General Store in town looking for something special to prepare for the big meal.

Cat had given her a very nice pearl comb earlier in the year, to Cora's great surprise, and she wanted to make today's meal something special to pay her back for her kindness. She saw several bottles of wine on display and thought, why not?

"Can you help me?" She asked the man standing nearby.

"I know a little bit about wine." The man said. Cora soon got the impression the man knew a great deal about wine, and she appreciated his modesty.

"My husband and I are having a get-together with another couple today, and I was wondering if you could suggest a wine for us."

"You can never go wrong with this red wine." He said as he showed her a bottle. "It goes down easy and still packs a punch."

"Alright, if you think so."

"I've got a special going on today. Buy one bottle, and the second one is half-price. A second bottle might come in handy for four people."

"That sounds fine."

"Good for you. I'll even throw in a free corkscrew."

"What's that?"

"You use that to take the cork out of the bottle."

"Yes, of course." She paid for the wine, then went looking for a few blueberries.

She walked around the store for a while. Out of the corner of her eye, she saw a quick movement, like someone had just dashed behind an aisle. Curious, she walked over to where she had seen the movement and looked around the corner. There he was, hiding. "What are you doing back here, Raymond?"

"Looking around the store, just like you."

"You're acting strange. I don't like it.

"I'm not acting strange."

"Then why are you hiding back here?"

"No particular reason, ma'am; besides, who says I'm hiding?"

She looked at him hard and said, "I hope you're telling me the truth. Promise me you won't cause any trouble."

"I promise. Don't worry."

Cora left him, knowing he was up to no good, and reminded herself how glad she was Junior had stopped running around with Raymond.

Samuel rode out with Cat on their way out to the Martin's cabin. He was surprised when Cat told him they had been invited to an early supper. He had no time to prepare for the encounter and wasn't sure if he was ready. He needed to stay calm.

Killing Junior would come later. For now, he had to find a

way to control his emotions. The plan he had in his mind would come together soon. He just needed more time. He couldn't get ahead of himself today. He had to stay focused on the big picture.

They rode up to Martin's cabin, walked up to it, and knocked on the door. Cora opened the door.

"Hello," Cora said with a big smile. She hugged Cat. Samuel, it's so good to see you. Please come in, you two. I'm almost finished with the meal. I hope you both like it." They exchanged more pleasantries and then sat down.

Samuel loathed the boy more than anyone except for his father, Oscar. He was with Cat, so he had no weapons - no club, and no gun. He expected to have a knife and a fork available with his meal. He hoped he wouldn't be sitting next to Junior. He had to stay in control and stick to his tried-and-true methods. He didn't need the temptation. He was no good at spontaneous vengeance.

"Cora, you always have one of the cleanest homes in the Territory. It's such a pleasure to come here."

"Thank you. Can I get you anything?"

"Just a glass of water, thanks," said Cat. Cora got Cat and Samuel a glass and filled it with fresh creek water from a pitcher.

Paul poked his head around a corner and said, "Hello, Cat. Hello Mister."

"Hello to you too, Paul," Cat said. She looked at Cora and said, "Well, something smells good."

"It's almost ready - chicken stew with mushrooms and vegetables. I hope you like the seasonings. We're eating out on the porch today. I'll go fetch the men." She left to go round them up.

A minute later, Will, Junior, and Lee came in from the fields and went inside the cabin to clean up. They came back out, and soon, everyone was sitting at the table set up outside on the covered porch.

Things have become too complicated, too fast. Now, three boys have been added to the mix. It would be easy to end Junior's life, but there would be too many other people to deal with. Cat would try to stop him. Will looked like he could be a force to be reckoned with.

Samuel looked down at his silverware and saw only a spoon and a butter knife.

"Samuel, do you want to say grace?" Cora asked.

"Uh, I must confess I don't know how…I never learned one."

"That's OK. We don't always say grace ourselves. Will?"

"OK." He said grace, then everyone dug into the food, especially the two younger boys. Cora smiled at them.

"Please ignore my two younger boys, Cat. There will be plenty of time to teach them manners later when the time is right," she said.

Cora turned her attention to Samuel. "Cat tells me you live in town and have some sort of inheritance. What do you do with your time?"

"Ah… nothing special, but I still find the days go by quick."

Samuel watched as Cora stole a glance at Will. He looked at her with a sour expression as though he thought Samuel was lazy or wondered how his days could go quickly if he had nothing special to do. *They have no idea, but they'll see what I do with my time soon enough.*

"He's a keeper, I can tell you that. He's very handy around the house." Said Cat.

Paul chimed in, "What's for dessert?"

"Blueberry pie, of course. Can't you smell it?"

"I guess I can." He said slyly.

"Why don't you and Junior go get the pie and bring it to the table?" Paul got the pie, and Junior got new silverware. Then, they brought everything back out to the table. Junior brought over a knife to cut the pie with.

"My ribs are still sore, and I only have one arm to use, but I'm glad I can help out with a few things, even if it is just carrying silverware. I've been trying to help in the fields but still can't do much." Junior said.

Junior sat down where he was before, directly across the table from Samuel. "Junior, what happened to you? How did you get hurt?" Samuel asked.

"Broke a rib several weeks ago. Last week I broke my arm. Still recovering. Hurts some." He said.

"I can see that, but how did all this happen?"

"I got into a little dust-up with that evil son of a gun they call the Ghost. I think he's a coward, really - he never seems to finish a fight. But that's good for me because otherwise, I might not be here today."

Samuel stopped talking, only vaguely becoming aware he was suddenly shoveling the pie into his mouth. He looked up and saw Cora smiling at him.

Not today, patience, not now. I must stay invisible.

"Boys, why don't you go inside for a while and let us adults talk," Cora said. The three of them left. Cora went into the cabin with them, then returned with two bottles of wine and the corkscrew. "Who knows how to open a bottle of wine?"

"I do," Samuel said, then removed the cork from the first bottle and poured everyone a glass.

"Where'd you learn to do that?" Will asked.

"Must have picked it up somewhere along the way. I got into a lot of trouble when I was younger."

"I can believe that," Cat said with a sideways smile. Soon, the second bottle was opened and poured, and their tongues got a little looser. Even Will started to talk.

"Junior and I have had issues over the years, but he's coming around now. I'm proud of him." Cora smiled broadly at Will.

Samuel looked at Will and then over at Cora but said nothing.

"Sometimes we don't know what things are 'til later," Will said.

It took Samuel a quick moment to understand what he meant, but then he got it. *At least I won't have any trouble outsmarting Will.*

The afternoon wore on. With only a few hours of daylight left, it was time to go. "You want to come home with me, Samuel?" Cat asked.

"I would love to, but I've got to get home. I need to clean my place up, or I'll probably catch some disease from living there. I'll be over this week to work on your windmill." He said.

Cat looked disappointed but kissed him on the cheek and said, "OK, Sammy. I'll be waiting for you. Cora and Will, thank you." They left, and Cora and Will began to clean up.

On his way back to his house, he was unsettled and angry. Cat acted like it wouldn't be long before she wanted to get intimate. He didn't know how to be intimate. He'd have to end their friendship, but he wanted it to last for as long as possible because she was such a good cover for him.

His hate for the boy intensified. *Why did he call me a coward? I was being smart by not getting caught.* I'm going to pound him senseless, then pound him some more. Cat and the boy had bothered him that day, but he expected them to do that.

Something unexpected, something new, was getting under his skin now - Cora and Will. They seemed to have a connection, a bond, that he knew he would never have with anyone in his life. Their connection couldn't be real, could it? Maybe, but he would never forgive them for their disturbing display – all designed to make him feel bad. What was wrong with these people?

Junior will be dealt with just like the others. Everyone will pay the same price to see the show, and they will pay with their lives. Samuel was still undecided about who he would kill first but looked forward to killing Junior last.

Chapter Thirty-One

Samuel began preparing to finish Junior, Will, Cora, Cat, Raymond, and anyone else who got in his way. He didn't care if doing this was an assignment to achieve justice. These people were all in his way. He was beyond frustration now - it was an obsession. His plan was becoming more crystalized now. There were some problems to work out, but he had no doubt he could pull it all together.

He knew he had a gift, but ultimately, he wanted nothing more than to feel like an ordinary man who did the right thing. He wanted to be nothing more than a soldier for justice. After all, he was one of the special ones who could make a difference in this unjust world. He looked forward to the day that he could return to his main goal in life.

It was Saturday, and Junior was working at the Farmer's Market, selling vegetables. It was a great day. The sky was clear, and the temperature was perfect. When it came time for his break, he was more than ready and started for a walk. He walked a few blocks toward downtown and entered the courthouse square. There were recently planted trees around the courthouse that looked like they were placed too far apart. Junior wondered if he would still be in Prescott many years from now when the trees would grow much larger, and their spacing would begin to make sense.

Several benches were scattered around the square, all facing the courthouse. These benches were popular and rarely empty. He was glad when he saw Raymond sitting on a bench, staring straight ahead, so he walked over to him.

"Hello, Raymond," Junior said.

"It's you."

"How are you doing these days?" Junior asked. Junior was glad he had his family to rely on and talk to, but Raymond was his only true friend roughly his age, just a couple of years older. He wanted to see if Raymond had changed his ways for the better - which he doubted - but he still held out some hope.

He needed some help in solving the Ghost murders, too, and thought Raymond could be a useful resource. "Raymond, I've concluded that the Ghost is insane. I saved a man's life twice, and the Ghost still tracked him down and killed him. He needs to be stopped.

"Why come to me?"

"I see the potential in you, Raymond. Mainly, I know you're smart. Not as smart as me," He said with a grin, "but for some reason, I think you can make something out of yourself if you want to."

"Good of you, but I prefer to work alone now. I don't want anyone to slow me down."

"It's more likely I would save you from doing something stupid, you blind fool, and you know it." Snapped Junior.

"What's your plan."

"First off, we need to start trusting each other."

"I trust you." Said Raymond.

"That's good, but I'm not sure I trust you. You need to prove to me I can. Everyone deserves a second chance, sometimes even a third chance. Are you ready? Are you ready for another chance to do the right thing?"

"So, you want to be the one in charge? Do you know everything now? Is it that important to you?"

"No. All I want is for you to be more honest with me. Then I could trust you more."

They were at an impasse. "Look," Junior finally said, "Let's talk about the Ghost. He's insane, so we can't know what he is thinking. The disguises he uses are confusing to me. Why does he use them?"

"Maybe to conceal his identity." Raymond deadpanned.

"Yes, I know, but it's so unusual. Nobody I know has disguises like he does. Where did he get them from?"

"No telling." Said Raymond.

"The Ghost is probably someone who recently moved here— just before the killing started," Junior said. They both thought about that, but neither one responded.

"A vigilante killer who wears disguises is new to the area, and now you say he is a madman. How very strange." Said Raymond.

Junior added, "I think the vigilante aspect could mean the Ghost was beaten as a child, and now he's trying to get justice. Not only that, but he was beaten often enough and no doubt hard enough that it drove him insane. But how could a madman possibly get the idea to use disguises in the first place and then be so good at using them?"

They both thought about that, and Raymond said, "Maybe the Ghost grew up around actors and saw all the costumes and make-up they used."

"That makes good sense, but I must admit knowing that doesn't help us right now."

They were stuck again, but Junior felt that progress had been made. "Thanks, Raymond. Let's keep thinking about this. We'll figure this out if we keep trying. Be good. See you around." Junior said, and then left.

Raymond's conversation with Junior had raised an important point. He needed to think about where he was, where he was going, and where he wanted to go.

He doubted Junior would be so hopeful about him if he knew everything he had done and the damage he had caused over the years. Junior couldn't understand where he came from. He never would understand his parents, how poor and desperate they were, and how hopeless they made him feel. Still, Junior's confidence in him felt good, even if it was misguided. People never said good things about him, ever.

He was glad the Ghost stopped him from burning down the Emporium. Although he couldn't be entirely sure, he thought his life as an arsonist might be over. This was a surprising revelation to him. Was he changing, or had he moved on to bigger and possibly more destructive things?

Junior showed up out of nowhere, complimented him, and showed confidence in him. Why? Junior had the perfect family; how could he expect me to be more like him?

On the other hand, it was also true that Junior left home for a time. He never said anything good about his father. He seems to want me as a friend. Maybe he understands me more than I gave him credit for.

Raymond knew one thing - He didn't like owing the Ghost a favor. He wanted to be in control, and doing the Ghost's bidding significantly drained his time and energy. For now, as long as the Ghost held the Emporium incident over his head, he had no choice but to do what he was told.

His assignment at the store with Cora was a waste of time, so the Ghost told him he would have another assignment ready for him, the details of which were supposed to be coming soon. He knew the Ghost would keep giving him assignments until Raymond put his foot down. He had to put a stop to it as soon as he could because if he didn't, sooner or later, he would end up being connected through some terrible crime to this out-of-control murderer.

Junior offered him a ray of hope, a possible way out. He was sure of it. Raymond liked the idea of a second chance and then a third chance. He wondered if he could ever change. He didn't think it was genuinely possible. He would need a fourth chance and a fifth.

Junior needed help and a friend. Raymond would use this to his advantage just as soon as he could break away from the Ghost. He might need twenty chances because his life had gone so far away from Junior's. If it took him twenty chances, it would be too late for him. He didn't relish the idea of dying young or spending the rest of his life wasting away in some far-away prison.

Chapter Thirty-Two

Junior saw something completely unexpected. Sharlot, his mother's friend, was riding up the long, straight road adjacent to the vegetable fields and headed towards their cabin.

He was in a section of the fields next up for watering and had an irrigation gate halfway opened. When he saw her, he stood up for a moment, then let the pain in his ribs subside. Junior finished opening the gate, yelled to Will to let him know he was going in, and started walking up to the cabin.

He had never seen Sharlot ride to their cabin before. He was sure she must have visited here sometime, but he'd never seen it. Sharlot was a busy woman, and only something important would cause her to come here. She must have some news for him.

As he continued to walk towards the cabin, he saw his mother come out and greet Sharlot. The two of them talked briefly. He tried to stay calm and hide his curiosity about Sharlot's rare visit.

"Good morning, Junior. I want to talk to you for just a minute." She said as he got closer.

He heard his mother ask if Sharlot needed anything.

"No, thank you, I'm fine. I'll wait here and have a quick talk with Junior." Cora nodded and went back inside.

"Morning," she said as Junior arrived.

"Good morning." He answered. They both sat down.

"Junior, I've been talking to Father Donovan, Pastor Taylor, and others. Yesterday, I talked with Pastor Taylor, who told me he had spotted a family with all the tell-tale signs you were looking for." She told him the family's last name was Mueller and where they lived - Just outside of town in a forested area with no close neighbors.

She explained the Mueller's situation to him and asked, "Do you think I should tell the sheriff?"

"If you see him, sure, but I will talk with the sheriff today. You don't need to go out of your way to talk to him." Junior said.

"Thanks. I do have other things planned for today. How's your rib? I see you hurt your arm, too."

"They're both healing, getting a little better every day. Thanks."

"You're young, that helps. I need to go. Tell your mother I'm sorry I couldn't stay longer. You take care of yourself."

"I will."

"Promise?"

"Promise."

She smiled at him, then left.

Junior thought about the situation. He needed to warn Mr. Mueller that he was in imminent danger. For all he knew, the Ghost had already struck the man down, but for some reason, he didn't think so. He had no idea how much time Mr. Mueller had before the Ghost visited him, but he was keenly aware that time was not his friend, and he had to get moving. He went into the cabin, told his mother where he was going, and began the ride towards the Mueller's house. He wanted to get moving right away, and once he was on his way, he would have plenty of time to think about what he would say when he arrived.

He had a little difficulty finding the house, but after he rode around the area long enough and used a process of elimination on a couple of options, he eventually settled on what had to be the correct house based on Sharlot's instructions. He rode over to the house. It was similar in design and construction to most of the homes in the area: single-story, chimney on the side, front porch, and maybe three or four rooms. He walked up the porch and knocked on the door. There was no answer, so he knocked again and waited.

"You lost?" Junior heard the voice to his left, turned, and looked in that direction. A man was standing at the front corner of the house with a rifle pointed at him. He did not look at all like what Junior expected. He was young, maybe twenty years old. Junior thought he couldn't have been much older than that. He also looked surprisingly clean for someone who lived outside of town.

"No, sir, I don't think so. My name is Will Martin Junior, but people call me Junior. I have a very important message for Mr. Mueller."

After a moment, the man asked, "What's the message?"

"Could you lower your weapon, please? I assure you you'll want to hear what I say."

Junior was slightly surprised when Mr. Mueller lowered his rifle and said, "Let's sit on the porch." They both sat down. "Sir, I have reason to believe you are going to be the next target of the Ghost."

The man blinked, then asked, "Why do you say that?"

"I don't have time to go into the particulars, Mr. Mueller, but I did want to come here to warn you as soon as I got this new information."

"How do I know you aren't the Ghost?"

"You can't know that, but I am not the Ghost. I've been working with Sheriff Lewis and Detective Matthew Williams to help them find the Ghost. My next stop is to go talk with them, and later today or possibly tomorrow, one or both of them will come here to talk to you."

"Is that right?"

"Yes, sir." In the meantime, for your safety, do not answer your door if a stranger comes knocking. I'd stay inside your house as much as possible, too.

"Fair enough. I think it's time for you to go."

Junior asked Mr. Mueller again to please be careful, then left.

"I'm busier than a barkeep on half-price beer night," Sheriff Lewis said. The boys at the saloons seem to drink more and more all the time, and it's starting to get out of hand. I'm spending a lot of time there wrestling drunks. I won't have time to help you, Junior, but Detective Williams here can. Do you still think this Ghost is a madman?"

"Yes, I'm sure of it. Junior said. He remembered telling Sheriff Lewis and Detective Williams about this when they came to tell him that Mr. Murphy was killed.

Sheriff Lewis looked down at his desk and shuffled some papers around, suddenly looking completely involved in his work. That was quick, Junior thought. He knew the sheriff would be useless to them, at least for now. He looked over at Williams.

"What do you have?" Detective Williams asked.

Junior explained what Sharlot had told him about the possible next victim, that he went to his house and warned the man, and he told Mr. Mueller he could expect a visit from one or both of the lawmen today or tomorrow.

"What's his situation over there?"

"Sharlot said it's just him and the boy that lives there. The wife left him a couple of years ago."

"Still goes to Church. Wants his sins forgiven, maybe?" Detective Williams hinted.

Junior shrugged his shoulders. "I don't know."

"Let me think about it while I make some coffee," Williams said.

Junior thought about it, too. He wanted to be one step ahead of the Ghost.

"We need to get him out of there, at least for a few days," the detective said, handing Junior a steaming mug of coffee. "If Mr. Mueller and his son were gone, I could stay at his place and nab the Ghost if he shows up."

"Where could they go?" Junior asked.

"Mr. Mueller could stay at my place for a while, or we could put him in a jail cell. The problem is that if he is in town, there's always the possibility that someone will spot him. The Ghost is probably looking for him. The best thing we could do would be to get him out of town for a few days."

"I suppose there are different ways we could do that."

"We need to work on a plan, Junior," Williams said.

"You're going to need some help at the Mueller house. What if the Ghost doesn't show up on the first day? You can't be watching for the Ghost day after day, all day and all night."

"You want to help?"

"Yes. I can at least be a lookout for you."

"OK. What do we do with Mr. Mueller's son?"

Junior took the question as a good sign, demonstrating that he had finally earned the trust of the detective. He already had an idea for hiding Mr. Mueller's son, but he needed to see if it would work. "I have an idea. Give me an hour or two, then I'll be back."

"OK, Junior."

Junior knocked on Charley's door, and Elizabeth answered. "Junior, Come on in." Once inside, Junior saw Charley, who stopped sharpening a knife and stood up from the table.

"What can I help you with, Junior?"

Junior reviewed the recent events and explained the need to hide both Muellers.

"I'm going on a hunt tomorrow." He said. "Do you think this Mr. Mueller has any skills I could use if I took him with me?"

Don't know for sure, but he looked comfortable with a rifle when he pointed his at me."

"Is he dangerous?"

"No way of knowing. I don't think he's any more dangerous than most people, other than he seems to be a child-beater. He should work out for you if you take it easy with him, and he doesn't get too wound up about anything. I think he is in serious danger if he stays at his house."

"I can watch the boy here. It might do him good to feel safe for a while," Elizabeth chimed in.

Charley thought about it for a while, then said, "Alright. Why don't you, me, and the detective visit Mr. Mueller tomorrow morning? You two can do most of the talking at first, and I'll watch him to see if I can trust him enough to take him along with me on the hunt. It won't take me long to make a decision."

"Sounds good, Charley."

The three men rode to the Mueller house the following morning. Junior led the way. Mr. Mueller was outside, sitting on his porch. Junior said hello to him, and then the three got off their horses and walked up to sit on the porch. Junior said, "Mr. Mueller, this is Detective Williams, and this is Charley, a good friend of my family."

"Mornin' to you." The man said as he looked the three of them over.

Detective Williams started the discussion, "I'm afraid what this young man here told you yesterday is true. We think this criminal, the Ghost, is going to come here sooner or later, and he aims to kill you." He's very dangerous and unpredictable and very likely belongs in a mental hospital. We have a plan we want to propose to you."

"Why in the world would this Ghost want to hurt me, of all people?"

"I can't tell you my sources for this information, but you need to believe me. You are in grave danger."

The man looked to be in disbelief.

"The information came from a very reliable source," Junior added.

The man turned to Detective Williams and said, "I want to see your identification.

"Certainly," he said as he took his badge out and showed it to the man.

Mr. Mueller looked at the three visitors again, one at a time, then lowered his head slightly and said, "I'll do anything you ask of me."

Charley added to the conversation, "Do you hunt, sir?"

"Hunt? Of course, I have, since I was a young boy, but why would you ask me that now?"

"I have a business in town that provides guided hunts for greenhorns. "I'm leaving on a hunt tomorrow, and if you go with me, the detective could stay here at your house and wait for the Ghost while you are safely out of harm's way."

"I can't leave my boy here, and he's not old enough to go on a hunt."

"The boy can stay with my wife. We have two children about the same age as your son, and your boy would fit right in." Charley said.

The man looked at the detective again. "I can't believe this, but you seem sure about what you say. When do we start?"

Charley answered, "Tomorrow morning, early. We'll come here, you'll ride out with my group, and then my wife will take your boy back home with her."

"I'll be with Charley's wife and your son tomorrow to see that they make it back into town safely." Detective Williams said.

Charley looked at the detective and said, "I guess it's all set then. See you all first thing in the morning. In the meantime, keep your guard up and don't answer the door. You can't take that chance. It may very well be the Ghost who is paying you a visit."

Chapter Thirty-Three

Junior opened the front door to Mueller's house. The inside was about what he expected - very basic, and the place needed a good cleaning. They brought enough food for five days, just in case, and they brought their personal necessities, such as bedrolls, extra blankets, clothing, and grooming items.

They got organized and settled in for the ordeal.

"The Ghost will probably come here during the day, but we must be ready for anything." Detective Williams said.

Junior nodded. "He'll be in a disguise, too. How should we handle it if he shows up and starts knocking at the door?"

"Good question." Williams gave it some thought. "You will stay inside, and when he knocks, you say you're coming to answer the door. Make sure you are loud enough for him to hear you. Keep saying that, but don't open the door. Have your gun out with the safety off. Meanwhile, I'll go out the rear door, work my way around to the front, and confront him. If he comes at me with his club or starts to run away, I'm going to shoot the son of a bitch. No more drama. I want to end this."

"That would end the drama, that's for sure. Can't say he didn't have it coming."

"Junior, when I first came here, I was new to the area and didn't have a good feel for things. Since then, you've been a big help. The sheriff and I owe you a debt."

"I just want to catch the Ghost." Junior then told the detective about Raymond's idea that the Ghost grew up with, or around, actors.

"It makes sense. Don't know how it helps us, though." He said.

They devised a plan to split guard duties so they could both get enough rest. It was also agreed the detective would be the only one to deal with the Ghost if he arrived. It was Detective William's job. He had the experience and a gun, and Junior still hadn't healed completely. Williams gave Junior a gun and said, "Use this as a last resort, only if you are under attack, and only if you have no other choice but to fire the weapon to save your life."

They took turns watching out the front window for movement but saw nothing for the rest of the day and the rest of that night. The next morning, Junior asked, "Are you married?"

"No, I never had the time. My job and marriage don't work well together. Do you have a girlfriend?"

"No, but I want to. When I find one, I don't know how she could resist me." He said, half-kidding.

"I like your confidence, kid."

"You mentioned this boy named Raymond. The sheriff tells me he's bad news - always getting into trouble."

"That's true, I know, but I want to think he can still amount to something if he decides to. He's smart."

"There's more to it than just being smart, Junior. You need to be careful when he's around you."

"I will."

The detective kept talking. "There is a new science in the law-enforcement world. It's called fingerprinting. I tried to use it once in Phoenix, but it's too new and hasn't been accepted yet. Everyone has a unique set of ridges on the tips of their fingers. After a criminal leaves a trace of his fingerprints at a crime scene, his prints can be copied from his fingers using ink. The copied fingerprints from the criminal are compared with those found at the crime scene."

"Did the Ghost leave these fingerprints at one of his crimes?

"Unfortunately, no, none we've found. When I found you with his club in your hands, standing over Mr. Murphy that day, I looked at the club to see if there were any markings, but there weren't.

The detective continued, "Right now, we're trying to prevent a murder, not find evidence to prove who committed a murder. I would love to be the first in the Territory to introduce fingerprint evidence in court. Someday, I will, but that's probably a few years away. Right now, we must focus on what we're doing here because we need quick, decisive action if the Ghost appears."

Another day passed with no activity, then another. Junior went to the well the next morning to get fresh water while Detective Williams made breakfast.

Junior returned inside and asked, "What if he sneaks in the back door? We wouldn't be ready for him."

"Stay calm, Junior. He prefers to knock on the front door to get close enough to his victim to surprise him and use his club. Besides, the rear door stays locked all the time. Don't worry." Detective Williams said.

"Alright, my turn to sleep, the detective said. See you at two o'clock." Junior sat and watched out the front window - the same view as the last few days. He learned to watch the birds. It helped keep his interest up, to keep his eyes engaged, and it helped him look for movement.

Just before two o'clock that afternoon, he woke the detective up. It was time for a shift change. Junior went to his bedroll to get some rest. After a couple of hours, he felt a gentle kick in his leg. He looked up to see the detective whispering to him.

"Come to the front of the house. I thought I saw something," he said. Junior went to the front window for several minutes but saw nothing. "I saw movement by that pine tree on the right," Detective Williams explained. They kept observing.

Junior whispered, "I saw it. It looked like the side of a head peeked out from behind the tree. The man is wearing a big floppy hat. I've seen the Ghost wear a hat like that before."

"Let's watch and see what his next move is," Williams said.

They waited and watched. The Ghost did not approach the house. An hour passed, then another. The Ghost showed himself out from one side of the tree for a quick moment, and then a few minutes later, he showed himself from the other side. They could not see much of his face because of his floppy hat. Junior knew he would be in disguise anyway.

"Maybe he's waiting to see if Mr. Mueller is home, then he'll come up to the front door," Junior said.

"Maybe."

"I could walk across the window a few times with my face turned back so he wouldn't recognize me. That might bring him to the door."

Detective Williams thought about that, then said, "Alright. Start a fire in the fireplace, build it up good so there's plenty of light in here, then casually walk across the window. Don't show your face. I'll keep an eye out from here. If nothing else, the smoke from the fireplace will get his attention."

Junior lit a fire, let it grow, then walked in front of the window. He walked across the window again and waited. Nothing happened.

"What's going on?" Junior asked.

"I'm not sure."

They continued to wait and watch. The Ghost continued peeking out from one side of the tree, then another.

"Damn, I hate the Ghost. He must be waiting for Mr. Mueller to come outside for some reason. Maybe he suspects Mr. Mueller has been warned not to answer the door." Williams said.

"Could be. He might have been watching me when I first came here to warn Mr. Mueller. Almost anything is possible with this Ghost."

"OK, it doesn't look like he will do anything unless he sees Mr. Mueller open the front door. I'm tired of waiting. I am going to sneak out the back door, go where he is, and confront him. I hope he surrenders peacefully, but I'm not counting on it."

"Grab your gun, just in case, but stay here." The detective quietly opened the back door and went outside. Junior watched him leave and then relocked the back door. He remained still for a moment and listened for any noises that may have been coming from the rear or sides of the house. He heard nothing, then went to the front window and watched.

The man behind the tree thought he heard something, so he lowered himself closer to the ground and listened. There it was again, barely perceptible, a snapping sound, but a sound not in harmony with the other sounds of nature he had grown used to hearing that day. He waited and watched, and then he saw him.

The man was trying to sneak up from behind, on his right side. It was time to move.

He picked up a rock and threw it behind the man, who turned around and looked in the direction where the rock landed. That was the moment he needed. He began to run down the narrow dirt road from the house. He could hear his pursuer and realized that throwing the rock only gave him a few seconds of head-start. He kept running. He could hide behind a bend in the road and some bushes there.

He got behind the bushes and looked for a branch he could use. Luckily, he found one. It was not ideal, but it would work. His pursuer was running hard after him, coming towards the corner and ready to make the turn with the road. When the man got close, he lunged out and hit him in the back of the head with a branch. The man fell to the ground, out cold. "Sorry, Mister," Raymond said. He started to run until he realized no one was following him, then he slowed down and walked back home. On the way home, he removed the ridiculous floppy hat the Ghost had insisted he wear.

Junior waited one hour, then two, without seeing or hearing anything since the Ghost and the detective ran away from the house. It was starting to get dark, and Junior needed to investigate. He cautiously exited the front door, looked around, and started walking down the road. He walked for a few minutes without seeing anything, then turned a corner in the road and saw the detective lying on the ground, moaning softly. He went over to look him over and noticed there were a couple of spots near the top of his head that were still moist with blood. He gently rolled him onto his back. His face was covered in dried blood, he was dazed, and he looked to be in pain.

"Guess you're lucky the Ghost was looking for someone else today." He lifted Detective Williams from under his shoulders and slowly dragged him safely back to the house.

Chapter Thirty-Four

Samuel realized he was losing track of large amounts of time - one hour here, two hours there. It was troublesome, and there didn't seem to be anything he could do about it. He used a handkerchief to wipe the sweat from his forehead.

He had important work to do, the most important work of his life so far. He needed to stay focused and ensure every detail was taken care of - every last detail. His next move, the one that would eliminate all of his problems at once, would start soon. He patted the remaining sweat from his forehead.

The coded knock sounded on his back door. He opened the door and let Raymond in. "What happened?" He asked Raymond.

"They were waiting for you, that's for sure. I think I saw two people inside the house. They started a fire in the fireplace and were probably trying to get me to come up to the front door, just like you said they might. Then one of them came out of the house and tried to catch me. I ran for a spell, then stopped and waited, and when he ran past me, I clubbed him on his head."

"He didn't see you?"

"Never."

"I don't understand how they knew I would show up there.

There was no way for them to know that." Samuel said. He looked sideways at Raymond for a moment, then discarded his suspicions.

"Junior must have been inside. It's the only thing that makes sense. He seems like such a nice boy, but don't let that fool you. He's evil, with evil powers, and now he's working with Oscar."

Raymond gave him a confused look. Samuel ignored it.

"Good work. We make a good team, you and me." Samuel said.

"Not for much longer. I've done enough for you. We're even now."

"You're getting closer to being paid up, young man, but we're far from even. I want you to keep an eye out for this, Mr. Mueller. I don't think he is at his house right now, so you'll have to look around to find him."

Raymond frowned, turned around, and left.

Samuel once heard someone say fortune favors the bold, but he doubted if that was always the best approach. The boy called him a coward because he never finished a fight. Try as he might, Samuel couldn't stop thinking about that. He knew it was better for him to escape and live to fight another day, but the boy's insult, said almost directly to his face, kept festering inside him.

One minute, Samuel knew he was right. The next minute, he was full of anger, hatred, and doubt. It was that old, familiar feeling he had when he was young.

Carving wood always seemed to calm him down. It was time to carve a new club, not that he needed one - he didn't, but he needed the hands-on feeling of doing something.

His design was perfected by now. He had some mesquite branches stashed away, and he looked for a suitable piece that had a knob that was once the base of an off-shooting branch. He was proud of this design idea - the knob would be the first thing that struck the evil-doer. He found a good-looking branch and began to carve.

As he was carving, he was glad he had not chosen the Manzanita branch. Normally, the red bark excited him and put him in the mood for his work, but not today.

It was a critical time for him. He had to stay calm so all the pieces would come together. *Stay calm, and justice will prevail.*

He opened his eyes and realized he had lost track of more time. His half-finished new club was lying on the floor near his feet, along with his carving knife. He wiped the sweat off his forehead again, got up, and walked around to stretch. He had no choice but to change his tactics now that he had to fight both Oscar and Junior, the two malevolent forces working in league against him. They were getting closer every day. He could feel it. He had no choice but to move forward with his plan. Otherwise, it was only a matter of time before they found him. *Fortune favors the bold.*

His new plan was genius, with only a few nuances left to work out. The new approach he was planning would be something unexpected, something bold and daring. He would be in control, one step ahead, and call all the shots.

Raymond wasn't sure where to start. He didn't want to go back to the Mueller house. Someone could be waiting for him at the house. Besides, Samuel didn't think they were even there. Where could Mr. Mueller and his son be hiding? Were they at the hotel? Had they left town? Was he staying with a friend? Did child-beaters even have friends? Not many, he decided. His first stop would be the hotel. If the two of them had left town, there was nothing he could do about it. He'd keep thinking about who else would let the two of them into their home for a few days.

Samuel was starting to worry him. The man lived in his own world and clearly lost his way somewhere along the line. Raymond mused. he must have lived like this for years.

Raymond started his search at the hotel. "Good afternoon," he said to the man behind the counter. I'm looking for a friend of mine. He's with a small boy."

"Let me see. That sounds like Mr. and Mrs. Anderson and their son. They are scheduled to check out soon, if you don't mind waiting in the lobby. Raymond didn't expect to be given a room number, so he nodded, thanked the man, and then sat in the small lobby to wait.

He saw the couple coming down the stairway a full hour later, with their boy tagging along. They looked too happy and too young. This was a dead end. He waved his thanks to the confused clerk and left the hotel.

He had some time to think while he was waiting in the lobby. Mr. Mueller probably didn't know anyone who could hide him, but the people hiding him would have friends. He knew Junior was working with the Sheriff on the case but didn't know any of the sheriff's friends. The detective was new to town. He might know someone, but it was not very likely. It was unlikely Will would risk opening up his home to a child-beater. Who else, then? He immediately thought of Charley. It was time for him to start watching Charley's house.

He found an out-of-the-way place to hide and watch the house safely. He waited and watched until it was nearly dark, then saw them. Two tired-looking men on horseback slowly approached and stopped in front of Charley's house. "Give me a minute, and I'll go fetch the boy," he heard Charley say. Soon after, Charley came out with one hand on the boy's shoulder. The boy kept his head down the entire time.

The man, who Raymond suspected was Mr. Mueller, got on his horse. Charley lifted the boy to him, and the man thanked him for all his help. The two of them rode away in the direction of the Mueller house. Charley went inside his house, and then Raymond followed the two until he was convinced they were headed home. There would be something good to report to Samuel.

Chapter Thirty-Five

He heard the coded knock on the back door, then let Raymond in. "What did you find out?"

"The man and the boy are back at their own house now. It looks like Mr. Mueller went with Charley on one of his guided hunts, and the boy stayed with Charley's wife."

"Mueller is back at his house with the boy; that's perfect. This Charley - I forgot about him. You'll do me one last favor, and then I promise we're even." He told Raymond what he wanted him to do, handed him the floppy hat, and watched him as he went out the door.

Sheriff Lewis had both of his jail cells double-booked with guests. Two drunks in each cell, with only one bed per cell. The whiskey saloons were all on Montezuma Street, and he went to each saloon there at least twice a night. Tonight, he was getting ready to go back for the third and final time to see if he would have to put three drunks in a cell tonight. He didn't like doing this. The more drunks, the harder it was for him to clean up after they left.

The sheriff opened the door that connected the front office to the cell room. Everything looked normal—four men sleeping. One of the drunks sat up, rocked his torso back and forth, and loudly mumbled something completely incoherent. Wonderful, he thought sarcastically. It's too late for him to make a career change - he was way too old to start over. He left the Office, locked the door, and rambled over to Montezuma Street.

He heard loud talking at the Emporium and then walked that way. "What's goin' on here, boys?"

"This one's sauced. Causin' trouble too. He's all yours."

Sargent Lewis saw the man stagger and fall to his knees. "Let's go, Mister. Off to jail for you. Lay on your stomach and put your hands behind your back." The sheriff cuffed the man, hauled him up on his feet, and took him to jail.

"Watch your step." The sheriff told the man as they negotiated the steps to the porch, the office, and finally into the cell room. The man stood in front of a jail cell, trying hard to remain upright. The sheriff opened the cell door, took his cuffs off, and pushed him toward the inside of the cell. "In ya' go, Mister." The sheriff locked the cell, turned, and headed towards the front office.

"I told him…leave me alone, son of a bitchin' Ghost."

Sheriff Lewis was halfway through the door when he heard the drunk, then turned around and went up to his cell. "What did you just say?" He asked but got no answer. The man was sitting on the floor with his back to the wall, and his head hung low. He opened the cell, went over to the man he had just put in the cell, and shoved him in the shoulder. "What did you say?" There was still no answer, and the sheriff realized the man had blacked out.

The following morning, Sheriff Lewis arrived at work early to question the drunk who had mentioned the Ghost. He went through the front office, opened the door to the cells, and took a look. It was the usual, he thought. Nobody was moving, and they all looked dirty and miserable. He went to the cell, pulled the man out, and led him to the front office.

"Want some coffee?" he asked. The man raised his head and nodded yes. Sheriff Lewis started to make the coffee, and he used the time to size the man up. He looked like many of the men he saw in Prescott—most likely dirt-poor and with a slightly desperate look about them. Honest or dishonest, cooperative or not, he had no idea. "What's your name?"

"Joe"

"Joe, I'm Sheriff Lewis. Here, have some coffee."

"Thank you."

"I brought you to the front office because you mentioned something about the Ghost killer last night.

"Ghost? Oh yeah, I remember. The damn guy kept buying me drinks. That's why I ended up here."

"I'll make you a deal, Joe. If you tell me everything I want to know about the man you talked to who mentioned the Ghost, I'll let you go free this morning with no charges."

"That sounds good. Let me think for a minute," Joe said. They both took a big gulp of coffee, and Joe did his best to gather his thoughts.

"I was having a drink by myself, enjoying the evening, and this man came up to the little table where I was sitting. He offered to buy me a whiskey, which I thought was a fair payment for taking up some of my space, so I said yes."

"And yeah, I said yes." He repeated as if he was trying to remember what he had just said. The man told me he had a job waiting for me if I wanted it. He bought me another glass of whiskey and said the job was at two in the morning. Not this morning, but tomorrow morning - after midnight tonight. Now, I'll be honest with you. I could definitely use five dollars, but I'm not dumb. There was something not right about all this. He bought me another whiskey, which I remember tasted very good, and I tried to learn more about his assignment, but he wouldn't tell me anything else. I might have had another whiskey or two after that, but I don't remember exactly."

He continued, "Finally, I told him I wouldn't do it, and the man got mad. He hissed at me. Yeah, he hissed. He said I would regret the day I crossed the Ghost. It didn't hit me right away. Was he the ghost? Was he working for the Ghost? It seems like a dream now, thinking about it. Anyway, then the man started saying things that made no sense. He mentioned someone's name a couple of times…Oscar, I think. Then, suddenly, I looked up, and he's goin' out the saloon's front door."

"I stood up and followed him, but that didn't go so well. I kept bumping into people and tables. Then, someone grabbed me by the arm and pushed me outside. The next thing I knew, you were hauling me here to put me in a cell."

What else do you remember?"

"Could I have some more coffee?"

"Sure."

The man took a fresh mug of coffee, sipped it, and momentarily thought about the sheriff's question. "I've told you everything about the man I can remember. Sorry"

Sheriff Lewis believed him and handed him a slip of paper. "Alright, write your full name and address on this piece of paper in case I need to talk to you again. If you remember anything more about what was said last night, you come to see me. Understood?"

"I understand."

"Then you're free to go." The man wrote down his name and address, took another sip of coffee, then left.

Sheriff Lewis considered what he should do with this latest piece of information. Detective Williams was temporarily out of service with a lump on his head, and he knew he was too busy dealing with all the drunks to spend any time chasing after the Ghost.

Joe's story was believable, but the Ghost's motivation for talking with Joe bothered him. It seemed like the Ghost was overexposing himself by asking a stranger for help. He had always worked alone and relied on surprise attacks. Why was he looking for someone to help him now? Was he changing his tactics?

At the moment, he had a jail full of drunks to process, and he would work on a plan to deal with this latest Ghost development later. Two o'clock the next morning was a long time from now.

Chapter Thirty-Six

Junior had just finished lunch when he heard a knock on the door. He went over to open the door, and was surprised to see the apprehensive face of Sheriff Lewis staring back at him.

"Junior, I need to talk with you and your father."

"Sure, let's go to the porch. I'll get Will." Soon, the three of them were sitting on the porch. Sheriff Lewis began to speak.

"Gentlemen, I have a problem. Last night, I brought in my last drunk of the night. He surprised me no end when he said something about a meeting he had that night with the Ghost or someone working for the Ghost. He wasn't sure. The man blacked out before I could talk to him last night, but I got him talking this morning, and I need to go over what he told me with both of you.

This caught Junior's attention. Will's eyes got a little larger, too.

The man claimed the Ghost needed help, what kind of help he did not know, at two a.m. the next morning – two in the morning, tonight. The drunk told me the man talked him into drinking too much, but despite that, he still turned the Ghost down, and then the Ghost, or maybe his front-man, got mad and left."

"What do you make of it?" Asked Junior.

"I don't know. It's a new approach for the Ghost, making me a little suspicious. He's always worked alone, and now he is looking for help. There's a good chance something is off, but I can't quite figure it out. But, on the other hand, it could also be that he's getting desperate. We're getting closer to finding him, and he must know that."

"When someone hit me and broke my rib, I always thought it was an accomplice of the Ghost and not the Ghost himself who hit me. Maybe the Ghost is looking for a new accomplice now for some reason?" Junior proposed.

"I don't know what is going on or what the Ghost may or may not be doing, but I am in no position to take a chance when a man's life could be at stake. Someone needs to be at the Mueller's tonight. It makes sense for the Ghost to be there at two in the morning tonight. I think the Ghost has identified Mr. Mueller as his next victim, and he must be stopped. This man's life could be at stake.

Sheriff Lewis continued, "Detective Williams is recovering well but not ready yet. He can't help me, and I'm too busy. I feel bad about asking, but I need your help tonight. I don't know who else to ask." Sheriff Lewis looked at Will and Junior and gave them both a hopeful, pleading look.

"I have been involved in this from the start, and I'd like to be involved in finishing it too. You can count on me." Junior said.

"I'm not lettin' you go over there alone, son." Will looked at him, then Sheriff Lewis, and said, "Junior and I want to help. What do you want us to do?"

"The man's a killer. He wants me to help him because he wants to kill someone. I'm not a killer." Raymond mumbled to himself as he rode over to his assignment. After tonight, he will be rid of the Ghost forever. He would put his foot down, and that would be that. He had done more than enough to be free of that madman forever.

He got off his horse, tied it up, and started walking the rest of the way. The sun went down a couple of hours ago, and fortunately, there was enough moonlight for him to navigate his way to Charley's house. He found a spot behind a storage building where he could watch the house. He could see some light coming from inside the house, and all was quiet. He almost forgot to put on the big, floppy hat and the fake mustache, but he remembered to do so and put them on. He waited, watched, and listened. No sounds from the neighbors, no sounds came from Charley's house. It was time.

He picked up a rock, stood up, stepped out, aimed, and threw it at Charley's only window. He missed low, and the rock bounced off his house. He went behind the storage building again and heard nothing. Raymond then cautiously looked at Charley's house and again saw nothing unusual. He stepped out and threw a second rock. This time, his aim was perfect. The rock hit the window with a smash, and the glass shattered into little pieces.

If Charley had come running out of the house now, Raymond would have had nowhere to hide. He didn't think that would be his reaction, however. He thought most people would take a moment to assess a situation like this before doing anything. He was right.

He hurried to hide behind the storage building and waited. Raymond peeked around the right side of the building and saw Charley looking directly at him. He ducked out of sight again, grateful the floppy hat and mustache covered much of his face. After another minute, he took a peek around the left side and saw Charley pointing a rifle in his general direction. He quickly moved his head back behind the cover of the building. He had done what he had been told, and it was time to leave. He had to crawl about fifteen yards to find more cover; then, he stayed low for about ten more yards until he could stand up. He was in the clear.

He could finally relax. It felt very, very good for him to be free of the Ghost's clutches forever. His work tonight was done. He knew Charley would spend the rest of the night at his house protecting his family.

The Ghost waited to see who would show up at the Mueller's house. He saw nothing right away. He pulled a twig off a bush and used it to clean his teeth as he looked left and right. Then he saw them. Will and Junior were trying to be very sneaky and moved as quietly as possible, but he still heard them as he watched them approach the house. Junior stayed in the front and went to one side to hide behind some bushes. Will went around the closest side of the house to him, and then he disappeared behind the rear. He wondered if Oscar and that poor boy were inside. There was nothing he could do about that now. First things first. His trap had been laid.

He waited for half an hour and saw no change, then slowly and quietly exited the area using his planned escape route. A half-hour later, he mounted his horse and started riding. His plan had worked perfectly so far. He needed to focus and keep alert because the next step was the payoff for all his efforts. It was time to get Cora.

The boys were finally in bed and hopefully asleep, so Cora started to unwind after the day's activities. She sat in front of her small mirror and combed her hair. Will and Junior were going to be out of the house all night, but she felt safe inside the thick log walls of her cabin.

She loved combing her hair with her special ivory comb. This was her time of the day to settle down and have some time just for herself. She had properly combed her hair and didn't need to keep combing it, but she did. It just felt good.

When Will left after Supper, he gave her strict instructions not to open the door to a stranger, no matter what - like she would do that anyway, she thought, although it did make her feel good that Will wanted her to stay safe. It was about bedtime for her when she was startled to hear the knock on the door.

Who would knock on her front door at this late hour? Had something happened to Will and Junior? She took a peek out her window and relaxed a little. It was just Samuel, but what was he doing out her way so late at night? She thought of Will and Junior again, then hurriedly put on her robe and opened the door.

"Samuel. What in the blazes are you doing out here? Is everything all right?"

"Everything is fine, Cora. I need to talk to you briefly. Can I come in?"

"Yes, of course, come in and get out of the cold."

"Where are Will and Junior? Where are the boys?" He asked her.

"Will and Junior are not here right now. The boys are asleep. Please tell me, why are you here at such a late hour?"

Samuel said nothing. He stepped closer to Cora, pulled out his pistol, and pointed it at her. "Don't make a sound. You're going with me. Now, slowly and quietly walk out the door."

She was stunned but said nothing and started moving towards the door. Samuel had always seemed strange to her, but now he had crossed the line. She had the comb in her hand when she opened the door to let Samuel in, and she was still holding it now.

On her way out, she pretended to drop it accidentally. "My comb."

"Leave it, let's go. I'll shoot you if you make me. Then I'll shoot your boys."

Chapter Thirty-Seven

Junior struggled to stay awake. He tried, but boredom was setting in. He sat there, jerked his head up, and realized it was not the first time he had started to fall asleep. He needed to keep trying. He was responsible for staying awake and looking for the Ghost, and he was not about to be surprised, captured, or killed. Another jolt of energy kicked in.

When he noticed that dawn had nearly arrived, he cautiously got up and went over to talk with Will, who was awake but didn't look alert. "If it hasn't happened by now, it's not going to," he whispered to Will, who stared blankly at him for a moment.

"Have a seat, Junior." Will motioned to a space next to him. Let's at least wait until dawn. We can't finish anythin' 'til we see it through." They sat there until dawn came and helped each other stay awake. When dawn finally came, there was no activity around the house.

"We got some bad information. I don't think he's coming." Junior said.

"You're right. If he hasn't shown up by now, he's not goin' to. Let's go home."

They rode home, bone-tired. Will looked forward to a hot breakfast followed by a serious nap. He opened the door and immediately sensed something was wrong. Lee and Paul were sitting at the kitchen table, looking sad. He could tell Paul had been crying. "What's wrong, boys? Where's your mother?"

Paul started crying, and Lee looked down at the table and said nothing. "Lee, I'm asking you, where is your mother?"

"She's gone, Father. We woke up this morning, and she was gone."

"What? She's gone?" He stood there, not believing, not understanding. He quickly searched the cabin and told the boys, "Stay here. I'm going to look around outside." On his way out, he saw Junior walking towards him after securing the horses.

"Junior. Your Mother is missing. Help me look for her."

"Missing. What do you mean?"

"She is not in the cabin and hasn't been there all morning. Help me look for her. Let's look in the barn and shed together, then you look in the fields, and I'll look in the creek…" He started to choke up and couldn't talk anymore. Cora had disappeared once before, many years ago. What followed her disappearance was the most miserable year of his life.

He needed to stay calm and slow his breathing. He searched for several minutes and then found himself wandering around, calling out her name. He tried to slow down and realized he was looking for her in the barn - for the second time. It hit him that he was putting off what he dreaded most. He needed to look in the creek. "Oh God," he mumbled. There are so many bad things that can happen in a creek."

He searched up and down the creek and around the trees but

found nothing. He looked around for what must have been another hour, then headed back to the cabin. He saw Junior sitting on the porch with his head in his hands. *I need to be strong now for Junior and the boys.*

He slowly walked up the steps to the covered porch and sat beside Junior. Neither said anything. Will felt like all of the world's burdens were on his shoulders.

"We'll figure it out. There must be a simple reason why she's gone. I saw no signs of a struggle anywhere. Did you?" Junior asked.

"I wasn't lookin' for it. Let's go inside and see how the boys are doin'," Will said.

Will opened the door and noticed Cora's favorite comb was lying on the floor. Junior saw it too. Will said, "That's odd. Cora prizes this comb. I've never seen it on the floor before."

Will picked it up and put it on her dresser.

"Boys, get dressed. We're going to Charley's." Will would be the first to admit his best friend Charley could be relied upon to come up with good solutions in crisis situations. Getting Junior to work with Charley would help, too.

Charley wondered why he was visited by the Ghost last night. The Ghost threw a rock through his window, then ran off as soon as he saw the rifle. There was a chance the Ghost was trying to draw him out of the house and away from his family, but he discounted that because the Ghost could have caught him and attacked him at any time when he was outside of the house, on any day, and at almost any place he wanted to. He had waited and stood guard all night, just in case.

He heard a few bats flapping around, and closer to morning,

he heard an owl hooting. That was all. He heard nothing else that aroused his suspicion. He couldn't take a chance on leaving, so he waited inside the house to protect his wife and two children. Somehow, he knew. He knew in his bones he had done exactly what the Ghost wanted him to do. The Ghost was calling the shots now. If the Ghost was one step ahead of him, then there was a good chance he would be one step ahead of the others, too.

Junior rode into town with Will and the two boys. On the way to Charley's house, they saw Raymond walking towards them.

"You all look like you could use some help. What's wrong?"

"My Mother's missing. We're going to Charley's to work on a plan." Junior said

"I want to help." Junior knew Will did not trust Raymond one bit, so he spoke quickly.

"Good. Get your horse and meet us at Charley's.

They all arrived at Charley's at about the same time. "Mornin' Charley, Elizabeth," Will said, then saw they looked as tired as he was. "What happened to you two?"

"We were visited by the Ghost last night."

Will instinctively gave them another look to see if they had any injuries. They looked OK. "What happened?"

"Elizabeth and I were sitting here talking last night when a rock came through the window."

Will looked at the window and saw there was no glass in it.

"I went to the window and saw a man with a mustache and wearing a floppy hat hiding behind the storage building. He hid when he saw me. I got my rifle and showed it. Then he looked out from the other side of the building. He must have seen me with the rifle because he ducked behind the building again, and that was the last I saw of him. He was teasing me. Playing a game. Makes no sense."

The conversation paused as they all seemed to be trying to decide what had actually happened last night.

"OK, Will. You showed up here with your three boys and Raymond. What is going on with you?"

"Cora is missing," Will said.

"What? When did that happen?"

"Last night. Yesterday, Sheriff Lewis came to see us. He had heard from a source that the Ghost was planning to attack Mr. Mueller this mornin' at two o'clock. The detective is nursin' a lump on his head, so the sheriff had no one else to turn to, and he asked us if we would be willing to help. Of course, we said yes. We were outside Mr. Mueller's house all night, but the Ghost never showed up."

"We came home this mornin', and Cora was missin'. We looked for her in and around the cabin, but she wasn't there."

Charley stared at Will in disbelief. "Was there any damage at the Cabin? Were there any signs of a struggle?"

"None."

Charley thought about the situation for a minute. Then he said, "This is how it looks to me. First, I was deliberately detained here at my house. The Ghost must have realized I would not leave my family. Then you two were sent away from your cabin, all the way to north Prescott, on a fool's errand. Then Cora leaves - or is taken by someone, God forbid the Ghost - and we're sitting here with our tired heads spinning, wondering what happened. The way I see it, we were all played like strings on a fiddle. Elizabeth, would you take care of Lee and Paul? The four of us need to figure out what to do next."

"Of course. Come here, boys. Have you had breakfast yet?"

"No, ma'am."

"Let's see what we can do about that."

Will and Charley sat at the table first, then Junior and Raymond sat down across from them. No one said anything, and it was apparent to Junior that no one had the slightest idea what they should do next.

Chapter Thirty-Eight

Charley looked at the others seated at his kitchen table but didn't know what to say.

Junior started the conversation, "Sheriff Lewis sent us off to Mr. Mueller's house, and all we did was lose a good night's sleep. Can we rule out the sheriff as not being involved?" Junior asked, to no one in particular.

This question caught Charley off guard. Junior looked tired. He didn't think Junior suspected the sheriff, but it was as good a place as any to start the conversation. It must have been the only thing he could think of to say.

"He was just trying to protect Mr. Mueller," Raymond said. "He got word of the potential danger and had no other way to protect him. He had no choice. I think he was played, just like we were."

"I think so, too." Said Charley.

"I know him. He's honest." Will added.

"Rocks are thrown through my window, and I'm tricked into staying inside. Then Cora is abducted. The Ghost is behind all of this," said Charley.

Will spoke up, "Before Junior and I left last night, I told Cora not to let in strangers. She wouldn't anyway, so how did this happen?"

"The Ghost is very good at using disguises. He could have been pretending to be you, Charley, Detective Williams, or one of her neighbors in distress." Raymond said.

Everyone took a moment to think about that.

Will was the next to speak up. "Cora was taken. This I know. She would never leave her boys alone."

"We have no idea where she is. We'll need to let the Sheriff know she's gone. Maybe Detective Williams has recovered enough by now and can help us. We can check with the neighbors, and if that doesn't work, then I don't know what else to do. Charley said. He looked over at Will, who looked very pale and dejected.

"Wait," said Junior. We found her ivory comb on the floor when we entered the cabin. She valued that comb and would never leave it on the floor. What if she left it there as a clue?"

"You may have something there, Junior. We need to think this through. We could use a fresh pair of eyes to look at all this. It would help to ask someone who's not so close to the situation. Let's go over to see the sheriff. We need for him to get involved anyway." Charley said. Everyone agreed, and the four left to visit the sheriff.

Cora was marched out of her cabin and to the barn, then waited as Samuel tied her hands behind her back. She watched as he put a saddle on Feather, her horse. She wondered if this was the time for her to try to stop Samuel, but he still had the gun, and she was still feeling stunned. He helped her onto her old friend Feather, then put a thick bag on her head. Feather did not move nearly as fast as she once did, but she was still dependable, and Cora knew Feather would follow Samuel's horse without a fuss.

They rode off for about one hour with Samuel in the lead, then stopped. Cora's bag was ripped off her head, and she saw she was outside Cat's cabin. Samuel got off his horse and helped her off Feather. "Inside. Now," he said with his pistol pointed at her.

She went to the front door, waited for it to open, and stepped inside. Cat was sitting up against the far wall, with her wrists tied behind her back and her ankles bound.

Cat gasped, "Not you, Cora. I'm so sorry."

"Not your fault," Cora said.

Samuel led her over to where Cat was, pushed her down, and tied her ankles. "Why are you doing this?" Cora asked.

"I have my reasons. You two are going to sit there. Don't cause any problems. I don't want to hurt you, but I will if you make me."

Cora knew beyond all doubt now. She was not only looking at Samuel - she was looking at the Ghost. She thought back to several years ago when she saved Will's life. She hoped against hope he could return the favor and save hers, and soon - somehow.

The four men went to the Sheriff's office. "Cora is missin', Sheriff." Said Will.

"Missing? How did that happen?" Will and Charley explained the recent activities and Cora's disappearance from her cabin.

"The Ghost is behind this, but what is he trying to accomplish?" Asked Sheriff Lewis.

"He may be getting desperate. It's hard to tell with him. He doesn't think like we do." Junior said.

Sheriff Lewis said, "He's trying to draw you people out. He wants all of you to do the things he planned ahead of time for you to do. That's his advantage over you. Before you know it, he'll be there, waiting, so he can ambush you. That's what I think. Unfortunately, my duties here limit how much I can get involved right now. When we know where the Ghost is, I will be the only one to take the lead in bringing him in, dead or alive."

The sheriff paused, looked at Junior, and said, "Junior, you've stopped him from killing more than once. The motives and actions of a man like this are hard to predict, but I know for sure that he is angry at you. He has to be. You need to be especially careful now."

Junior nodded soberly at the sheriff without saying anything.

The sheriff continued, "Normally, in these situations, I try to put myself in the criminal's shoes. That may not work here with an insane man. Plus, he is getting you all to do exactly what he wants. Somehow, if we can start to out-think the rotten son of a bitch it might make enough of a difference in this sick game he's playing. We need to consider every possible action we need to take and do so quickly. If we fail, people we know and love will start dying."

Chapter Thirty-Nine

They were a long way from having a plan. An idea had been suggested that Cora had left her ivory comb as a clue, but Sheriff Lewis was not sure he believed it. It seemed like Will and Junior wanted, or maybe needed, for it to be a clue and read too much into a comb found on the floor. Their judgment was affected - they were tired, and everyone was anxious about what was happening.

Unfortunately for the sheriff, it was the only idea anyone had. The sheriff thought it was better to do almost anything than to feel lost and waste time. The group needed to keep moving. He would explore the possibility that the comb was a clue, and in so doing, a more promising idea might come to light.

"OK, let's go with Junior's suggestion that the comb was a clue Cora deliberately left us. What was she trying to tell us? I'm not sure how it helps us. It doesn't tell us much, does it?" said Sheriff Lewis.

"Cat is the connection. She gave Cora the comb as a gift." Said Will.

"But I don't see her as the Ghost. It doesn't make sense," said Sheriff Lewis. What about her brother, Happy?"

"I've known Happy since he was a teenager. There's no way he could be the Ghost." Charley paused briefly, then added, "It is still possible the Ghost took Cora to Happy's house. Think about it. Nobody would expect to look there."

"What about Samuel, Cat's latest man-friend? I don't think we can rule him out completely. The clue leads to him as much as it does to anyone else," said Junior.

"It's a possibility. What about the Mercantile? I'm sure Cora buys soaps and beauty creams there. Maybe there is someone who works there she was trying to lead us to," said Raymond.

They had exhausted their list of possibilities, and the discussion slowed considerably. Sheriff Lewis got things started again. "Time is not on our side here, men. I have an idea. We need to split up. You'll each take a lead and check it out. I have to stay here. Will, you go to Cat's house. Charley and Raymond, you go to Samuel's house. Junior, you go to Happy's house. On your way over, check with a few of your neighbors in case Cora had to hide out with one of them for some reason. Detective Williams, based on what you told me earlier, you're not completely on your game yet. You go to the Mercantile. It's the easiest job. Are you up for it?"

"Yes, I've got it."

"Where does Samuel live?" Charley asked no one in particular. No one spoke up right away, and everyone looked at each other.

"I know where he lives," Raymond said. Everyone turned and looked at Raymond. Detective Williams did not attempt to hide his surprise at this new revelation.

"I followed him home one day. I was curious to find out where he lived, that's all." From what Sheriff Lewis knew about Raymond, his explanation was odd enough to be true, so he said nothing.

"OK, it's settled then, right?" Sheriff Lewis said as he looked at Junior.

"How is your rib and your arm? Can you use a gun?" he asked Junior.

"My side still hurts, and my arm is much better, just tender. I can shoot a gun, but I don't have one."

Sheriff Lewis went to his desk, opened a drawer, pulled out a pistol with a holster wrapped around it, and handed it to him. "All right, men, this is it."

"Once you get into position, turn your safeties off. Be alert. Remember, this Ghost is a cold-blooded killer, and he may be in disguise. You are only authorized to use your weapons for self-defense. This is strictly a search-and-observe operation for all of you.

If you see Cora and the Ghost, do not try to apprehend the Ghost by yourself. You wait there until the rest of us come to help you. Don't let them out of your sight. If they are inside a house, try to position yourself where you can see both the building's front and rear. Use your best judgment on how to do that. Return to the Sheriff's Office if you determine Cora and the Ghost are not with the person you are assigned to observe. Time is critical."

"Everyone has three hours. If everyone except for one person or group returns after three hours, we will all go to where that person or group was assigned and assist in capturing or killing the Ghost. I will lead all of us at that time. That's all. Remember, I am the law and the only one responsible for apprehending the Ghost. Don't take on more than you can safely handle. See you all soon. Stay alert and be careful, men."

Detective Williams didn't think that there was much of a chance that anyone at the Mercantile was involved in Cora's disappearance. His suspicions were confirmed after talking with the owner and his two workers, who appeared to be as down-to-earth as people could be. On the way back to the Sheriff's Office, he got a little dizzy and slowed down to take a breather.

Charley didn't trust Raymond one bit. On the walk over to Samuel's house, he tried to stay behind Raymond so that he could keep an eye on him. Charley didn't say much, either. He much preferred that Raymond did the talking and hoped he could catch him in a lie.

When they got to Samuel's house, it was deserted and quiet. They watched for about one hour, then turned around and went back. Raymond said little on their way to the Sheriff's Office.

Junior talked with a few of his neighbors, but none had seen his mother recently. They all became concerned about Cora, and he felt terrible about bothering them. When he rode up to Happy's house, he knew he didn't want to talk to him. He saw no reason to concern Happy and his family by asking about Cora. Happy was doing some work outside, and his children were playing nearby. With everything that was going on, Junior decided to observe from a distance. Everything looked normal.

He continued to watch them, but more than anything, he was worried about his mother. The Ghost had captured her – several hours ago. This dominated his thoughts, and he felt a strong urge to punch something - or someone.

Chapter Forty

"People must know by now that I am missing. They will come here looking for me. I know they will. We need to do everything we can right here and right now. We need to try to escape if we can. If we can't, we must be ready if the opportunity presents itself. Maybe Samuel will make a mistake." Cora said. Samuel was outside, somewhere. They had no idea what he was doing.

"You're right. I was so wrong about trusting Samuel." Cat said.

"We can't do anything about that now."

The door slammed open, and Samuel entered the house. When Cora looked at him, he had the most evil-looking smile she could ever imagine. The coldness of it chilled her to the bone. He was a monster. The Ghost walked over and stood in front of Cat.

"I don't want to hurt you, but you give me no choice."

"I didn't do anything to you except care for you, you fool."

Cora cringed. Her response was vintage Cat - never afraid to fight back - but she should have stayed quiet. She should have been terrified. Samuel untied Cat's ankles. She tried to kick him but missed. He reached around her, grabbed the rope that tied her wrists, and yanked her to her feet.

"Let's go. Out the door." He forced her to get moving. Cora saw him pick up something off the kitchen table. It looked like a long, floppy, rubber kids-toy. As they walked away from Cat's house, their voices gradually became more distant. She could hear Cat complaining and Samuel commanding. "Stop. Stop. That hurts." Cora heard Cat say. Then she heard the real hits, the hard hits. Cat screamed after each one. Cat screamed one last time, and then there was silence. Cora knew Cat would soon be dead.

A few minutes later, the door opened, and Samuel entered the cabin. He looked dazed, then went to the kitchen table and sat facing Cora. His gaze bored right through her, so she looked down, not knowing what else to do. *Am I next?*

Nothing happened for the next five minutes, which felt like a half-hour to Cora. She looked up, and he was still looking at her, so she looked down again. After another few minutes, she slowly moved her eyes up and looked up at him, trying not to move her head too much. He was looking in her direction, but his eyes were closed. He had not moved since he sat down. She raised her head entirely, but he never changed his position. He was not far away physically, but his mind was somewhere else, somewhere far away, and she could never know where his thoughts had gone.

He stayed that way for at least two hours, two hours of agony. She couldn't move or make much noise. It was bad enough that she had to listen to her friend being beaten to death. Now she was the one tied up and totally at the mercy of this killer, who chose this moment to leave her and go on some emotional journey on his own. Her life was hanging in the balance – swaying in the wind. She watched him as his face twitched occasionally. From time to time, he made little jerking movements with his whole body. How strange. She wanted to scream. Then, without warning, he started to rouse himself back to life.

"Let's go. Out the door. Somebody will come looking for you soon." He untied her ankles. "Up you go." Cora gave him no reason to be angry with her. He pushed her out the front door, over to and inside his barn, then pushed her down, re-tied her ankles, tied her to a huge log post, and gagged her. "Don't give me any trouble. Stay here and be quiet until I come back." She nodded and didn't move. She was in no position to argue. After he left, she was so exhausted that she briefly fell asleep.

There was a knock on the cabin door outside. Two men were talking. She recognized their voices and was suddenly wide awake. Her hope spiked.

Will approached Cat's cabin and took a minute to take in the surroundings. All was quiet. He waited and watched. Nothing caught his eye as being out of place, so he rode up to the cabin. He got off his horse, walked up the porch, and knocked on the door. After a few moments, Samuel opened the door. "Good morning, Samuel. I'm looking for Cat."

"She had to leave to help her brother Happy with some emergency. I don't know when she will be back."

"Can I come in?"

"Of course."

Will walked into the cabin and looked around. Everything looked normal. He was so tired. Thinking was an effort, and everything was happening slowly. "Can I sit down?"

"Have a seat, please."

He sat down and then looked at Samuel, who looked back at him with a serious expression but said nothing.

Finally, Samuel said, "Would you like some coffee?"

"Yes, that sounds good." In no time, Will was staring at a

steaming mug of coffee.

He drank the coffee until it was about half-gone. It tasted good, and he felt a little more energetic. "Why are you here?" Will asked.

"Cat wanted me to stay here. I don't know why. Women, you know."

That made some sense to Will, so he let it drop. Neither man said much. Will looked down at his coffee, took another sip, and then looked at Samuel, who was looking back at him with that same serious expression he had before. He never liked Samuel, but Cat was a little different and odd, too, so maybe they were good for each other.

He needed to keep moving. There was no Ghost or Cora here. "Thanks for the coffee. I best get goin'." He stood up, walked over, opened the door, then turned and said, "You ought to be careful. Strange things are goin' on these days."

"I'll be careful," Samuel said with a smile. Will walked to his horse, got on it, and began the ride back to the Sheriff's Office.

Cora heard the knock on the door and began to listen intently. She recognized Will's voice, but he was too far away for her to understand what he was saying. She recognized Samuel's voice, too. Then the door shut, and she heard nothing. There was not much she could do to help Will if it came to that. She could make some noise but couldn't yell loud enough or even talk through the gag.

Cat never had any good sense about men. What a strange man this Samuel had become. Despite her shortcomings, Cat was her friend, and they shared many laughs and some sad moments, too. Cat was almost family to her, and she would be missed.

Cora knew Cat was physically stronger than she was, but in the end, her strength didn't help her. If Cora were to survive, she would have to rely on her wits. Understand your enemy, she thought. The problem was that there was no way she could ever understand the Ghost.

She heard Will talking again, and then she heard the sounds of Will's horse leaving. She listened until the sounds became faint and soon heard nothing more. Maybe Will doubled back to rescue her? She waited another hour, and then she began to lose hope. She couldn't escape without help, and now her time there was starting to run very short.

Chapter Forty-One

Charley, Raymond, Junior, and Will arrived at the Sheriff's Office about the same time. Everyone was there, including Detective Williams, and it became apparent that no one had seen the Ghost.

Sheriff Lewis pushed on, regardless, "Anyone see anything useful out there?"

"Raymond and I watched Samuel's house the whole time. He wasn't there, and there was no movement at his house." Charley said.

Detective Williams added, "The mercantile was a dead-end, no suspects there."

"Happy and his family were at their house, and it looked like they were having a normal, quiet day. Not even a hint of the Ghost." Junior said.

Will added, "I went to see Cat. Samuel was there and told me Cat had just left for Happy's. He said Happy rode over to get her because there was some emergency over at Happy's house he needed Cat's help with."

Sheriff Lewis listened, then said, "I don't like the sound of that. We must go to Happy's house to see what this emergency was all about." He surveyed the group - a tired and listless bunch.

Raymond was the only one interested in talking. "Maybe some coffee would help everyone." He said.

Sheriff Lewis took a few minutes to make the coffee. With mugs full of coffee in his hand, he turned around and walked towards the group, then stopped. Will was asleep in his chair. Charley and Junior were almost asleep, bobbing their heads up and down, eyes closed.

Raymond shrugged, took a mug, and said, "How about a three-hour nap? Then we can get started again."

"Looks like they need it. Three hours it is." Everyone except for Raymond began to fall asleep in their chairs.

Raymond was tired of sitting around the office. Sheriff Lewis had left about an hour previously. Everyone was snoring, and it was the perfect time for him to go outside and take a walk. As he walked, he started to think about what people had reported about their trips earlier. The group had decided the next thing to do was return to Happy's to see what his emergency was. Something about the timing of it all did not fit cleanly in his mind.

Junior went to see Happy, and he came back in just under three hours. Will went to Cat's, which was the most distant of anyone's trip, yet Samuel said Happy had already come to get Cat because he needed her help. Happy would have had to leave to get Cat immediately after Junior left and make it to Cat's cabin in record time. Junior said everything was fine with Happy and his family while he was there.

The likelihood of Happy leaving to go get Cat didn't seem likely at all. The timing was off, way off. The whole scenario seemed fabricated and unrealistic. Raymond didn't think Happy left his house to get his sister. What could Cat do at Happy's house that Marie couldn't do? What could have happened in such a short time? He returned to the Sheriff's Office to talk to Junior about it.

He would neglect to mention to anyone that he knew all along Samuel was the Ghost. Samuel was outnumbered now and would have fewer and fewer places to hide. Cora would be a burden to him and one he wouldn't want to carry for long. That bothered him.

The Ghost would be a formidable opponent for the group even though he was outnumbered. He knew how cunning Samuel was, and Samuel seemed to be implementing a well-thought-out plan. Raymond wasn't sure who had the advantage right now.

If Samuel was captured, he might blame him for participating in the Ghost's wrongdoings. Raymond wasn't that worried. Samuel had no proof, and nobody would be inclined to believe him.

When he returned to the office, he nudged Junior, who didn't move at first but finally raised his head to look at him. Raymond pointed towards the door and went outside. Junior followed.

"I was having a good sleep. What is so important."

"The group's decision to return to Happy's is a complete waste of time. We need to go to Cat's cabin. I'm sure I'm right." Raymond explained the timing of the events, and Junior agreed.

"Let's leave a message for the group when they wake up. Sheriff Lewis is still out on patrol. Detective Williams got bored and left over an hour ago. You and I need to get to Cat's right away. There's no time to lose."

"Agreed." Said Junior. They left a note and started the trip to Cat's cabin.

Detective Williams was relaxing in the restaurant on Cortez Street when he spotted Raymond walking. This was not a surprise because it was a beautiful, overcast day and perfect for a walk. The problem was that anything Raymond did made him suspicious, so he followed him back to the Sheriff's Office and waited. Raymond came out of the office with Junior. He saw them talking, then they went back inside. A short time later, they came back out again and left. What were they up to now? The three-hour rest period was only about half-finished. Something was up, so he followed the two young men.

Sheriff Lewis returned to his office after leaving the group alone for three hours. When he went inside, he saw Will and Charley snoring loudly. Junior, Raymond, and the detective were gone. He walked over to his desk, saw the note, and read it. He walked over to Will, shook him, and then did the same to Charley. "Wake up. You can't sleep in the Sheriff's Office all day."

Will and Charley were groggy but started to come to life.

"Junior left a note. It said he and Raymond went to Cat's house on a hunch. The note doesn't say when they left. We can't rely on hunches. I still want you two to go to Happy's and see if there is some kind of an emergency there. Unfortunately, I have to stay here for a while. If you see Detective Williams, tell him I could use his help here." said Sheriff Lewis.

"Let's go then," said Will. Charley nodded, and the two men left to visit Happy.

Chapter Forty-Two

He knew that people would be coming to Cat's cabin soon. Today, tomorrow, maybe the next day. He would be ready. His bait was in place. It's always better to fish with live bait, he thought, as long as she cooperated. He smiled to himself.

His life changed when Cat had to be punished, but he wouldn't miss her. His thoughts turned to Junior more than anything. Junior was the source of all his problems. How wonderful would it be if Junior was no longer interfering with his efforts to make Prescott a safer town and to help the helpless ones who desperately needed him? Junior would be punished. He smiled broadly this time. He needed to give Cora water and a little food. Then, he needed to proceed with his plans.

Charley and Will approached with caution. They found some bushes and small trees that provided enough cover for them to observe Happy's house, and they waited. Some sounds came from the house, people were talking, and smoke came out of the chimney. Everything seemed normal.

"I'll go to the front door. Will, you go just past the corner on the side. If something goes wrong, you'll be able to act fast." Will nodded, and they both moved into position.

Charley knocked on the door, and after a few moments, Happy opened the door and smiled. "Charley, it's good to see you. What's going on?"

"I'm sorry, but we had a report that Cat came to see you earlier because you had some emergency. Was she here?"

"No emergency here, and I haven't seen Cat for over a week."

Will heard this and walked over to the front door. "Hello, Happy. It looks like we got some bad information. Let's sit on the deck for a minute and think this through."

The three sat down, Will and Charley in deck chairs and Happy in his rocking chair. He sat and rocked slowly and waited for someone to speak. Charley started. "I'm damn tired of being messed with like this. Samuel lied to Will. There's no other explanation. The only question is whether the Ghost forced him to lie."

"It's hard for me to tell. He's a strange one, that Samuel. He don't say much. He could have lied all on his own, or he could have been made to. I don't know which one," said Will.

The two men thought this out, while Happy just looked at them, back and forth, not really knowing what they were talking about. Finally, Charley said, "Alright. I will stay here, just in case, until we know what is going on. Happy, can you put me up here for a while, at least overnight?"

"Sure, and then you can tell me what in the blazes is going on."

"Gladly. Will, can you go to Cat's house and check on Junior and Raymond?"

"I'm on my way."

"Good luck, and be careful." Will nodded, then left to go to Cat's.

"Think about it. He moved to Prescott just before the killings started. He doesn't need to work, so he had enough time to plan his attacks. And, you have to admit, he acts strange most of the time." Said Raymond.

Junior didn't know when Raymond would have had a chance to talk with Samuel, but Raymond rode his horse around town most days and could have met Samuel somewhere. He tossed the question out of his mind. They had more important things to do now. Junior gave him an appraising look, then said, "It does make sense, now that you mention it. What's the best way to catch the son of a bitch?"

The two developed their plan of attack on the ride to Cat's cabin. "We should split up. If one of us gets into trouble and makes a little noise, the other can move toward the noise and surprise Samuel. I don't think he would expect us to split up. I'll approach from the front, and you go around to the back. Go slow, and be as quiet as possible, safeties off. They were within walking distance of the cabin, so they stopped, tied up their horses, and began their approaches.

A few trees were scattered around the front of Cat's cabin, but mostly, it was a flat, open space dotted with low bushes. Raymond had to crawl up to the cabin most of the way to avoid exposing himself. When he had no other option but to be seen from the front of the cabin, he would move behind a bush, then stop and lie still to see if he had been noticed. If there was no response after a few minutes, he kept going.

He saw a solitary oak tree ahead, large enough to easily hide behind, and decided to take a breather there. He made his way to the back of the tree, relaxed, and took a deep breath. Next, he peeked around the side of the tree and never saw the club that hit him on his head. The club made a smacking sound, and he cried out, "AHH," and then collapsed at the tree's base, out cold.

Junior saw that Raymond was progressing slowly due to a lack of cover. He didn't want to get ahead of him, so he slowed and increased the distance between them to a good one hundred yards. That put him in the pine forest. No one would spot them together. He thought he heard a smacking sound, followed immediately by an odd guttural sound. Did he step on a twig and snap it, or was it Raymond? He wished he had been paying closer attention.

The noise came from the direction of where he thought Raymond should be, and he decided he needed to see if Raymond was OK. He carefully approached the forest's edge and looked at the area in front of Cat's cabin. He took a few moments to look for Raymond, then saw him lying at the base of a large oak tree. He looked hurt.

He could have, and should have, taken his time and slowly worked his way over to the oak tree, but Junior didn't know how badly Raymond was hurt. He ran over to check on him and was glad nobody was shooting at him as he ran. When he reached the oak tree, he saw Raymond had been clubbed. His head was still oozing blood, and he wasn't moving. Junior didn't know how to help him.

Then he saw something at the edge of his vision and looked towards the barn. Someone was waving franticly to get his attention. It was Will. What a sight for sore eyes - good old stubborn, dependable Will. Then Will started to wave in earnest for him to come to the barn quickly.

Junior decided to break cover and ran towards the barn. When he was about fifty yards from the barn door, Will continued to wave him over, then went inside the barn. Junior approached the door, went inside the barn, and immediately saw Cora bound and gagged.

The door closed behind him, so he turned around and saw

Will pointing a shotgun at him - no, it was the Ghost pointing a shotgun at him - no, it was Samuel.

"I don't have to hurt you now, Junior, but I'll blow a big hole through your chest if you make me," Samuel said with a strange hissing sound. "Slowly drop your handgun on the ground, then get on your belly. I'm tying you up here with your mom. Don't make any noise.

Junior dropped the gun the sheriff had given him, then slowly laid on his belly. Samuel tied his wrists up so tightly that they immediately hurt, and then he proceeded to gag Junior and tie him up next to Cora on the large log post. I'll be outside but not too far away." He pointed the shotgun at Junior, then Cora, then back at Junior. "I'm going to wait outside for more of your friends to show up."

He looked at Junior and hissed, "When everyone is here, I'm going to put on quite a show, and you are all invited. Don't worry; admission is free."

Chapter Forty-Three

The Ghost left the barn. Junior wanted to kick himself, but his ankles were tied together. His first big test as a man, he thought, *and he failed.* He had been tricked by the Ghost.

"Uh why we." His mother said through her gag.

He didn't get it. She kept repeating herself - not loudly, but excitedly – and then he nodded at her. He got it. His mother wanted him to untie her. He thought about how to do that. Their wrists were tied together behind their backs. There was another, larger rope wrapped around the outside of both of them that tied them to the post. The ropes were cinched very tightly. He tried to position himself so his fingers were close to her wrists. He couldn't do it. The ropes were too tight.

He used a back-and-forth, sideways motion and made some progress, but the rope that tied them to the post burned his skin when he moved against it, and he was drawing blood.

He looked at his mother and exhaled as much as he could - several times. He repeated this, and then she nodded yes, indicating she understood what he wanted her to do. They both exhaled at the same time, and he made gradual but painful progress. His hands got a little closer to hers with every try. They repeated this back-and-forth motion several times. By now, he could see his mother was bleeding, too.

"Op. Op." He said. They stopped and took a break.

Something was going on, and Detective Williams intended to find out what It was. He wondered why Junior seemed to trust Raymond. The ignorance and naivete of youth, no doubt. He saw the two young men split up. Raymond was going towards Cat's cabin so he decided to follow him. He then watched in shocked surprise when someone appeared out of nowhere at a large oak tree, clubbed Raymond, and then disappeared again behind the tree.

He was concerned for Raymond because he wasn't moving, but he also did not want to be shot if he exposed himself. Nothing happened for several minutes, and he was getting ready to go check on Raymond when Junior ran out of the pine trees on his right, lowered himself, then stood up again and ran as fast as he could over to the Oak tree.

He watched Junior pause briefly, kneel, and look at Raymond. Junior looked over at the barn and started to walk towards it. Then, he began to run towards the barn. Someone was there, waving him over. It looked like Will was at the barn, but he knew when he left town that Will was still at the Sheriff's Office. The Ghost was making a move.

The detective needed to get involved in what was happening. The first thing to do would be to see what condition Raymond was in. He slowly worked his way to the Oak Tree and checked Raymond's pulse. He was alive and still breathing but unconscious. It was out of his hands. All he could do was to position Raymond in a comfortable-looking position, with his head slightly elevated. He got ready to move to the cabin, then heard the unmistakable sound of a gun cocking.

"Don't move, and get away from that man."

"Will, is that you? It's me, Detective Williams."

He turned to face Will. The detective was cautious and wanted to make sure he was talking to the real Will. He had just seen another Will at the barn. He looked at the man and recognized him as the real Will.

"I was following Raymond and Junior when I saw someone club Raymond here. A little later, Junior came over to check on Raymond, then ran behind the cabin and into the barn."

"Someone is tryin' to cover up horse shit, but I can still smell it. Can't you?"

"Sure can."

"Let's walk to the cabin gradually to sneak up on whoever is inside," Will said.

The detective lowered himself slowly. He still felt the effects of being hit on the head. "OK. I'll move towards the left corner of the front, and you go towards the right corner." Will nodded.

They stayed low and were getting close to the cabin when Samuel cautiously opened the front door and came halfway out. He had a shotgun, pointed straight out, but not directly at the detective or Will.

"I've got a gun. Don't make me use it. I've seen at least two of you sneaking around out there. Stand up and identify yourselves, or I'll start shooting."

The detective and Will stood up tentatively. "We don't want any trouble. We're the only two out here," said Will. We've got some questions for you."

"Questions? Alright. I understand. Come in, and I'll answer your questions. The detective and Will walked up to Cat's cabin, and went inside. Will motioned for Samuel to sit at the table, and then he and the detective sat opposite Samuel.

Junior reached the rope that tied his mother's wrists, and then he started the difficult task of blindly untying it from his awkward angle. He had no choice but to twist his torso to get his fingers in the best position to work on the rope. This put pressure on his ribs, which had stubbornly refused to heal completely. He soon found out the pain that he felt from the pressure on his ribs was much worse than the pain he felt from the rope burns. This hurt.

Samuel got comfortable in his seat. He had anticipated the questions they would ask him and practiced his answers repeatedly. He was ready - excited even. He was a master of deception and took great pride in it. He would enjoy toying with these two.

Detective Williams asked, "Where is Cat, and why are you here?"

"This morning, I was working on Cat's windmill again - it needs a new part—when this man seemed to pop up out of nowhere. He demanded I go inside the cabin here, where Cat was. What could I do? He had a gun. I went inside the cabin here. When we got inside, he said he was the Ghost."

"When I heard that, I have to tell you, I was scared. Even Cat was so scared that, for once, she didn't say much. This Ghost started talking, almost to himself, but it didn't make sense. Something about needing more bait, having bigger plans, and such. I couldn't make much sense of it."

"The Ghost tied Cat's hands behind her back and walked her out the front door, but before he left, he told me if anybody came here, I was to tell them she just left with Happy because of some emergency at Happy's place."

"You lied to me today because the Ghost told you to?" Will asked.

"Yes. I'm sorry."

"That doesn't answer why you are here, in Cat's cabin," the detective said.

"He told me if he saw me anywhere outside of this cabin, he would kill Cat. Until a minute ago, when I went out to the deck to face you two, I'd been inside here all day, worried sick."

He measured their responses and was gratified. They were starting to believe him. *They are such simple people.*

"I took a chance when I saw you two. I had no choice but to confront you before shots were fired. I think the Ghost is long gone by now, anyway."

The detective wanted more convincing. "Have you seen Junior or Raymond?"

"Not for days, why?"

"They came here this afternoon. Someone hit Raymond on the head a few minutes ago. He's still breathing but unconscious. He's lying out at the base of that big oak tree out front.

Samuel didn't realize Raymond was still alive. *Damn it.* He would have plenty of time to finish the job later - *patience, patience.*

"Oh no. I hope he's OK. The Ghost is still out there, and Junior's out there, too. I had no idea."

Will and the detective looked at each other worriedly. Samuel did his best to look weak and innocent.

Junior hadn't felt anything pop, so he was hopeful he hadn't re-broken his rib. His fingernails had started to crack and break from the pressure he put on them by trying to untie his mother's knot. The pain from his hands was a distraction from the pain from his ribs, and he was strangely grateful for that.

It seemed nearly impossible for him to figure out how to untie her wrists. He had no idea what kind of knot Samuel had used. All he could do was try to loosen every bit of rope he could and keep at it until he could feel something loosening. Finally, it happened, and he began to loosen the knot.

Will knew he had to stay calm. His wife was missing, and his oldest son was outside somewhere. The Ghost was out there, too. *Junior was smart enough to stay safe, wasn't he?*

Detective Williams said, "We've got to search for Junior and Cora."

"Cora?" Samuel asked.

"Yeah, she's missing too. It's the Ghost against us three. The odds are in our favor."

Everyone got up and started to move. The detective was the first to walk towards the front door, but then he stopped suddenly. "What's that?" He asked as he pointed at something propped up against the wall in the back corner of the cabin. He walked over and picked it up. Will and Samuel watched him with great interest.

Cora's wrists were untied. She was glad Junior untied her first because his hands were stronger than hers and could work faster than she could. Now that her hands were free, it was her turn to try to untie the rope on Junior's wrists.

She went to work on untying Junior's wrists and soon found out how difficult it was. It hurt her hands, but she kept trying.

Samuel had finally made a mistake - thank God. He had tied them up too close together. He had no idea what type of people he was dealing with. *We're the Martins of Prescott, for God's sake.* Will was somewhere outside, but she hadn't heard his voice for a few minutes.

She knew, and worried, that it would all be meaningless if she couldn't untie Junior's wrists quickly enough. She heard a gunshot.

"It's a club…With fresh blood on it…What's it doing here?" The detective seemed to hesitate briefly, then turned towards Samuel as he began to draw his pistol. He was too slow. Samuel produced a gun Will hadn't seen before. He shot the detective and spun him down to the floor.

Will reached for his gun, but he was too late. Samuel turned and pointed his pistol at him.

"Put it down on the floor, then stand up slowly."

Will had no choice but to comply with Samuel's demand, and he surrendered his weapon.

"Very slowly get the detective's weapon, hold it by the grip with two fingers only, and put it there." Samuel pointed his gun at a spot on the floor several feet away from where Williams was lying. Will slowly walked over, picked up the pistol, and carefully placed it where Samuel had pointed.

"Good. Now go see if he's still alive."

Will walked over to check on the detective. He had a fresh wound in the arm, but he was quickly roused. Detective Williams sat up, groggily looked around the room, and then became aware of what was happening.

"Stand up." Samuel hissed.

"He's groggy from being hit on the head a few days ago. Can I help him stand up?" Will asked.

"Hurry up. I'm losing my patience with you two." Samuel hissed again, this time a little louder.

Will helped Detective Williams stand up, and they both turned and faced Samuel.

"Who else is coming?" Samuel asked.

"I don't know." Said Will.

"No matter, I can wait for them. Right now, I want you two to slowly walk out of here and around to the barn behind the house. Stay where I can see you. There are some people there I want you to meet for the last time."

Junior noticed his mother was becoming frantic.

"Calm down. Concentrate." He said.

"You're right. I'm concentrating now."

He could feel her work on each little piece of the knot. She methodically pulled and twisted every part of it, trying to find some piece of the rope she could work loose.

She found a small piece of the knot she could loosen slightly, then she kept working on it until she pulled a piece of rope out, and he could feel the knot begin to loosen. Soon, his wrists were free.

The rope wrapped around them, and the post became a little slacker because their arms were no longer behind their backs. They were able to painstakingly raise both arms, one at a time, above the rope. Junior then turned the rope until the knot was directly in front of him and untied it. They were free of the post, and they both removed their gags.

Junior took a quick moment to listen for any sounds coming from outside the barn. He heard nothing and decided to risk it and untie the rope around his ankles. After his feet were untied, he looked at his mother, who pointed at the door and whispered, "Go!"

He needed something to defend himself with. He looked around and saw a pitchfork. He grabbed it and went to the door. Junior stopped there and waited again to listen for any sounds. He heard none, so he slowly cracked open the door. He saw nothing, opened the door fully, stepped out, and looked around.

He saw nothing and worked his way to the back of Cat's cabin. He had a vague sensation of pain coming from his ribs, arms, and hands but paid it no mind. Will, Detective Williams, and the Ghost were nearby. He wondered about the gunshot but had no time to dwell on it.

"Keep going. All the way to the barn." Junior heard Samuel hiss. Junior had no idea how any human could become the kind of evil monster Samuel was. He started to shake and worked to calm himself. The sound came from his left, so he moved in that direction and waited behind the corner of the cabin.

He saw Detective Williams first. The detective jerked his eyes over to look at him but kept walking. Will was next. Will hesitated briefly as he came around the corner and saw him, but he did not turn his head, which would have given away Junior's position. Junior knew Samuel would be next. He got the pitchfork ready to strike.

"Keep moving, damn it!" Samuel yelled.

The moment came. Samuel looked to his left as he stepped behind the corner of the cabin. He saw the pitchfork coming and reflexively twisted his torso to his right to try to evade being stabbed. This exposed his back, and he was struck.

Junior lunged and then gave it everything he had. He pushed the pitchfork into Samuel's back. He expected it to go straight in, but it hit bones first before plunging deeper. The force of the strike knocked the gun loose from Samuel's hand, and he fell on his stomach, with his face turned to his left.

Junior felt numb. Samuel yelled when hit with the pitchfork, but he didn't move or make any sound once he was on the ground. Junior pulled out the pitchfork. There was a lot of blood.

"I got his gun," Detective Williams said.

Samuel still wasn't moving. Junior moved over to his left so that he could see Samuel's face. He was grimacing, and his eyes were closed.

"Samuel, do you have anything to say?" Detective Williams asked.

Still grimacing, Samuel opened his eyes slightly and looked at the detective. He looked at Will, then moved his gaze to Junior. He opened his eyes fully when he saw Junior still holding the pitchfork.

He was mortally wounded and seemed to know it. He still had not moved since he hit the ground. He looked at Junior for a few moments; then Junior saw a faint smile creep onto Samuel's face. Samuel continued to look at him, and Junior watched as the light slowly left his eyes. A few moments later, it was suddenly over. The Ghost was dead.

"That son of a bitch ain't goin' to kill anymore. Good work, Junior." Will said.

He was still in a state of shock. It was hard to watch a man die, even if it was the Ghost. "Mother's in the barn," Junior said.

Will went into the barn and then emerged with Cora by his side. She walked over and saw Samuel, and she looked to be at a loss for words. Junior realized he was still holding onto the pitchfork, so he threw it to the ground. She walked over to him and gave him a quick, admiring look and a big, hard hug.

"Where's Cat?" He asked.

Cora looked at the ground, shook her head, and seemed to be fighting off tears. The three of them left the barn, both happy and sad.

"Raymond was hit in the head by Samuel. He needs our help.

Let's take him home with us tonight. Tomorrow, we'll get Raymond more help, then drop by the Sheriff's Office to explain what happened here." Junior said.

Everyone nodded a somber agreement. Will and Junior collected Raymond as carefully as they could, and then they all left Cat's place and headed home.

Chapter Forty-Four

Will was still tired when Lee and Paul woke him up. He nudged Cora, who got out of bed stiffly and put on her robe.

"Boys. Go wake up, Junior." Will said.

By the time breakfast was served, the sun had already been up for over two hours.

"Junior, you and I need to take care of a few things this morning. We need to decide what to do to help Raymond. Then we've got to see the Sheriff and explain to him what happened yesterday, and then I'm sure we'll need to ride over to Cat's cabin." Will said.

Cora had been busy making breakfast and hadn't had a chance to check on Raymond. "Will, how is Raymond doing?"

"He's restin' but still hasn't woken up."

"We should get him home where his mother can watch over him. Right now, he's still unconscious, and I'm a little worried."

"It's out of our hands now. Let's finish eatin' our biscuits and gravy, drop off Raymond, and then go see the Doc downtown. He'll want to make a house call at Raymond's as soon as possible," Will said.

They went to Raymond's parent's house. Will carried

Raymond up to the front door, and Junior knocked. Raymond's mother shrieked when she saw him.

"He's alive, just hit in the head, ma'am," Will said.

"That boy gets in as much trouble as ten other boys put together. What did he do now?"

Junior spoke up. "Let's get him to a bed, then we'll tell you." Junior continued after Raymond was put on a bed, "You should be proud of him. He played a key role in bringing down the Ghost. The Ghost is dead now, ma'am. Raymond was very brave, and it's even possible his actions saved at least one life."

"My Raymond? For sure?"

"Yes, ma'am, for sure. We'll get the Doctor and have him come here to look at Raymond as soon as possible."

"I can't thank you enough for bringing him here and for your kind words."

"Junior and I need to go into town now. Take care." Will said.

They left and went to the Sheriff's Office after a quick trip to see the Doc. Once inside, they explained to the sheriff what had happened, and then the three of them left to visit the scene at Cat's cabin. Two of them were on horseback, and Sheriff Lewis drove a wagon.

They could smell an unpleasant odor as they got closer to the cabin. Cora had told Will that she thought Samuel had taken Cat somewhere north of the cabin. They spread out to search for Cat, and it didn't take long for them to find her. Will spotted her first.

"Junior, go fetch a blanket from the wagon." Cat had been badly beaten, and Will didn't want Junior to see that. When he saw Junior bringing the blanket, he walked out to him, took the blanket, and said, "You'd better wait for us at the wagon." A few minutes later, Will and Sheriff Lewis brought Cat, rolled up in a blanket, and put her in the wagon. Next, they picked up Samuel and put him in the wagon.

"Two for the undertaker," the sheriff said. They were in no hurry on their way back into town. Later, Will split off and went home. Sheriff Lewis went to visit the undertaker, and Junior went to the newspaper office.

The weekly Prescott Prospector newspaper added the following short article just before publication.

'GHOST KILLER' STRUCK DOWN

Our sheriff, Herman Lewis, recently reported the infamous 'Ghost' killer met his maker at the hands of W Martin, Junior. A few local men were organized in a bold plan to take down the Ghost. 'The sheriff orchestrated his plan to perfection. I just did my part. The sheriff put it all together,' Mr. W Martin Junior is reported to have said. More details will follow in our next edition.

Chapter Forty-Five

Junior had been closely monitoring Raymond's condition over the past two months. He remained unconscious the entire first week. When he finally came to, he was still in bad shape. His head hurt all the time, too much light made him cry out with pain, he couldn't sit up in bed without feeling dizzy, and eating anything was an adventure.

As the weeks went by, he gradually improved, and now, a couple of months later, he was almost back to normal. The Doc told everyone it was a miracle. His youth was the only thing that saved him, he said.

A day didn't seem to go by that someone in the family didn't mention Cat. She was Cora's friend, and despite her quirks and failings, over time, she had become a family friend, too.

One day, Cora said, "Why don't we get everyone here to celebrate Cat? By everyone, I mean Happy and his family, Charley and his family, Lillian and her family, Sharlot, and Detective Lewis if he wants to come. Raymond seems to have turned his life around, so let's invite him, too. He needs to get out of the house, anyway, now that he's feeling better. We can make room for everyone. We'll pick a time far enough in advance so we can get ready, and our guests will have plenty of time to plan for it."

He knew his mother was officially only suggesting this, but she had probably been thinking about it for a while and was already set on doing it. He looked at Will, who had a resigned look on his face. This discussion was over.

Word was sent out, and everyone gladly agreed to be there. Work began on the preparations. For him and Will, that meant building a long table with bench-style seating. Cora wanted all the adults to spend time together on the porch, eating and talking.

Junior designed the table so it could be quickly taken apart, compactly stored, and easily reassembled for future use. A few wooden pegs had to be used, but gravity held most of the table together. Junior and Will planned for what they needed, went to the lumber mill, and then came back and started to put it together.

Cora, meanwhile, was preparing for a feast. She planned to harvest extra vegetables, including sweet corn, which was in peak season. She was going to have beef and chicken and was designing recipes for the meats to make them extra tasty. Some liquor, including several bottles of wine and beer, were also to be purchased.

Finally, the big day came, and people began showing up around noon. Happy, Marie and their two children were the first to arrive. They were greeted warmly by everyone. Marie went inside the cabin to talk with Cora, and their children ran off to play with Lee and Paul. Junior found himself with Will and Happy, trying to come up with something to say.

Will broke the ice, "How's the livery business these days?"

"My business grows as the town grows. It's good. Me and Marie are saving-up to buy a new house someday."

"Good for you. I may need to ask you for a loan, as good as you're doin'." Will joked, then left, and Happy was alone with Junior.

Junior was proud to know Happy so much that sometimes, Happy felt like an uncle to him. Happy had made something of himself. He had a good family and owned the best livery in town - not bad. He felt terrible about having had words with Happy when he tried to take Will's horse.

"Happy, I know you didn't mean to tell me Will wasn't my real father. So you know, I don't hold anything against you. I'm not proud of the way I acted, either. It was an accident that happened in the heat of the moment."

"Thanks, Junior. That day has bothered me from time to time."

They both had a beer. Happy suggested Junior only have one beer. "The first time I drank alcohol, it was whiskey, and I got real sick afterward. I felt awful for a whole day. You don't want to go through what I did."

"Good advice, thanks." Said Junior.

I thought something big was up that day when Will and Charley came over. What a day that must have been." Happy said.

"I think we were all fortunate. It could have been a disaster. I'm glad you didn't have to get involved in it."

Junior noticed Charley and his family, Lillian with her husband Frank and their children, had all arrived. Frank walked over to talk to Charley. Junior thanked Happy for his advice on drinking, then walked over to where Charley was standing. Frank was already talking with Charley, and he watched Junior approach.

"Hey there, Junior. You're a hero now." Frank said.

"Thanks. I'm just glad it's over."

"Where's Raymond?" Charley asked.

"I told him we were going to eat around three this afternoon. I can't see him missing a meal like this one." Junior said. He looked around and saw Detective Williams walking their way.

The detective walked up to them, and Charley spoke to him, "I talked with the sheriff last week. He told me you have been permanently assigned to his office here in town. I guess your bosses thought this area had enough criminals to keep you busy."

"It was a mutual decision. I didn't want to go back to Phoenix. I have some ideas I want to experiment with, new ideas that I know I couldn't work on back in Phoenix."

"That's amazing. Progress never stops. The future is coming, and the only thing we can say about it is that it will be different from the past," Charley added thoughtfully.

The mood had become too somber for Junior's taste, especially for a day like today. He looked over Charley's shoulder and saw Raymond walking their way with a beer in his hand. He made it over to their little group.

"You've finally recovered now, haven't you, Raymond," Frank said.

"I'm feeling much better, and I've had a lot of time to think. For me now, it's all about restoring the natural order of things, like me besting Junior on a more regular basis, for example. All above board, of course."

Junior smiled slightly. He noticed Charley, too, seemed to know Raymond was boasting, but it looked to Junior like Charley was glad to see Raymond's renewed confidence.

"Raymond, I've got some news. Sharlot was able to use her connections to find out more about Samuel. Turns out his father worked in the circus. His father's name was Oscar, and he is reported to have died in an accident. He fell and hit his head. Samuel was in a mental hospital in Santa Fe and was under suspicion for his father's death. He was released from the hospital a couple of years later due to good behavior." Junior said.

"They should have kept him there. I thought he might have grown up around actors, but growing up around a circus makes sense, too." Raymond said.

"The sheriff searched the house Samuel was renting and found one room completely full of disguises, face paints, and other unusual items. It was very strange," Junior said.

"Time to eat." Yelled Cora.

Everyone except Junior moved toward the long table on the covered porch. Junior wanted to check in with the children, who were going to eat inside, so he walked in and saw that Sharlot had arrived. "I volunteered to eat with the children to keep them under control, if that's even possible," she said with a smile.

He looked at Paul, who was obviously having trouble getting used to having so many people at the house all at once. He was looking down at his plate and fiddling with his silverware repeatedly.

"Hey, Paul." He said.

Paul looked up, and Junior contorted his face into a 'funny face'. Paul giggled and seemed to relax. Junior patted him on the shoulder and knew he would be just fine. Everything else was good with the children, so he went outside to sit with the adults. Everyone had settled in, and he found a place to sit beside Raymond.

Cora, Marie, Elizabeth, and Lillie swarmed the table, laying down food and drink. He followed Happy's advice about alcohol and switched to water for the rest of the day. He noticed Raymond had switched to wine.

"Thank you all for being here. Will and I are extremely proud to have such good friends. I wanted to have everyone here as soon as Raymond recovered to celebrate the end of a sad chapter in our community's history and to especially thank those of you who helped to safely bring it to an end. Unfortunately, we lost Cat, a true friend." Cora paused briefly, then continued, "Let's all raise a glass and toast to Cat."

Everyone raised their glasses. Cora looked directly at Happy. "Happy, you and I have been through some tough times together over the years, and many good times. I knew your sister well, and I know how very proud she was of you. The fact is, we all are."

Happy could barely talk but managed to say, "Thank you."

"Now it's time to eat. Will, would you say the blessing?"

Will said his short blessing, and everyone started in on the feast.

There was a noticeable quiet for a few minutes, and then the conversations started to pick up and become a little louder. "Lillian, my goodness. I love your potatoes," Cora said.

"What did you do to the beef? It's the best beef I've ever had." Lillian replied.

"It's a secret."

Detective Williams added, "Well, it's no secret your little town is not to be trifled with. I'm impressed with all of you."

"Junior never gave up in his hunt for the Ghost. I'm ashamed to admit it now, but I wasn't quite sure what was going on after he broke out of jail." Said Charley.

"I didn't really know what I was doing back then myself. I got lucky, I guess."

Raymond corrected him, "Luck had nothing to do with it. You would not stop. You never gave up, like when you tripped and turned your ankle on the old Mill Road. You just got up again and kept on running. You refused to be stopped." Raymond took another sip of wine.

Junior didn't move but stopped chewing briefly, then slowly

started to chew again. He recalled that day and remembered never telling anyone he had a slight ankle sprain. Raymond had no way of knowing that unless he was there and saw it. *He must have been there.* Raymond had to have been the one who clubbed him and cracked his ribs. What else had Raymond not told him?

"It was a team effort. Everyone helped." Added Charley.

Junior nodded, then looked around the table and added what he had been thinking for a while. "We all helped."

Junior continued to speak, only with a more serious tone. Everyone stopped eating and looked at him. "The past few months were hard on everyone. We were under a lot of pressure, and I guess our true natures came out. It is safe to say that we are all part of an exceptional family and blessed to have exceptional friends."

He paused for a moment, then looked at Will with a sincere expression and said. "I'm proud to call you my father."

Junior noticed Cora's head jerk slightly. He looked over at her and saw she was smiling at Will. He looked over at his father again. Will didn't say anything, not that Junior thought he would. He watched as his father took a sip of wine, eyes twinkling, then lowered his head. Junior thought he saw Will's eyes mist up some.

Paul came out to the porch. "Anyone still hungry? I thought for sure I smelled strawberry pie."

Author's Notes

Thank you for reading this book. This is a work of fiction. It is not intended as a work of historical fiction, although an effort was made to convey a feeling for the time and place of the story. The locations and events in this novel are invented or modified to suit the story. Any similarities to historical facts are purely coincidental. The character of Sharlot in this book is loosely modeled after Sharlot M. Hall. All of the other characters are fictitious.

Sharlot M. Hall had an important impact on the development of northern Arizona in its formative years. The following is summarized from the book Arizona Legends and Lore, tales of Southwestern Pioneers: Sharlot was an avid reader as a youth, although books were hard for her to come by. She was an intelligent woman who wrote poems and articles and worked hard to do her part to help make her parent's ranch near Prescott remain a going concern. She thought of herself as an 'outdoors woman.' She wrote articles for a newspaper based in California and garnered national attention for her work. Her mother became ill and needed assistance when Sharlot was in her thirties, and Sharlot decided to stay with her to care for her.

Sharlot collected stories and artifacts of the early pioneers and the Indians in northern Arizona. Eventually, her collections became the Sharlot Hall Museum, which still thrives today. If you find yourself in downtown Prescott with some free time, I encourage you to visit the Museum and look around.

Printed in Great Britain
by Amazon